WHALE MUSIC

WHALE MUSIC

Paul
Quarrington

VINTAGE CANADA
A Division of Random House of Canada

Canadian Cataloguing in Publication Data

Quarrington, Paul
    Whale music

ISBN 0-679-30868-7

I. Title.

PS8583.U334W48 1997   C813'.54   C96-932612-2
PR9199.3.Q37W42 1997

Cover design: Stray Toaster

To Dorothy and Carson

"I like the Walrus best," said Alice, "because he was a *little* sorry for the poor oysters."

"He ate more than the Carpenter, though," said Tweedledee.

— *Lewis Carroll*

There is a toe sticking out from underneath a green blanket on my living-room sofa. A lovely toe, a pale and dainty toe. A toe that has never tested dirty bathwater. I am fond of pretty toes like this, because my own are so ugly. My big toes are huge and flat like ping-pong paddles. The rest are deformed midget toes, little squirmy grub toes. The nails are hard and horny and for some reason have turned bright yellow.

Apparently I've received a visitor. This strikes me as highly unlikely. Oh, certainly, people come to see me from time to time — executives from Galaxy Records, reporters from magazines, my mother on a weekly raid-and-pillage — but this is some form of *house guest*, because the owner of this toe has decided to spend the night! I don't know how I feel about this.

Into the backyard then, for a refreshing dip in the pool.

Let me see how large a splash I can make. Immense, a monster. This is not just my weight — that helps, but size alone does not ensure a fine splash — it is a matter of maximizing surface contact, making sure every available square inch of naked pale flesh slaps the water simultaneously. Danny was great at this, which proves that size is nothing, because Danny never achieved my proportions, although towards the end my brother was quite corpulent and bloated.

1

We were all of us born too late, that's a sad fact. This age is a strange new neighbourhood, cheaply constructed and stuck out in the middle of nowhere. None of us belongs. Daniel should have been a medieval warlord. Dan-Dan should have wandered throughout the barren earthworks, a butt of malmsey in his paw, tweaking the bosoms of handmaids, shooting the boots to the snivelling turnspits. When he passed out in the shadowed hallway, there would be minions aplenty to haul his carcass off to bed.

My brain is a little leguminous, I make no bones about it. Indeed, I worked hard for this brain, put in the years and squandered millions. So, let me just ask, what's this about a toe? A pale, dainty one poking out from beneath a green blanket? I see. This is impossible, people do not come to visit me. Sometimes record executives (even President and Chairman of the Board Kenny Sexstone himself, the bizarre, puppetlike creature), magazine people or fraudulent psychiatrists knock on the door, but I pretend I'm not home. I hide behind something and wait for them to go away. My mother doesn't fall for this, she unlocks the door (as many keys as I come up with, she comes up with more) and barges in. My mother makes vague inquiries as to my health, she sticks her hand between the cushions on the sofa and ferrets out uncashed cheques. Ergo, this alleged toe on the sofa couldn't belong to a visitor, because I would not have opened the door. It could not be my mother's, because my mother's nail is always painted a garish red. I probably imagined this toe on the sofa, it is too unlikely a thing. But, if you insist, I will go back to the living room and take one more gander.

Ah, here we are in the music room.

Look at all this equipment! I have synthesizers and recording modules, mixing boards and otherworldly musical machines, everything interfaced with a Macintosh computer. I'm pretty sure that I could get the house to lift off if I tried hard enough. The world is going down in flames, it is a flushing conflagration, but technology has kept pace. Do you see that over in the corner? That hulking assemblage of wires, circuit boards, plastic and wood? That is the Yamaha 666, the most advanced keyboard system ever invented. Tread softly, we don't want to wake it.

I love Science. Look at the astounding toys it's produced, consider the wonders of pharmaceuticals. The future has arrived, as promised in those little films they showed us in grade school. You remember those, don't you? The film would slip off the take-up reel, before long celluloid would be roiling about the floor, your teacher would panic and start screaming for the A.V. man.

I must work on the Whale Music. The Whale Music is very important to me. It's the *only* thing that's important to me. Don't try to stop me from working on it like Mom and Fay and Kenny Sexstone and countless record executives have tried to do. The record execs say the Whale Music isn't commercial. I say it's not my fault if whales don't have any money.

A low note on the pianoforte machine. Don't you love low notes? Don't they tingle in your privates and send electrical juice spurting to your brain? Of course they do. And now rhythms, layered as the sea, slow and powerful near the bottom, clear and sparkly on top, whitecaps catching the sun. I need, I need — I need a saxophone! Do you play the sax? I need, it is absolutely imperative that I have, a sax — a *soprano* sax — to do the dolphins. I never learned how to play the sax, a costly oversight. What I must do is hire Mooky Saunders, unless he's dead.

Into the living room, then, to use a telephone, although I have a nagging suspicion that I don't own this instrument of torture. Still, there's no harm in checking.

Do you see what I see? Toes, five of them, attached to a foot, a pale ankle, a calf, a slender calf, a calf that has romped through clover in Switzerland. This is a very strange thing to be poking

3

out from underneath a green blanket on my living room sofa. This is some form of intruder. What could they be after? Despite popular belief and overwhelming evidence, I am not paranoid. At least, I don't believe that anyone is trying to kill me. My friend John Lennon was assassinated, but I cannot imagine someone doing that to me. What would be the point, other than a bravura display of mental imbalance one-upmanship?

Wait a moment. I suppose there's some chance, a slim one but a chance all the same, that I've killed someone. Oh my goodness, I hope not. I may have killed a record executive or magazine reporter, one of the main reasons I don't let them through the front door. I may have strangled them, or smothered them within the foul-smelling folds of my body, then covered the corpse with this green blanket.

All is well, because the form underneath the green blanket just moved. Now it's rolling, and the green blanket is falling away to reveal . . . nakedness.

Into the backyard, into the pool. Look how big a splash I can make! Colossal, improbable.

It was Danny who taught me the technique. He was seven, I was eight, when the father had a pool put into the backyard on Whitman Avenue. The father had made a bit of money from a song called "Vivian in Velvet", which you might remember if you're quite old and have ridiculously bad taste in music. My mother had wanted the pool, apparently as a backdrop to her tanning activities. The first thing Danny did, as soon as the pool was full of water, was announce that he was going to produce the most humungous of splashes. He spent quite a few minutes telling me the technique involved. "You don't gotta run," he pointed out. "Running is for shits. Two, three steps maximum, and then you got to lay your body *over* the water and drop. Think *down*. Try to get as much of your body to hit as you can. Now, I'm gonna go first. Watch me." Danny took two determined steps towards the deep end and stretched into the air. As he hit the water he produced a beautiful thing, liquid pyrotechnics. Then it occurred to me that Danny didn't know how to swim. I managed to fish him out with the handle of the skimming net.

My house is high on a cliff, and from the edge of my property, pressed against the fence (barbed wire running along the top, eight feet in the air), I can see the ocean. From time to time I will spy a pod of whales. They swim around the world, you know, whales circle the globe purposefully. They lunch off the Isles of Scilly, stop for idle chatter near Monrovia. I feel very fortunate to see a pod — a *family* — sail by in the water beneath me. I love to see that. What I don't love to see is a naked body on my living room couch. It is a female body, by the way. What am I to do?

Into the music room. I rewind the tape on the console, blast the song into the world octaphonically. Yes, yes! This is lovely and I must dance to the *Whale Music*. I throw off my bathrobe into one of the dark corners. I sing the "Song of Flight." The dolphins leap through waves, they swim through sunlight, and now I remember, what this needs is a saxophone. I'm going to phone Mooky Saunders, unless (a) Mooky is dead or (b) I don't own a telephone. So it's into the living room for a look-see.

Oh. Er. Um. There is a naked girl sleeping on my couch. She appears to be no older than fifteen — extremely bad legal news — and she is snoring lightly. Her hair is a golden colour, and it spills around her, it cascades onto the floor. I will cover her with the green blanket, which has likewise tumbled onto the living-room rug.

The girl suddenly sputters and twists her arms into the air. She makes an odd sound — *eeaagh!* — and her legs begin to kick in a petulant way. Then she opens her eyes — one of them, at any rate, the right — and sees me with the blanket held out in front. She is in the middle of another odd sound —

5

oooopphh — but she breaks it off in order to smile at me. How lovely of her. She smiles at me, digs her tiny fists into eye sockets. She says, "Good morning."

"Attire," say I, "is one of the hallmarks of civilization."

She is yawning. "You should talk," she mentions in the middle of her yawn.

I am without bathrobe. I wonder where it might be. It is no doubt in the last room I was in, a conclusion that should (you'd think) simplify matters. No such luck. The short-term memory is not all it might be. I cast a glance down upon my nakedness and, judging from the spectacular belly, I'd bet dollars to doughnuts that I've just been in the kitchen. Doughnuts. Follow me, we'll have some doughnuts and milk.

You see the hallway with all the gold records on the wall? Platinum records as well, which means sales of multi mega-units. Platinum means shipping crates to the Dogons. There used to be more of these gold and platinum records, but one night Danny got especially drunk and frisbeed many of them into the ocean. Anyway, if we follow this hallway, we get to the kitchen. I think. Sometimes I voyage throughout the manse equipped with chart and sextant, but I'm pretty sure that this passage leads kitchenward. And here we are! You get the milk, I'll get the doughnuts. I hope you like jelly-filled. I hope you like rock-hard jelly-filled with one or two bites taken out of them.

"Hey, man, is this any better?"

The formerly sleeping girl has put on a pair of panties. They are almost invisible, I can see little curls of hair pressed like flowers in a high-school yearbook. Her small breasts are bouncing, because this formerly sleeping girl has become very animated.

"So," she asks, "do you have any coffee or what?"

Do I have coffee. I support the country of Colombia almost single-handedly. "Look in that cupboard," I say through a mouthful of doughnut.

She opens it, whistles through her teeth and announces,

"Coffee." The girl sets about preparing it.

"Make lots," I tell her. "I'm not supposed to have any."

"Okee-dokee."

Do you think she might be some sort of housekeeper? I've had them before, although they have tended to be much older and stouter creatures, Teutonic, more given to the wearing of clothing. The girl has freckles all over her body, little bits of sunlight.

"Where do you come from?" I ask.

"Toronto," is her curious response. "I told you that before."

"Toronto." I believe it's a planet in the Alpha Centauri galaxy. This makes sense, this seems to me the most logical explanation for her presence. She is not a house guest, she is a scientist from beyond the sun, conducting some sort of interplanetary survey. "Pretty cold up there," I add conversationally.

"You speak truth."

"Care for a doughnut, a staple of the Earth diet?"

"Ugh."

What terrible manners they have up on Toronto. All the more for me.

She has managed to get a percolator merrily bubbling on top of the stove. It is producing lovely polyrhythms. I never noticed that household appliances were so funky. I rush to the music room to grab a little tape recorder. While there, I decide to have a quick listen to the Whale Music. Listen, in the background, do you know what that is? It's the anguished bellow of a bull whose mate has been harpooned. The cow has been chopped up and stuffed into little perfume bottles. I wipe tears from my fat face. It is some time before I get back. The brewing machine has stopped, the girl is peacefully sipping coffee from a large mug.

"Do you know Mooky Saunders?" I demand.

She shrugs. "Sure. He plays on a lot of albums."

"Is he dead?"

"Why would he be dead?"

7

"It seems to me," I tell her, "that if you don't keep track of people, they die."

"He's not dead."

"I'm going to call him on the telephone. He must play the dolphins."

The girl nods, shrugs. "Coffee?"

"Yes, certainly, please. Sometimes, though, coffee makes me behave a tad oddly."

She fills up another mug. Her golden hair hangs down all the way to her tiny waist. "I just want to say, it was wonderful last night."

"Well, this is certainly good news," I tell her. "For the longest time I've been unable to . . ." Various phrases fill my mind, all of them spoken in Danny's voice (actually, the voice of his alter ego, Stud E. Baker, High Prince of the Greasy Geeks), things like *charm the one-eyed snake*. They all sound too strange, and I am at a loss for words until I remember a phrase from the divorce proceedings. "For the longest time," I begin again, "I've been unable to have intimate relations."

"Oh." The girl seems embarrassed, her entire body reddens slightly. "That's not what I meant. We . . . we didn't. I meant, it was wonderful when you played me the Whale Music."

"You liked the Whale Music?"

"It was fantastic. It was the best thing I've ever heard."

"Do you have whales on Toronto?"

"Er, no. I saw whales before, though, when I used to live on Galiano."

She gives me a cup of coffee. It is hot and sweet and I drain the mug in a few short moments. "May I please have more?"

"For sure."

"I'm glad you liked the music, because you are the farthest thing from a whale I could imagine. I was a little worried that it would appeal only to whales."

She giggles and has to sweep golden hair out of her face. "You say some pretty strange stuff."

The coffee has gotten me all jumpy, it has attached itself to some residual pharmaceutical mother lode. I leap about, I must do something. I must work on the Whale Music, which this strange creature from Toronto thinks is wonderful. "Do me a favour," I tell her. "See if I have a telephone. If I do, find Mooky Saunders. See if he does dolphins. Tell him he gets quadruple scale. I'm going to the music room. Can you do that for me — Um, what's your name?"

"Claire."

Ouch. I'm forced to drive my forefingers into my ears. I suffer from tinnitus, to put it mildly. Some clown with crash cymbals is stuck inside my head. I wait for the noise to go away, and remove my fingers with an audible pop. "Claire," I add conversationally, "is my mother's name."

"So you mentioned."

"Claire" was also the name of a song the father, Henry Howell, wrote. There's a recording of this, the artist a man named Beany Poacher. To call this tune bouncy would be like calling me fat, or my brother Danny dead.

> *Claire, the way the moonlight sparkles in your hair,*
> *The way my mind goes blank when you are there.*
> *What do I care that the world is not exactly fair?*
> *When you are there, fair's fair, my lovely Claire.*

Mind you, song-writing wasn't the father's only job. He was also a sales representative for a company called Universal Party Favors. They carried such standard items as plastic ice cubes with flies inside and whoopee cushions. They also had some rather inventive stock, for example an automatic card shuffler. I still have three or four of these devices, and it really is amazing how well they shuffle the deck, although about every five or six times they chew it up and spit out little pieces of cardboard. Henry Howell had a reputation as a hard seller, not that it did him much good. When the big item is rubberized doggy-do, the last thing you want to be is an obnoxious, pushy salesman, but this was the father's style. "You think this won't go?" he'd scream. "You think this won't be the single most *numero-uno* party joke throughout the nation? You, my friend, are sadly mistaken, you are living in a fantasy world!"

The father Henry Howell was a large man, stocky in his twenties and flat-out fat from then on. He had bland features that, given the right lighting, could pass as a kind of handsomeness. This I inherited from him. Danny got my mother's looks, hard and chiselled, dark and deep-set eyes, lips a bit oversized. My mother is, and my brother was, beautiful in an odd and unsettling way.

My mother's beauty was such that when Claire Graham was seventeen she found employment as a Kirby Sweater Gal. What she did was, she'd go to various department stores and model Kirby sweaters. My mother would stand among the mannequins. She'd push her small perfect breasts forward, a miler trying to break the ribbon. She'd lift her hands awkwardly, her fingers splayed in what she hoped was an elegant manner. And then my mother would freeze. Four hours on, half an hour for lunch, back to the stand until four-thirty in the afternoon.

One day the much older (thirty-four years to her seventeen) Hank Howell came blustering through the doorway of the department store she was working. The father no doubt had some hot item he wanted to pitch, for example gum that turned your mouth black. The father thought that mouth-blackening gum was the greatest thing since sliced bread —

and it is a good indication of the limits to his intelligence that he never thought to invent mouth-blackening bread, which has just occurred to me now. At any rate, the father went into the department store, took his place in the centre of the floor and cast his little eyes about for the mouth-blackening-gum purchaser. As the father did this, some portion of his mind noted the mannequin he was planted next to, and he reached out with his thick, horny hand and patted its bottom.

My mother loved to tell this story, she'd hoot or gurgle. (The hoot was her natural laugh, the gurgle a sophisticated little chuckle she's worked on over the years.) The father would come close to blushing and deny it. "I was just," he'd explain, "tapping the ashes of my cigarette." He never came up with the same lame story twice. "I was just," he might say, "feeling the material in that skirt."

Danny was always bewildered by the story of how our parents met. "I don't see why you'd pat the fanny of a dummy," he'd say to the father.

"Aw, I wasn't patting her fanny, Dan-Dan. My hand had gone numb and I was trying to beat the blood back into my fingertips."

The father got the blood beat back into his face, that's for sure, because the young Claire Graham produced an uppercut from somewhere near the floor and collapsed Hank Howell's nose. Blood spilled forth in biblical quantities. (I inherited the Howell beak, a snivelling little creature it is; any sign of danger and it starts bleeding profusely.) Claire Graham was instantly remorseful. She leapt off her pedestal and took the father's chubby face in her hands. "Tilt your head back," she told him, "and lie down." The father was too shaken to do anything but obey. After all, only a few seconds had elapsed since he'd absent-mindedly reached over and tapped the bottom of a department store dummy. Claire Graham wanted to keep a close eye on the damage she'd done, and the most expeditious way was by hiking her skirt and straddling the father's wide

11

chest. And then Claire began cooing. "There, there," she whispered, "don't be such a big baby." She was a great cooer.

The upshot of all this was, Claire Graham lost her job, Hank Howell unloaded his entire spring line and, more importantly, was inspired to one of his greatest near-misses.

Claire, missing you is more than I can bear.
When you're not with me I go on a tear
And everywhere that you're not there
Cannot compare to the lair of Claire!

You get the idea.

Sometimes I suspect that the father fell in love with my mother because it was easy to find rhymes for *Claire*.

The question is, why did Claire Graham fall in love with Hank Howell? My mother claims, after one or two lemon gins, that it was this very song that did the trick. I doubt it. I've tried the Routine countless times — indeed, it accounts for some of my biggest hits, "Sandra", "Mary Mary", "Kiss Me, Karen" — and not once has the subject ever fallen in love with me. The one woman who did love me — came close to loving me, at any rate closer than you might have thought possible — was always a little insulted by my inability to address a song to her, but to me the word *Fay* always sounded a touch whiny.

My mother was born too late, or perhaps it was her misfortune to have been born at all. Claire Graham should have existed in a fairy tale, one where frogs are princes. She was born into a world where frogs are frogs, this is perhaps why she fell in love with the father.

There is more to it. I have a theory that my mother fell victim to the father's virulent hucksterism. He spun lies of elaborate fancy, all of which had to do with money. Awesome amounts of the slime, great deserts full of greenbacks. "When a song hits big," was something my father said often — even now I hear it spoken in his voice, a sound like a rusty saw going through a wombat — "When a song hits big, you'll be sitting on Easy Street."

My mother wanted to sit on Easy Street. It has been suggested by these fraudulent doctors, by these wormy lawyers, by my ex-wife, *ha-ha, she should talk,* that my mother is a greedy, avaricious woman. They don't know her, they don't love her. My mother only ever wanted to sit her perfect bottom on Easy Street.

So the long and the short of it is, Claire forced herself to fall in love with the father. They married, and in a year I was born — six pounds, six ounces, about the same as my thumb weighs now — and a year after that came Danny.

Do you like earliest memories? Considering the state of my short-term retention, I find it amazing that I still possess an earliest memory, but here it is. We lived in a two-storey house on Whitman Avenue, in a town named Palomountain, California. Danny and I shared a room on the second floor (we shared this room until we were seventeen and sixteen, at which point we went *on the road*) and this one day my mother was dressing us up. It seems to me that as she did this my mother's eyes were filled with tears, but I can't be certain that this is part of the memory. My mother stood me on a chest of drawers and put me in a little blue suit, complete with jacket, vest and short pants. Then she set me on the ground and started working on Daniel. I was three years old, and it was certainly the first time in my life I had ever been well dressed. I immediately began to strut up and down the hallway outside our room. I was concentrating more on my style than my course, and what happened was, I tumbled down the stairs and crashed my head into the wall at the bottom. This split my head open — I still have a misshapen, rather lumpy brow — and also did something to my hearing. I suffer from tinnitus, a ringing in my ears (*ringing* might be putting too fine a point on it, it's the earwig equivalent of J. P. Sousa and the American Eagles), and part of my love for music, especially very loud music, is that it drowns out this strange sound inside my skull.

Danny's earliest memory, which he recounted on many occasions, is of climbing out of his crib and crawling slowly and painfully into the living room, where the parents were having a cocktail party. My mother confirms this, even though Danny was only ten months old at the time.

A fairly early memory goes like this. One day my mother brought home a recording, placed it on the little turntable. (I was colouring a picture of Captain America, *shizzam*. Danny was playing with a Dinky toy.) The record was made by a failed country-and-western yodeller who was trying his hand at something new. The record began like this:

> One, two, three o'clock, four o'clock rock!
> Five, six, seven o'clock, eight o'clock rock!
> Nine, ten, eleven o'clock, twelve o'clock rock!
> We're gonna rock around the clock tonight!

My mother stood with her back pressed against the living-room wall, for some reason short of breath. When the slap-bass began she wheeled into the centre of the rug, twirling about in an alarming fashion. Her skirt lifted until her underwear was plainly visible. Danny abandoned his toy truck and joined her, and those two danced (I stared at them) until the father descended from the den upstairs and broke the record over his knee. "Twaddle!" shouted the father. "That stuff will never sell. It's got no *schnooze!*"

Don't even ask about this schnooze business. That's just the way the father viewed music. It either had schnooze or it didn't. Most of my stuff, according to the father, lacked schnooze in a big way.

Bill Haley has been called the father of rock and roll, and while that may not be true, he certainly got things going for us chubby white boys.

Danny and I met Bill Haley, you know. This was some time in the seventies. We were in Mexico, I forget why, but we were in a motel on the dark edge of a town, and all of a sudden Danny remembered that this is where Bill Haley lived. Danny was flying pretty high, whiskey and cocaine, a nice little combo if you care to feed your soul to intergalactic vultures. Danny got it into his mind that we must go visit Bill Haley. Dan's then-girlfriend was about fourteen. She shrugged, assuming, I think, that Bill Haley was simply an old friend. I didn't want to go, of course, it must have taken all of Danny's persuasive powers to get me to Mexico in the first place, but Danny prepared some pharmaceutical concoction that encouraged socializing, and I agreed. (A recipe: cocaine, cocaine, the garrulous drug, a little mescaline to fill the night with portent, alcohol to heat my Celtic blood, to make me feel like boozing with the gobbers at the nobby. Danny and I shared a very alchemical attitude towards intoxicants.) The four of us — I had a girl with me, back then I wasn't half so fat, and there was a rumour going about to the effect that I was a genius, which some women find attractive — piled into the rented Jeep and drove into the heart of this desert town.

Bill Haley answered the door dressed in his old cowboy yodelling clothes, a ten-gallon hat and sequined shirt. He was paunchy, the last few pearl buttons were popped open, and his belly shone in the gloom of his bungalow.

"Howdy!" Haley said. He still had the little kiss curl plastered onto his forehead. Bill Haley was blind in one eye, and that eye was cocked at nothing in particular. The good one was bloodshot and pointed at us.

Danny told him who we were, but I don't think it meant anything to Haley. It meant something to him that we had women with us. He grinned. He still had that famous grin, like he was trying to hook the edge of his mouth over his ear. "Come on in, pardners," he said. "Do you want something to drink?"

"That's what we're here for," said Danny.

"Do you know George Jones?" demanded Haley suddenly, stopping on his way to the little coffee table that held his bottles of liquor.

"The cowboy guy, George Jones?" asked Danny.

"Yeah. That fuck."

Danny nodded. "Sure."

"You know that song of his, 'She Thinks I Still Care'?"

Danny nodded, I believe his then-girlfriend even hummed a few bars.

"Well, listen to this here." Haley stumbled over to a little hi-fi. Danny, who hadn't had a drink in several minutes and was going through withdrawal, stumbled over to the coffee table and helped himself to the mescal. There was a little worm in the bottom of the bottle. Haley put on a forty-five and bounced the needle into the grooves. "There!" he shouted as very strange stuff started coming out of the tiny speakers. "What do you think of that shit?"

"What is it?" asked Danny. He was chewing on the worm now.

"That is me singing that song in fucking *Spanish!* It's going to be a fucking hit!"

Danny nodded, listened to the song for a while. "Good feel," he announced.

"Yes," I agreed. At least, it seemed as though the band had come to a consensus regarding liquor and/or drug intake, and whatever downer they were on, they were on it each and every one.

"Spanish people have feelings, too," announced Haley.

"Absolutely," said Danny.

"I'm going back on the road," Bill Haley told us. He put his arm around Danny's girlfriend. "I'm going back to England. I'm still tops there. Biggest thing that ever hit." Haley let his hand fall onto the girl's chest. "There's only one little problem, man. Rudi is *el morto.*"

"Rudi Pompilli?" I asked. That was the Comets' sax-player, the little guy who wore glasses.

"That's the cat, Jack." Haley took off his cowboy hat and covered his heart ceremoniously. "Chewed up by the Big C, man. And the babe never even smoked or drank or did nothing. His funeral is today, up in Chester, you know, but I said like fuck it. Fuck *it*. Because, I have got better things to do. Like, getting back into this yodelling. I could have been one of the great yodellers of all time, dig, but then this rock'n'roll stuff happened and I got side-tracked. Listen." Bill Haley began to yodel, and he was good at it, but being a good yodeller is, I think, a little like being a good mass murderer. Haley yodelled the name Rudi over and over again.

I've overdone it on the coffee. My fingers are shaking so much that they miss the keys. Black clam notes tumble into the Whale Music like leaves and twigs into a pool. This is not good. To calm myself I need, for example, a Librium. Not that I have any. If a doctor in California prescribes so much as an Aspirin to Des Howl, I believe they snatch away his licence, no questions asked. Or perhaps I could do a toke or two. I seem like the kind of guy who'd have some grass or hash, don't I? It's just a matter of finding it.

Now, if I was me, where would I hide drugs? Taped to the underside of the toilet tank lid? Hidden in a dirty sock? In hollowed-out books? None of this sounds like me. A guy like me would leave his dope *lying around*. Probably, and this is just a wild guess, lying around on something like the living-room table.

North by northwest, into the living room, and on the table we find a little plastic bag full of twiggery and tiny lumbers. A smell of peatmoss, bogs, the scent of Lithuanian swampland. I *am* a genius. Now comes the hard part. Papers. My dope I would leave out in the open, I've proven this, but a fellow like me would hide his rolling papers so that he could never find them. Absolutely. I'd toss them into a kitchen drawer, bury them under a pile of salad forks and egg beaters.

An easterly furtherance, down the gold and platinum record hallway, into the kitchen.

There's the alien Claire, preparing something that looks like food. "Hello, Claire."

"Do you like pasta?"

This of a man who nauseates other gluttons. I ignore the question, intent on my quest. I select the biggest kitchen drawer, haul it open.

"I'll just make a big pot anyway. If you don't want to eat any, that's okay."

Salad forks, egg beaters, plastic spatulas — Fay liked a well-equipped kitchen, it gave the illusion that she could cook — and three or four automatic card shufflers. This is really a handy little device, quite the best unit that the father ever fobbed off on the public. Allow me to demonstrate. We take a deck of cards — in this case, a mixture of Tarot and Swedish nudies — we open up this little slot here . . . and out tumbles a pack of cigarette rolling papers. This machine works even better than I thought.

Towards Orion, back into the living room. I take a paper, toss in a few seeds and twigs, and even with my fat fingers I manage to roll a number. I stick it into my mouth and I fire up the joint. Ah. I think this is good stuff. It's hard for me to tell, what with the way the old brain operates even on standard mode. But my fingertips have ceased twitching, always a good sign. I have become mellow, if not a total dullard. I don't think I can work on the Whale Music now, unless I come up with something peppy. A little nose-candy, perhaps, or a yellow-jacket, even some booze. I am not supposed to drink, of course. Many people and doctors have told me this. I even was in a hospital where everyone from the chief administrator to the janitor kept telling me I shouldn't drink, but I say, what harm can one little sip do?

Claire comes into the living room. She is still dressed only in her panties, that appears to be her outfit, but I have grown used to it. Her belly-button reminds me for some reason of a sandbox. She holds a plate of spaghetti noodles, jumps cross-legged onto the couch, zaps the television on with the remote and begins to eat. "Plenty left, Big Guy," she says with her mouth full.

"You know what goes good with pasta?" I ask craftily. "Wine."

She nods. "You speak truth."

"Why don't you go get some wine?"

"What, like at a store?"

"A store. A liquor store. Like the one on the corner."

"Maybe you could go?" She gesticulates at her nudity. "I don't feel like getting dressed."

There are several things wrong with that plan. One, my bathrobe is not exactly street-wear, either. Two, I simply don't go outside, certainly not into the *world*, although I do flop into the pool from time to time. Three, there isn't a liquor store owner in the state who would sell me a bottle of wine, and when you consider the morality of your average liquor store owner, that's going some. I inform Claire of points number one and two.

"Well, okay. Just wait till I finish this."

Hot-diggity-dog.

So I join Claire on the sofa to watch television while she eats. Actually, her spaghetti looks pretty good. I think I'll trundle on down the hallway here, bearing by the Pleiades. Look, there's the album *Grin*, my erstwhile masterwork, a mere fribble in comparison to the Whale Music, but all right in its way. And here's a single, what is it, oh, "Kiss Me, Karen", that famous song that got everyone in the United States laid except me. You people have a lot to thank me for. When you were thirteen and getting either (a) tiny tumescent bulges or (b) budding breasts pressed into you, I bet you never even gave a thought to the pudgy seventeen-year-old who wrote the song you were dancing to. Did you know that he existed in shadowed hotel rooms? Did you know that he was already baffled and perplexed? Nothing like I am now, of course. For instance, here I am in the gold and platinum hallway, and I have no idea why. I'm pointed in this direction, so let me bravely barge on ahead. Aha! The kitchen! I must have been hungry (that's an easy bet) so I grab a box of jelly-filleds. Now what? Listen. A faint sound. People talking with music in the background. You know what that is, don't you? Television. If you start to talk and you hear music in the background, you're likely on television. The television is in the living room, unless I redecorated — one time I tossed the machine into the pool — so it's back down the gold and platinum hallway and . . . ah! The alien Claire. Freckled nose and breasts. She reminds me of the roller-coaster on Coney Island. I sit down beside her and aim my eyes at the television, eager to discover what is going on out there in the real world.

"Good," I say, nodding at the screen. "You're watching 'Love Mountain', my favourite."

I'm pleased to see that not much new has happened in the real world. It's true that the program only informs me about the town of Love Mountain, Colorado, but if there was widespread annihilation or nuclear holocaust, Peter Mandrake, Cindy Winston, Kingsley Charlesworth and all those, they'd mention it, wouldn't they? Today Kingsley Charlesworth seems to be blackmailing Cindy about something. I am not sure what, but this is all right, Cindy seems unclear herself and even Kingsley is vague. Claire emits a series of small barks, what they must use for laughter in her neck of the galactic woods.

Claire is through her spaghetti. She pulls on a pair of bluejeans and a very strange blue sweatshirt with a big leaf on it. The Toronto Maple Leafs, her sweatshirt announces. Claire is number twenty-one of the Toronto Maple Leafs. "So . . ." Claire does a little patty-cake on her thighs. "You got any money?"

I knew there'd be a catch. I'm fabulously wealthy, but that doesn't necessarily mean that I can lay my hands on any actual money. "Well," I say, "take a look around. Check up in my bedroom."

"Okee-dokee." Claire flies up the stairs. They must be very energetic on Toronto. I watch Peter Mandrake. The man is a swine, he doesn't deserve the love of a woman so pure as Gail Gaynor, but that's the way things work out there in the real world. Besides, he is not so big a swine as Farley O'Keefe.

Claire is back. "I found about three thousand dollars."

"Buy *two* bottles of wine. And, um . . . say, do you like whiskey?"

Claire shrugs. "It's okay."

"Then by all means buy a magnum! Buy a jeroboam! Buy anything else you want. Buy more doughnuts, these are slightly stale. Buy me some cheeseburgers. Buy me a penny-whistle that can play in B-flat. Buy yourself some Earth clothes, number twenty-one. Buy some floppy disks for my computer. Buy an automatic card shuffler, what wonderful machines they are. Buy me a telephone—"

. Claire interrupts. "You got a telephone. It was just unplugged."

"Of course it was unplugged. What good would it be if it wasn't unplugged? And buy me a Mars bar."

Claire is giggling again, which has the effect of making her long golden hair dance. It is a very lovely sound, Claire's giggling, and gives me an idea. I stand up, flee into the music room. For this I must power-on the Yamaha 666, which I do with great trepidation. The Yamaha 666 is so advanced a keyboard that even Stevie Wonder and I have problems with it. I call it the Beast. Once I get it juiced-up it screams, the Beast

21

must be fed a handful of microchips and talked to softly. Finally it quiets. I start to combine frequencies and after some trial and error approximate the sound of Claire's giggling. I fly into the percussion booth and paint background, a dreary, sludging rhythm, monotonous whoppings on a marching bass drum. This is going well. It needs something, though, it needs a *trumpet,* which fortunately I know how to play. I lick my lips clean of icing sugar and blow. A melody pops out into the air, and it wants to be wrapped in soft chord structure. Back to the Yamaha 666. The readjustments make it howl, but then it is tamed, I am coaxing out soft major sevenths. Major sevenths make the bottoms of my feet itch, this is why I love them so much. This is good, this is a ballad, this needs words! I bolt into the control room, create about a baseball stadium's worth of echo, and then it's into the vocal booth. I put on the headphones and begin to sing. *"Claire, the way the sunlight bounces in your hair . . ."*

At one point I decide to take a refreshing dip in the pool. It is night, the sky is spotted with starlight. I look up for a long time searching for Claire's home.

I wonder if the world of Toronto evolved in a sensible way It's inconceivable that all planets are like this place. Sometime my confusion is such that my tummy will twist like a pretze my brain will grow fur and burrow into the dirt. I must accep some responsibility — I overindulged on the pharmaceutica front, I drank deeply of the rotgut of life — but I really don think it's all my fault. The randomness of our world mind-boggling. In my case the boggle is audible, I walk aroun with a ringing in my ears, a warning bell, a siren, *mayda mayday.*

This love business, for example, is prickly as a porcupin Even Babboo Nass Fazoo backed away from that subject. H bandied the word about quite a bit, plucking a flower, waftir it beneath the shrivelled mushroom he used for a nose, proud

22

exclaiming in that squeaky little voice of his, "Now, I am luffink diz floor, but is de floor luffink me?" I've come to my own conclusions. My mother didn't fall in love with my father, she fell in love with his P. T. Barnumisms. My father fell in love with a mannequin. My brother Danny fell in love with hundreds of women, all of whom took some piece of his heart away when they left. I fell in love with Fay, who went through life like a bowling ball.

Bowling was the one thing, as a youngster, that I could do better than my brother Daniel. If you could have seen the ten-year-old Desmond, you would understand. I was a born bowler. I was shaped like an avocado, which gave me the requisite centre of gravity. My arms were segmented with baby fat, giving me some strength and shock absorption for the joints. The feet, flat and wide, lent me stability and balance. And, most important, there was the dullness of the activity. How perfect.

Danny was good, though, powerful and keen-eyed. His delivery was flamboyant where mine was workmanlike. Dan-Dan threw the balls with a huge left-handed hook that often threatened to topple them into the gutters. But they would always at the last moment break away from that edge, catch that one-pin and send it reeling backwards.

Dan-Dan shot more strikes than I did, but he lacked finesse. I picked up more spares. And Dan-Dan went for the seven-ten splits.

Do you bowl? Do you know what I'm talking about? The deadly seven-ten split, where the corner pins are left standing on each side of the lane. Most people do what I did, take out one or the other with a slow, easy mow. Danny would attempt to catch the ten just to its right, to send it flying across the wood and into the seven.

It was next to impossible. He never made it.

God, I loved my brother Danny.

23

The father decided that Danny and I needed music lessons, and we started out on the accordion — or, as Danny called it, the titty-tickler. The father thought the accordion was a wonderful instrument, redolent of schnooze, and I have to admit it's got a lot going for it. It's not particularly hip (except if you wander away outside with the thing, playing a sort of jazz that would bewilder Ornette Coleman) and the number of accordion groupies worldwide is probably only about seven, and an ugly, dwarfish assortment they are. Still, it teaches one a lot about music, the accordion does, what with the right hand learning how to work a keyboard, the left hand busy as a beaver on those mystery buttons. Actually, you know, the buttons produce chords, so right there you have lead and rhythm, and the accordion is a handy thing to write songs on. Also, on *A World of Heaven* (two and half mill worldwide, they listened to that one in Paso de los Toros) there is an accordion solo. But here's a secret: that's not me playing, like everyone assumes. That's Danny.

Our teacher was an old man named Hermann Gerhardt. Danny identified him as an escaped war criminal and accused him of various atrocities including eating dead babies, but basically Dan was very fond of the guy. Hermann Gerhardt was slightly humpbacked and wore his trousers pulled up to just below the nipples. He had spectacles, but one of the lenses was blackened. Sometimes the glasses would slip over the bumps of his nose and we could see a yellow eye floating there, wet and fishlike.

We were very good students, Danny and I. Myself, let's not make too big a point of it, I was by way of being a child prodigy. Music simply became my language, probably because whenever I attempted to communicate in my mother tongue the father would make me feel like I'd said something stupid.

I practised constantly, sitting on my bed and drawing out all those lush Italian melodies. It didn't take long before I'd figured out the system of music, how sensible and mathematical it all was. People claim that I can play any musical instrument (which isn't true, I can't play the saxophone, is Mooky Saunders dead or what?) but once you've glommed on to what's happening, it's a simple matter to reason out how any particular fretboard or twisted piece of tubing works. A piano keyboard is, to me, a beautiful thing, the doorway to an orderly and rational universe. I can slip through when baffled by this sorry world we live in.

Danny never spotted the doorway. He was always more than happy to jump into whatever shitpiles littered his path. But he was an excellent accordion player, and here's the reason — more than almost any other musical instrument, the accordion is a *machine*. It's a contraption. It has to be pumped, the mystery buttons have to be depressed, and it's only as a sort of afterthought that your fingers stumble up and down the keyboard and force out schnoozy melodies. Danny figured out the mechanics of the accordion, but was forever baffled by the mechanics of music. Still, he was Hermann Gerhardt's pride and joy, even when, at his first recital, Danny pretended that every in-squeeze of the bellows was pinching his nipple. Dan didn't allow the music to be interfered with, but over and over again he would screw up his face and silently howl with pain. The audience, four or five sets of parents, stirred nervously in their fold-up chairs. I watched Mr. Gerhardt. He was laughing so hard that tears came even from his yellow, fishlike blind eye.

Of course, the father was very excited that he'd produced a

musical genius (Danny, that is — the father thought I was no more than competent) and he forced Danny to practise all the time. Danny's chief interest in those days, however, was the Los Angeles Dodgers, recently transplanted from distant Brooklyn, and between that and my father's badgering he lost all interest in the accordion. That was the first bad blood between those two. I tried to cheer my father up by practising very hard and achieving a level of excellence on the accordion, but he was not to be cheered. He didn't even notice when I played a piece called "My Dad," one I'd written especially for him. Granted, the melody was rather derivative, and the tune likely sounded like any one of a thousand schnoozy ditties, but all the father did was note in a disinterested way that my left hand was getting lazy. My mother liked the tune, it set her to dancing in the living room, so I changed the title to "My Mom" and never played it again.

Danny became a very good minor-league baseball player, the captain of his team of nine-year-olds, the winners of regional championships. The father decided that he'd sired another Ty Cobb. He bought himself an oversized glove and demanded that he and Danny spend long hours practising hitting and put-outs. Dan-Dan soon realized that practice with a fat and clumsy man could only erode his skills. Daniel abandoned baseball altogether.

So I decided to become a good baseball player. Danny decided to become a hoodlum. I never achieved my goal. In my entire little-league career I had only one at-bat, the coach putting me in out of desperation, and although I did manage to get on base (hit by pitch), I was lifted in favour of a pinch-runner. Danny, on the other hand, became a very good little hoodlum.

Danny discovered the great love of his life, speed. Not the pharmaceutical variety (although he was to develop a powerful fondness for that), but velocity and fleetness. Our home town of Palomountain nestled in some pretty ambitious foothills, the streets went up and down like a roller-coaster, and Danny took to finding anything with wheels and hurtling down the declines. When his rusty bicycle proved unworthy of the exercise he stole better ones, when he got bored with that he helped himself to go-carts and soap-box jalopies, and when that was no longer boiling his blood he got extremely ambitious and stole a car. That was when he was thirteen years old, and, although he tried to look older by donning sunglasses and smoking cigarettes, the local police soon became aware that a small child was bombing around town in a great big black Studebaker, and they shut him down.

Danny had to go to reform school for a year.

That was kind of a watershed year for the Howell family.

Let's review the pristine American upbringing, let's look at this childhood painted by Normie Rockwell. Here we see the Howells at dinner: the father, the mother, Danny and Desmond. What are they eating? No one knows. It was cooked by the mother, and she has the best insight, but she identifies all of her dishes with a kind of crippled continental French that the boys have long since given up trying to decipher. The father doesn't care what it is. The father eats with fork and spoon. Apparently he never mastered the knife, the knife is beyond him, the whole concept of knife goes over the father's flat, brush-cutted head.

Daniel picks at the meal. Desmond devours with gusto.

"This is good," Danny offers. "It tastes like in a restaurant."

Mother looks up dreamily. She names the dish. We are baffled.

"It is good," I say. "I'm having seconds."

"Hey, Dezzy-do," says the father. "You're turning into a real porker."

"He's big-boned," says my mother quietly.

" 'Sides," offers Dan, turning towards the father, "he's not as fat as you."

"Put a lock on it."

"Henry," says my mother, and that single word snaps the

27

father's head up. "What's happening with Jimmy Cohn?"

Cohn being one of many weasel-like men that my father had music-related business with.

"That guy," snarls the father. "He wouldn't know a smash hit number one socko boff if it came up and kissed his ass."

"Please. *Les enfants.*"

"I'm just saying."

"I think you should talk to this Maurice Mantle," says my mother.

"Maurice Mantle is chicken-shit. I want someone with know-how and savvy, baby, because when I hit, I'm hitting *big.*"

"Perhaps," suggests my mother, who has yet to see any evidence of the father hitting in any manner at all, "you should talk to Maurice."

"*Maurice,*" mocks the father. "I don't need him. When I hit, baby . . ."

"I'm hitting big," says Danny. Danny scrunches up his face. "So we hoid."

The father bristles, but finally allows a chuckle for his cocky son. My mother laughs gently, rubs his hair. I laugh, too, overjoyed.

It was hard when Danny went away to reform school.

Mother cried so much that I thought she might dry up and blow away like dust. The father sat in his study, the door closed, everything silent within. The one thing I remember him saying was — and wait, let's set the scene, because it's important to realize that the father had no logical reason to make this pronouncement, it wasn't a response to anything, he merely opened the door to his study one day and proclaimed — "My sons. What disappointments."

I decided to become one. That is, I did this to the best of my ability, but as things turned out, I was a failure even at becoming a major disappointment. I took my accordion, my trumpet, my English horn and my violin to a pawnshop and traded them in for an electric organ, one of those whiny little Farfisas that sound like a systematic arrangement of bee farts. I also purchased a small amplifier, one with a cracked speaker (so that squawking and howling was the best one could hope for), and I set up in the basement and began the most ungodly sort of racket.

The father was down in the basement within minutes, his face ashen. The composer of "Vivian in Velvet" was aghast. "Where's the schnooze?" he demanded.

"There is no schnooze!" I hollered above the music.

"You'll break your mother's heart!"

"Not likely!"

"You'll break my heart!"

"Now we're getting somewhere!"

"I got one son who's a criminal and another who's a musical maniac!"

I liked the description. I laughed ghoulishly, stabbed at an eleventh chord that I knew would sting the father right between the ears, make him feel like throwing up. "Stop!" he screamed.

"Do you want to hear the lyrics, Daddy?"

"Lyrics?" His hair was standing on end.

"Absolutely!"

"How could such a thing have lyrics?"

"Bam-diddle-oom-pow, she's my little pom-pom girl!"

"Aaagh!" The father covered his ears, doubled over.

"She's got big pom-poms, she knows how to bam-diddle-oom-pow!"

"Desmond, stop this!"

"I'm going to take her pom-poms, throw them all over this football field!"

Unnecessary cruelty? Perhaps. The father fled the basement, locked himself in his study. I didn't keep up the music for much longer, because I didn't care for it myself. I turned the volume down low, so that the father couldn't hear it upstairs, and began to play some soothing major seventh chords.

The father, the father, the great unruly man. He should have existed in a rainforest, before the recording of time. He could have gobbled up lizards, spilled his seed willy-nilly, covered the earth with dull-witted progeny. And they would have ruled the world, kings and queens all.

Danny came home after a year in reform school, and it made me sad because we had grown very far apart. He had taken to wearing T-shirts and bluejeans, his feet decked out in shiny pointed shoes. In a desperate attempt to make friends at high school I was wearing Pendletons, clam diggers and Hush Puppies. I was working hard at my music — at least, that's all I ever did. Danny was still obsessed with speed and machines, *cars* to put it simply, and his hobby was rebuilding old wrecks even though he wasn't old enough to legally drive them. He'd spend hours on their engines and bodies, and then he'd cruise them stealthily onto an old dirt track near our house, and he'd bomb around until the cars either gave up the ghost or were driven into trees.

One day when I came home from school I saw Danny out in the driveway underneath one of his old coupés. Danny was always preceding me home from school, which leads me to believe that he was not in fact attending. Anyway, he couldn't see me as he worked on the chassis, and I was surprised to hear him singing. He was singing a popular song of the time, I think it was "Teen Angel," and his recently changed voice was a very sweet and pretty one. Without thinking I joined in, adding a high harmony, and Danny scooted out from underneath the car with a big grin on his face. We finished the song, even locked our arms around each other's shoulders to add pathos. Then Danny laughed, gave me a little punch to the belly.

"Do you want to come down into the basement?" I asked. "We could sing some more songs."

Danny thought about it, but finally he shook his grease-spotted head, waved a monkey wrench in the air. "Nope. I got to work on this beast. It needs more torque."

"Torque?"

"Torque."

The strange-sounding word started bouncing inside my head. "Go like this," I said urgently. "*Torque torque. Torque torque.*" I gave Danny a note, jabbed in the air to set him on a rhythm. Danny made a rude sound, but I was insistent, and my brother finally started doing it, quietly at first and then with more power. "*Torque torque. Torque torque.*"

I falsettoed away up high, the better to swoop down on the melody like an eagle. "*The beast needs more torque!*" I sang. "*The beast needs more torque.*" I waved my brother up to another note, and he adjusted. "*I gotta uncork the cork, because the beast needs more torque!*" Up to the fifth, an idiot could see it coming. "*The pig needs more pork,*" I shouted, "*and the beast needs more torque!*" We laughed, Danny and I, and then we flew down to the basement. The Farfisa spat out the raunchy chords like that was what it had been waiting to do: Danny grabbed a tambourine, and without thinking he began to sing the melody, and I took over the undercurrent, "*Torque torque. Torque torque.*" The song was written in seven minutes, but we spent about four hours singing it over and over again.

We were finally summoned up to dinner. The father scowled at us and picked away at his *poule grappé*. He looked sad and distant, lonely in a strange world. My mother was very animated, though, and as she served us our food she sang softly under her breath, "*The beast needs more torque . . .*"

I have decided that I must go to bed. Not a radical bed-going, mind you, just a simple clocking of zee-time in order to rise refreshed and rosy-cheeked. This is a real step forward for me, mental-health-wise, and I *should* call Dr. Tockette and make him aware of this achievement. No way in hell I'd do such a thing, but it's a positive sign that for a fleeting moment I considered initiating discourse with the quack.

I have finished recording the song "Claire". I don't know how long it took, but I do know that my belly has lost some of its size and toning. My eyes are screaming eaglet arseholes, I have developed a pungency that only a long period without dips in the pool can produce. Speaking of which, I think I'll go for one now. Let me see how big a splash I can make.

Ah, here is Claire herself, sunbathing beside the pool. She is asleep. Talk about your restful slumber, this is napping in Connecticut, dozing by the fire while Aunt Dorothy makes plum pudding. This girl makes the oddest sounds when she sleeps, it's like her nose, mouth and throat decide to party down while she's flaked out, they sputter and whistle and make noises like tiny pink engines. Needless to say, Claire is currently naked. They have scant truck with clothes up on chilly Toronto, which is a bit surprising. Claire is lying on her stomach. I wonder if she realizes that her bottom is turning red as a lobster. This is going to be very painful for the creature. Beside her lies a tube of ointment, and I decide that I will add some to this sensitive area. I make a dab in one palm, rub my fleshy hams together and then gingerly press down on Claire's body.

"*Aaeeyah!*" There is a sudden bolt of awful electricity, and Claire is on her feet, staring at me, her hands twisted and clawlike. "What the fuck are you doing?"

I show her my greasy palms. You have to careful when you have an interplanetary house guest, you never know when you're going to offend some ethnocentricity. "Your bottom was getting burned, number twenty-one. I thought it would hurt you." I clamber to my feet, not feeling particularly well. "I have decided to go to bed. A great leap for mankind. I'm sorry I scared you."

"Where I come from you don't just go around latching on to someone's arse-end."

There, you see? How was I to know? I turn and lumber away. I wander down to the barbed-wire fence, I press my forehead against the metal, dig it into my fat face. Below me is the ocean. I hope I will see some whales. Baleen, humpbacked or sperm, it makes no difference. I am composing music for them, you know. When I finish the music, I will set up speakers, hundreds of them, I will play the music for the whales. They will gather beneath my house, they will nestle comfortably in the sea and smile upwards.

Claire is beside me. She has put on a terry-cloth robe. We watch the water. It is rough, tempestuous. Men will be lost at sea today, their widows will evermore wear weeds.

"I don't like being touched," Claire tells me. "I was touched a lot, for a long time, and now I don't like it."

"I don't like touching."

"I didn't mean to scream at you."

"Oh, think nothing of it. I've been screamed at many times. Fay was a great one for screaming at me."

"That your wife?"

"My used-to-be wife."

"Your ex."

"Ex, why and zee."

"How long were you married?"

"Many, many years. More than I care to remember. Or am capable of, for all that."

"Why'd you bust up?"

Now, to make matters truly nauseating, we have the daily Memory Matinee. See Desmond come home unexpectedly. See him mount the stairs, eager for the embrace of his life-mate. See him open the bedroom door. See . . . *agh*.

Fay, you know, was born too late. As are we all. Fay should have existed during the French Revolution. She would not have been bored. She could have led small peasant insurrections. She'd cheer dizzily as the heads rolled off the aristocrats, her ample bosom heaving. In that time of mayhem, there would have been wanton copulation.

"So what have you been up to, dude?" Claire is trying to be cheery, she even taps my flabby arm with a small set of freckled knuckles. "You been working away?"

"I've been working."

"On the *Whale Music*?"

"No. No, I've neglected the *Whale Music*. I'm going to go work on that now."

"Don't you think you maybe ought to go to bed?"

"If you have any questions on human behaviour — although I myself am stymied much of the time — feel free to ask."

"Huh?"

I wander into the living room. Wait. My fairy godmother has been here. Look on the table, what do you see? A bottle of whiskey. When brain cells fall out, you leave them under your pillow, and in the morning there will be a bottle of booze there. I unscrew the top, look around cannily (force of habit, I instinctively search for the despicable ex-footballer Farley O'Keefe), and send a shot downwards.

I blast back into the music room, retro-rocket into the control booth, power-on all my computers and machines. "Desmond to Earth, Desmond to Earth," I mutter into a squalling microphone. Apparently there is something evil up on the planet Toronto in the Alpha Centauri galaxy. I drink more whiskey. And now, the *Whale Music*. Yes! I must dance to the *Whale Music*. I must leap into the vocal booth and sing along, the "Song of Flight" and of "Danger". You know what this needs, don't you? A sax, absolutely, a sax to crackle like dolphins in the never-ending sun, a sax to rip life through the heavy water.

If Dan-Dan were here, he could play the sax. That was a

34

musical machine that he learnt to work, maybe not particularly well, but Danny could certainly play the dolphins.

It is not a good idea to reflect on my brother and consume whiskey.

It seems to me that I recently had some intention of going to bed. What a noble intention that was, wouldn't Dr. Tockette have been pleased. Now I'm going to sleep, but unfortunately getting to bed is more or less out of the question.

Oh, dreamtime. Peachy. There's nothing I like better than these little features. My mind has hired a really shlocky director, some asshole who affects a monocle and talks with a thick Brooklyn accent. He favours gratuitous nudity, graphic violence. Today the boor has decided to redo the death scene. "Okay, okay," he shouts at his underlings. "Light the car!" A silver Porsche is illuminated. My brother Daniel sits behind the wheel. Danny looks good, bright-eyed, rosy-cheeked. Women crowd the side of the road, fawning. A few faint. Slowly Danny depresses the accelerator. The Porsche rolls forward a few feet. "Cut!" yells Cecil B. "Good stuff, Dan-Dan!" Daniel climbs out of the car, goes over to stand with his adoring female public. "Stand-in!" shouts the director.

Stud E. Baker leaps forward. "Rock and roll!" he shouts, gyrating his pelvis. The outline of a thick monkey-dong causes much giggling along the sidelines. Stud E. Baker removes his Confederate Army cap for a brief moment of solemnity. "If I don't pull this off," he announces, "and I don't see how the fuck I *could*, I just want you all to know that it's been a gas."

"Stop!" That's me shouting. I am invited to my own nightmares, after all. "Don't do it!"

"Forgive me, Desmond."

I am silent.

"Okee-fedoke." Stud E. Baker climbs into the silver Porsche. He places his snakeskin boot on the gas pedal, works the revs up. "Quality machine," he announces. Stud places his right hand on the stick-shift. "It's one for the money!" he sings.

"Two for the show," I mumble.

"Three to get ready," chorus the scantily clad beauties along the roadway.

"And go, cats, go!" Stud E. Baker throws the machine into gear, the teeth bite with fury, a lion clamping its maw around the flank of a gazelle. He runs through second, third, fourth, within seconds he has the Porsche in overdrive. And then Stud E. Baker turns the wheel softly to the right. Through the guardrail. For long silent moments the silver car flies above the Pacific. The Porsche hits the water with a surprisingly soft sound. A moment later comes the explosion.

The whales surface cautiously, curious looks in their large sad eyes.

"*Fawk.*"

I sense a presence in the room. Moreover, I sense a shoe in my tummy.

"What is with you, Desmerelda?"

In my state it would be a mug's game to play along with every apparition that happened by. I decide to ignore this one, which is huge and black.

"You have accumulated some avoirdupois there, baby. You be doing me quite a favour if you would get un-nekkid."

Pretty pushy for a drug- and liquor-produced figment, wouldn't you say?

"Well, if I get quadruple scale for watching you lie curled up on the floor, I say fine by me. But I want to see the money."

Hallucinations have unionized. What is this world coming to? Before long we'll be as badly off as that ghastly planet that hurt something within the alien Claire.

"Fawk." The fabrication disappears into a shadow. I tumble briefly back to never-never-land (I don't sleep, I collapse into these bread-pudding comas, as restful as cattle-drives) until a reveille is sounded on a saxophone, the thirds all pulled bluesily flat. I leap to my feet and peer into the darkness. "You can play the sax?"

"Desmerelda, whom do you think it is?"

"I need a saxophonist."

"So the lady said."

"I was going to hire Mooky Saunders, but he's dead."

"The hell I am."

"You've returned from beyond the grave?"

"Des-baby, let's start at the beginning. Hey, Des, it's Mooky. The lady told me you needed a sax. She called me on the telephone. I am not dead, Des. I never felt better. Okay? Now, see if you can pick up that ball and run with it."

"Mooky!"

"Touchdown."

I pull on my bathrobe. I shake Mooky's hand, which is enormous, nails as big as playing cards. "It's good to see you."

"Quite the set-up you got." Mooky wanders around, touching all my equipment gently. "Quite the play-pen."

"I've been working on Whale Music."

"W-h-a-l-e or w-a-i-l?"

"And I need you to do dolphins."

"Dolphins. Fawk. I thought the lady asked could I do 'Dolphy.' "

I play Mooky what I've done so far. He tilts his head, his long fingers stroke the air. When it's through he grins at me. "You crazy."

"Can you hear the dolphins? They leap through the waves, five or six abreast."

"I can hear them motherfuckers."

"Soprano?"

"Absolutely, Desmond. Them is some soprano dolphins."

"It's in the key of F, Mook."

"Could have fooled me, Desmerelda. But if you say so."

Claire comes into the music room. She is trepidatious, she sets her feet down tentatively. Mooky is warming up, lines of music scoot around the padded walls. Claire comes into the control booth, where I am busy capturing sounds. "Hey," she says.

"Hello, number. twenty-one."

"Are you hungry, Des?"

"Probably. But I've got no time to eat. We're doing the dolphins."

"Oh, yeah." She watches Mooky through the plate of glass. "He sure is big."

"Echo!" I fire up a reverb unit, the sound opens, the music bubbles up from the bowels of the earth.

"Guess what?" asks Claire. "My butt is raw. I can hardly sit down."

"I guess you're just not used to the sun. Our planet is only three stones away, you know, perhaps a tad too close for comfort."

"You want me to split?"

"No."

"I just thought that maybe you figured that me and you, you know, and now you'd be kind of peed-off or something and want me to leave."

"Complete your mission, whatever it may be."

"My mission?"

Mooky puts on his headphones, sticks his finger into the air. "Turn that up," he speaks into the microphone. "Drown me in that shit, Desmerelda."

I crank up his levels until they'd be just about deafening. Mooky gives the A-OK. I rewind, start the tape from the beginning.

The dolphins begin to leap into the sun.

Claire begins to dance. She closes her eyes, extends her arms, and rhythm overtakes her body. Soon she too is leaping, obeying the command. Leap, flee, there is danger here! Jump! Leap! I join the alien and leap as best I can, although I am more earthbound. Wallowed by my lard and sorrow. Claire reaches out one of her small hands. I take it.

I stop leaping, though, when I notice a face pressed against the dark glass window that separates my music room from the rest of the world. The face belongs to my mother.

I don't know when or where my mother encountered Maurice, but I know she was the first to mention his name in our household. Mantle was the president of Mantlepieces Inc. My mother badgered the father for a very long while, and finally he crumbled, he and Mantle had a meeting, a deal was struck, and Maurice became the father's publisher.

Maurice Mantle was a tall man with a moustache, and he was bald in a manner suggesting not so much that he'd lost hair, but more that his skull had ripped skyward with determination. Maurice was the first adult male I'd ever encountered who was concerned with his personal appearance. Before that I had thought that most men were like the father, that jackets were meant to look as if they'd been borrowed from a brother-in-law, that part of the tie's function was to let people know what you'd had for lunch. Maurice Mantle was dapper, almost perfect, and the only reason I say *almost* is that Mantle was always judging himself short of immaculacy, constantly adjusting sleeve lengths, tugging at his stockings, brushing lint (fairly irritably, I might add, especially given the invisibility of the lint) from his trousers. I think now that these things sartorial were designed to distract the eye from Maurice Mantle's head, which was resolutely, profoundly bald. Still, I'd have to report that he was a handsome man, and certainly charming. Although I tried not to, I couldn't help comparing the father to Maurice Mantle, and the father invariably ended up seeming freshly dug-up, like he ate little furry animals and belched swamp-mung.

Maurice Mantle got into the habit of coming over to the house. He'd bring little presents for Danny and myself. I remember he brought me a chromatic harmonica, he brought Danny a baseball that had been signed by all the members of the Los Angeles Dodgers. My mother encouraged Danny and I to call him Uncle Maurice. This we could not do. I called him a respectful Mr. Mantle, Danny usually hailed him as Moe. I know full well that Maurice was coming to see our mother, but he could not set foot inside the house without the father cornering him, ushering him upstairs to the den, where the father would pitch his latest tunes the way he pitched his rubberized doggy-do. "Now this one, Maurice, this one would be perfect for that Presley boy." Then the father, with his fat finger on the musical pulse of the nation, would pull out a tenor guitar and play something like "The Legend of Pocahontas."

Pretty, pretty Pocahontas,
You could win a beauty contest.
I think I love you, I'm being honest,
Pretty, pretty Pocahontas.

Meanwhile, Danny and I were spending our time in the basement (my mother often coming down with milk and cookies) composing songs full of automotive imagery.

Foot on the floor, who could ask for more?
Screaming in the valley in my old four-door!

One day Maurice Mantle was effecting an escape from the
father's den when he heard a sound coming from the
basement. He cocked an ear at the top of the stairs, he watched
my mother dance around the kitchen. He stared at her
muscular calves. "The young fellows?" he asked.

"*Torque torque,*" sang my mother.

"That's catchy."

My mother did a bit of pelvic rotation. "*Torque torque.*"

The father joined them in the kitchen, waving his hands
dismissively. "Twaddle," he pronounced.

"I don't know," said Maurice Mantle. "I think we should
maybe make a demonstration tape."

My mother turned around and bobbed her fanny. "*Torque
torque.*" If she were not my own mother, I could say lots about
her fanny. Just picturing it in my mind makes me queasy.

"Not bad," said Maurice Mantle.

The father nodded glumly. "I'll take them into a studio next
week," the father said. "I'll produce the boys."

So we went into a studio, the father, Danny and I. It was in a
fellow's garage, and the fellow was distinctly odd, a fat young
man with glasses about an inch thick. He sported a brush-cut
that allowed plain view of his skull. He dressed in velour,
strangely coloured. He was the sort of guy who should
have a hobby like flying remote-control airplanes or collecting exotic poisonous snakes, but instead his hobby was sound
recording. He had a huge, cumbersome tape recorder and a
number of ancient radio microphones. His name was Fred
Head, and Danny called him Freaky Fred. So appropriate was the
name that Fred Head didn't seem to care or really notice.

On that first session, I played the portable organ. Dan
pounded away on his tambourine, and the father added a bit of

41

guitar, fey and limp-wristed strumming. Fred Head didn't much care for the music — he stared straight ahead, or at least he approximated that, because his eyes were sort of crossed — but he seemed to get excited when I mentioned before a run-through that there were two or three different harmonies I could do, that I was having trouble deciding between them.

"Do them all," he told me.

"I beg your pardon?"

"We can do over-dubs," he told me. "You can sing over and over again."

I felt like Van Gogh when he found out that paint comes in different colours. I sang one harmony, a straightforward one, sitting a third above Danny's melody. Then Fred Head rewound the tape and I added a bass, growling like an engine. Freaky Fred was having fun now, so we added a high falsetto swooper.

"Too much, too much," said the father.

We recorded "Torque Torque" and "Foot on the Floor" that day. Fred Head and I worked on the tapes for about nine hours. Danny mostly slept, or listened to the baseball game on a tiny radio. The father sat in a corner and made occasional mutterings, but he knew he was outdone. Fred Head and I had a like-mindedness that the father was powerless against. (Indeed, look at me now, a replica, a clone, of Freaky Fred. I am bloated, I am uninterested in everything but noise. Fred and I even have mental problems in common, although he has outdistanced me on this count: the State still has Freaky Fred locked in a soft white room.) The father was sputtering in his slumber when Fred and I finally finished. Then Freddy handed the father a small white box containing the tape recording. The father whipped out a pen and scribbled:

THE FABULOUS HOWELL BROTHERS
PRODUCED BY HENRY HOWELL

and he was at Maurice Mantle's office the next day at nine o'clock. The father dragged Danny and me along with him, even though we were supposed to be at school. On instructions from the father, Danny and I were dressed identically, pin-striped button-down collared shirts and dark trousers. Dan did his best to undermine the effect, wearing his old boots, filling his hair with grease and then letting it tumble over most of his face. My hair has always been a snivelly cringing thing, meekly lying down on top of my skull without having to be told. The father threw the tape onto a machine in Mr. Mantle's office and said, "I think you're going to like this, Maurice. If you don't, you're maybe not as smart a guy as I thought you were, and I think you probably are." Beside Maurice Mantle the father seemed the sort of guy that would sell a sheep's baby sister to a drunken marine. "Now, I was trying something new here. This is a new sound, you see, a whole new concept." What the father meant was that he himself didn't care for it, was prepared to join Mr. Mantle in denouncing the music if that's what Maurice wanted to do. "What we got here," the father lied, "what we got on a stick, Maurice, what we got enough to maybe fill the Grand Canyon with, is *schnooze*." The father punched a button, the tape started rolling.

It sounded weird to me, the music trapped by the machine's three-inch speaker. Danny was tapping his toe — mostly to draw attention to the mud on his boot — but then he started throwing up his shoulders and burying his head in his chest, a strangely rhythmic display of insecurity. "What's that?" demanded Maurice Mantle. "Is that a dance?"

"Yeah, yeah," said the father. "That's the dance goes with the music."

"That's good," decided Mr. Mantle. He placed elegant fingers to the knot in his tie, shoved it microscopically to the right. The father did likewise, that is, he grabbed ahold of the Jackson Pollock beavertail he had wrapped around his thick neck and made motions as though he were strangling himself.

43

"Why don't we listen through those big speakers?" I asked. "It would sound better through them."

"Probably," agreed Maurice Mantle. "But most people don't have big speakers, do they, Desmond? Especially kids. They have little rinky-dink pieces of shit and if music don't sound good through them, the music just don't sound good."

This was the first time an adult said the word *shit* in front of me. A coming of age.

The tape finished, and the only sound in the room was the loose end hitting the controls of the machine as the flange turned. Mr. Mantle crossed over to the tape recorder, whacked at the STOP button. He wiggled his leg, effecting a better draping of the trouser. "What does Claire think of this?"

My mother had listened closely the first time she'd heard it, bending over so that her ear was closer to the music. She seemed bewildered for a long time, confused by the harmonies. "Angels," she whispered. "It sounds like little angels." Then she'd listened again, and this time she wheeled out into the middle of the room, lifting her skirts, jerking her head so violently that I feared she'd give herself whiplash.

"Claire likes it," announced the father.

"Does she?" asked Maurice Mantle of Danny and me.

We nodded.

"Well, I guess Mantlepieces Inc. will publish the music."

The father brought one of his fingers up into the air. Even the single finger seemed coarse, you wouldn't care to know the places that finger had been. "We split, Moe. We go fifty-fifty on the publishing here and don't jerk me around because you know and I know what we got here is a hit song. And let's not be kidding ourselves or letting friendship — especially with my *wife* — get in the way of clear-headed business transactions. We go split, that's it."

"You want to keep some publishing for the young fellows?"

"I want to keep some publishing, Moe."

"I'll tell you the truth, Hank, I don't see why I should."

"Here's why you should, Moe. Because I'm the guy's gonna take this thing to the record companies. I'm the guy who's gonna make them take it, and when we got a record, I'm the guy's gonna take that record and shove it down the throat of every disc jockey in the country. You're the guy's gonna be sitting on your duff collecting money. So the deal is, we split, fifty-fifty."

Maurice Mantle thought for a moment, then shrugged. He had to immediately shrug again, because the first shrug disarranged his lapel. "What the hell."

They signed some contracts that morning, and what I didn't know at the time, although I sure found out, was that the father was doing some pretty strange things. For one, he made sure that the fifty-fifty split agreement was virtually etched in stone. The father insisted on safeguards, panoplied no-escape clauses. Thus, when he fucked Maurice Mantle over sideways, it would not be viewed as any kind of chicanery, it would be seen for what it was, a vicious and bloodthirsty attack. Also, the father did some fanciful crediting. That is to say, he claimed (while Danny and I assaulted a Coke machine in the hallway—Danny could boot the contraption right in its belly, make it issue frosty bottles without swallowing a dime) that he, the father, the great unruly man, was the sole author of the words and composer of the music.

I know why the father did what he did.

Danny told me. Danny had insight into the father.

It was an act of love.

I don't care.

I last saw the father at Danny's funeral, the tolling of the knell. The gods attended the inhumation and were angry. Thunder rumbled, the skies boiled.

The father brought a date.

He seems much smaller now, surviving mostly on smokes and mealy rum. The father's talent agency is not going well. He handles a few strippers and a magician who cannot afford a live rabbit and makes do with one long-deceased.

The father wept, though. Tears burned across his face. When the rains came, the father looked up angrily, spat on the ground. The one good thing about the father is this ill-conceived defiance.

The first two or three record companies tossed us out on our butts. The father was bewildered by the lack of respect given to Henry "Hank" Howell. "Haven't these people ever heard 'Vivian in Velvet'?"

"You know," said Danny, "here's what I think it is. We come in with these songs about cars. Big, fast cars. Quality machines. But they see us drive up in this piece of junk Buick here, they figure we don't know our asses from holes in the ground." (Danny cottoned on to the music biz lingo pretty good.) "So we gotta get like a T-Bird, dig, a mean and nasty set of wheels. That way we command respect."

The father gave me a little whack on the side of the head. "Why can't you be smart like your brother?"

A Thunderbird was acquired — the father was fearless when it came to hurling himself into debt — and we cruised up to the Galaxy Records building in grand style. Not a single record executive saw us do it, mind, not even the receptionist, because the parking lot was around back.

You've likely seen — or at least seen a photograph of — the Galaxy building, a huge white skyscraper that looms over the city of Los Angeles, California. They own that building thanks to me, and before they met me they were housed in a dingy low-roofed affair that looked like a vacuum-cleaner repair shop. Galaxy Records was mostly two people back then, Edgar Sexstone and his son Kenneth. The senior Sexstone was interested only in classical music, and he left everything else in the hands of his son. This could have been a mistake, because Kenny was certifiably insane. When I first met him he was sitting in a darkened office listening to a recording of rain. He had a stereo set-up that was for that time very futuristic, woofers and tweeters and all of that, and the sound was so realistic that when I entered the office I felt wet.

"Could we maybe get," demanded the father, "a little light in here?"

"Let there be light," said Kenny Sexstone, and in an instant the office was flooded with the stuff. "Hello, men," said Kenny. "Talk to me. Let's communicate. You speak, I'll respond." Kenneth was a scrawny little man, seeming to be no more than fifteen years of age even though he was then in his early thirties. He looked as though he'd been carved out of wood and then crudely painted, his hair blood-red and solid, his eyes two bright blue marbles. "This is a brother act?" He pointed at Danny and me. "Yin and Yang. Flip and flop. Sturm und Drang." Kenny Sexstone next aimed his marbly eyes at the father. "Speak away, kind sir. Be my interlocutor."

The father waved his arms grandiosely. "The Fabulous Howell Brothers."

"The *Howl* Brothers," said Kenny Sexstone. I've never known whether he misheard or extemporized.

"Desmond and Daniel Howell."

"Des and Dan. Danny and Des."

"The tape." The father held aloft the flat white cardboard box. "The music."

"The sound," said Kenny Sexstone. "The feeling." He threw the tape on to a huge machine and levered it into motion.

47

"Torque Torque" fell out of the huge speakers. It filled the room like a bad smell. I now longed for Maurice Mantle's tiny three-inchers, because Kenny Sexstone's monsters amplified every imperfection. Every time my harmonies fell off pitch — singing in the studio is a knack that takes time to acquire — it stung and made me feel ill. Kenny Sexstone winced as though someone were banging him over the head with a ball-peen. I didn't know then that Kenneth was saddled with perfect pitch, a sense of hearing so acute that he could tell an A 441 from an A 440. Still, Kenny was grinning at the end of the tune, and he smashed the STOP button and said, "Automotive imagery. The way to go. The kids have wheels. Genius at work here."

"Yeah, well." The father shrugged modestly.

"Danny and Des, the Howl Brothers." Kenny Sexstone started up the tape recorder, we all listened to "Foot on the Floor". It was again very painful for Kenneth, but at the end he was happy as could be. "Yes, yes. I'll get contracts. Name-in-blood type of thing. I'll sign you for eternity."

"I produce them," said the father. "That's got to be part of the deal."

"You produce?"

"I produced this, didn't I?"

"And," said Danny — *Danny?* Both the father and I turned to look at him — "and another thing is, we work with this engineer guy, Fred Head."

Kenneth Sexstone waved his hand dismissively. "Engineers are plebs, my son. Easily shanghaied."

"Yeah, well, *Kenny,* we only work with Fred Head. Right, Des?"

"Hey," said the father, "engineers are engineers."

"Des?" said Danny quietly.

"I would prefer to work with Mr. Head," I mumbled.

"Enough!" shouted Kenneth Sexstone. "No cause for inconsonance. Mr. Head shall be retained. Now." He rose from behind his desk in jerky little hops like a marionette. "It's tranquillity time."

"Aw, jeez," said the father, "I got things to do."

"Tranquillity time," Kenneth Sexstone repeated, unimpressed by the father's claims of business. He took a tape, put it on to his huge machine. "Desmond. Hit the lights."

I was off and moving before I'd fully realized what it was Mr. Sexstone wanted me to do. It certainly didn't take the two of us long to establish our relationship. I banged at the wall switch, plunged the four of us into blackness.

"Listen," whispered Kenneth.

A sound issued forth, the strangest sound I've ever heard, a howling from the dark side of the moon.

"Sperms," whispered Kenneth Sexstone.

Amidst inexplicable beepings, aquatic and metallic echoes, came another ululation, as sad as a sunken ship.

"Humpbacks," whispered Sexstone.

"Jeez, I really got to go." I knew that even in the darkness the father was glancing at his wristwatch.

"It sounds kind of like a constipated elephant," remarked Daniel.

Another sound, this one so low it rumbled in my loins and bristled my pubic hairs and will-nots.

"What *is* this?" I asked.

"Whale music," said Kenneth Sexstone.

Shall we play the game for Kenny? The game of best placement in the space-time continuum, seeing as none of us belongs here? Okay, okay, but here's the kicker: what we need for Kenneth is a whole other planet! One with, oh, chrome pleasure-bots. A planet where food doesn't exist, everyone survives on a regimen of megavitamins and liquid californium. A planet where popular entertainment involves sticking electrodes into the fat of the brain. Yes, Kenneth should live in such a place. For one thing, he'd like it. For another, it would get him far away from me!

The dolphins leap into the sun. We listen to them, Mooky, Claire and I. We are happy, the three of us. "Does anyone feel," I ask, "like a refreshing dip in the pool?"

"Let's do," says Mooky. "Leave us transmogrify and dolphinize."

"Doff clothing!" I command. Then it's out into the backyard, into the pool.

My mother sits in a chaise-longe with a lemon gin in her hand, transfixed by the spectacle of her bloated son, a huge Negroid and a gamine from the planet Toronto cavorting nakedly in the light-sprinkled water.

"Hi, Mommy," I say. "Do you care to join us for a refreshing dip in the pool?"

"I think not." My mother is dressed in a very businesslike outfit, because she is under the impression that she comes to my house to do business. Vultures and coyotes *do business* when they sit by·a lion-kill and drool. The thing of it is, I make money, even my oldest tunes make money. In fact, "Torque Torque" is on the hit parade once more, a smash for Lou Gruber, rocketing up the charts everywhere from New York to Papua New Guinea. I can't keep track of all the money I make, I am distracted much of the time, and my mother weekly swoops down to check under rugs and so forth. So, she is dressed in a business suit, but she makes some concession to the heat, she pays some homage to the sun, one of her lesser deities. She has hiked up the skirt. She has undone buttons on her blouse.

Mooky climbs out of the pool. "Desmerelda, I got to split. I got a session across town."

"Mr. Mooks, it's been a pleasure."

Mooky laughs. "Shit. Dolphins." He walks back into the music room, where he left his clothes. My mother watches him go. "Who's that, Desmond?"

"Mooky Saunders, the best dolphin-man in the world."

"Oh, yes. And who is this little piece of trash?"

Mom is in one of her moods, not that she ever isn't.

"Aw shit," mutters the alien Claire, climbing from the pool. "Just when I was beginning to enjoy myself."

"Don't let me stop you," says my mother Claire. "No doubt my son finds you in some way amusing. I like for my son to be amused."

"Mommy, she's on a mission from Toronto. I'm sure she's been given instructions not to interfere with the life forms here, and I think we should respond with similar courtesy."

"Oh, Desmond," sighs my mother. My mother aims deadly eyes at the alien. "What exactly is your mission?"

"Just crashing, that's all," she answers.

"Oh!" It all becomes clear to me.

"Hey, lady." The alien raises a finger, points at my mother. "Desmond and I are friends, okay?"

"Desmond has no friends," sighs my mother.

"I'm going in the house now," says the alien Claire.

"Make yourself at home!" yells my mother. "Take advantage of my son's weakened mental condition! Help yourself to whatever you need or want! See how much money you can cheat him out of!"

The alien Claire spins around. She places her hands on her hips and cocks her body. "Did you go to Bitch College, or is this a natural talent?"

"Oh, I went to Bitch College, my dear. I did post graduate work."

"I'm pleased to see you two getting along," say I.

"I just need to know one thing," says my mother, "out of

51

concern for my son's well-being. Exactly how old are you?"

"In earth years," I remind Claire.

"I'm twenty. How old are you?"

"I was twenty once."

"Hold it against me, why don't ya?"

"Run along and play now. I have to talk to Desmond about his treatments."

"Right."

I watch Claire as she runs along. Her buttocks are small and very firm. They are also bright red, unaccustomed as Claire is to the proximity of the sun.

"Dr. Tockette has been calling me," says my mother. She lights a cigarette. She takes a couple of puffs and then puts it out. My mother doesn't really like smoking, but she enjoys showing off just how elegantly she can light up.

"I have no need for Tockette," I respond. "I've made great strides. Why, just yesterday I almost went to bed. I almost got into my nappies, pulled down the covers and waited for Mr. Sandman."

"He says you won't let him in the house."

"People come and say that they're Dr. Tockette, but they're not, because the real Dr. Tockette knows the secret password."

"Dr. Tockette refuses to indulge you in this secret password business, Desmond. He says it's necessary for your treatment that you open the door and invite him in."

"There, you see, a Mexican stand-off."

"It costs us two hundred dollars every time you won't let him in."

"Ha! I could find people who would do it for half that."

"Desmond, Desmond," she sighs. "I found an empty bottle of whiskey."

"Yes?"

"You've been drinking."

"Perhaps a small sip. Forestalling a cold."

"Don't you want to get better?"

"I only want to be happy."

"Happy? What makes you think you have any right to be happy?"

"I am a life form. Watch the whales, Mommy. They're happy. They swim around the world in happy pods. They lunch off the coast of Peru, they gather for cocktail hour just south of Greenland. They sing songs. I'm throwing a big party for them, just as soon as I've finished the *Whale Music*."

"Enough."

"You're invited. Bring that husband of yours, what's his name?"

"You know very well what his name is. His name is Maurice."

"Yes, yes, Maurice. How is Maurice?"

"Maurice is very ill."

"I'm sorry to hear that."

"Are you? Are you really, Desmond?"

The ringing in my ears suddenly becomes deafening, the little hobgoblins have gotten hold of sousaphones and crash cymbals. I pull myself out of the water. I feel so uncomfortable on dry land. "Mom, come into the music room. Come hear the dolphins."

"Put on your robe, please."

I plod into the music room, locate the bathrobe in the control room. My mother enters the dim room, leans against the wall. She has a new lemon gin in her hand, they seem to materialize there. "Listen," I instruct her, although, what with the twenty or so speakers mounted on the wall, it's not as though she has any choice. I feed the tape into the module. The "Song of Flight", I announce, and then the music starts. Wait, though. This is not the "Song of Flight", this is something I've not heard before. A sound akin to giggling, an idiotic marching drum thud. Chords float throughout, juicy major sevenths. The soles of my fat feet start to itch. Then there is a voice — *"Claire, the way the sunlight bounces in your hair."* Good voice, whoever it is. Lush harmonies, the high voice gliding up to the ninth whenever it gets a chance, which, to my way of thinking, is as close as you can get to Heaven and still keep the change in your pocket. Pretty as this might be, it is not the "Song of Flight", featuring Mooky Saunders. I'm about to press STOP when I catch a glimpse of my mother. She is smiling. She is smiling the way she used to smile when Danny made a joke. Or when I made a joke for that matter. My mother is twisting her body back and forth, too, her hips connected to the heavy bass drum. I allow the music to continue. A trumpet solo now, savage and hawklike, keening through the soft clouds. This is all right, this music, whoever it is. The chorus. My mother joins in, finding the only available harmony, fitting her voice into the music like she fits her small hand into a satin glove. A tear rolls down her cheek, tumbles into her lemon gin. Just the single tear. The music ends, that is to say, it disappears forever to journey in the cosmos.

"Desmond," says my mother.

"Yes?" I speak into a microphone, amplify my voice twentyfold so that it echoes in the recording chamber.

"Desmond. You still got it."

"Did you think that was me?"

"Of course it was you."

"Son of a gun." Even I'm impressed.

"And you wrote it about me?"

"Claire," I point out, "is your name."

"Has anyone from Galaxy Records heard this?"

"Well, no. I've a policy of not allowing record executives in the house, except for purposes of committing ritual suicide."

"You won't even allow Kenny into the house?"

"Especially Kenny. He alarms me."

"I'm the first person to ever hear this?"

"As far as I know."

"It is very beautiful, Desmond. I'm proud of you."

"Do you want to hear the 'Song of Flight'?"

"I should be getting back. Maurice needs me."

"If there's anything I can do, you know."

"Could I have a copy of that tape?"

"Mommy, you can have the tape. It's not Whale Music." I rewind, hand her the inch master. My mother kisses me on the cheek. "I'm sorry I was rude to your little friend."

"It must be ghastly up on Toronto. She has something painful in her, Mom. She seems to be happy, but inside I think she's very sad."

"We could start a club."

"She likes the Whale Music."

"Goodbye, Desmond."

"Toodle-oo."

My mother disappears. I feel strangely energized. I think it is time to begin work on the last movement of the Whale Music, the "Song of Congregation".

Do you know what I find strange, besides most everything? Motherhood is biological, correct? God concocted this scheme, He thought it was mighty clever, a little egg monthly shoots down the pipe, if some male-making matter is at the same time going up, you get babies. (Well, most of the time. Fay, astoundingly, could not conceive, even though her whole body seemed to swell and burst with the full moon.) But here in the War Zone, this process becomes unbelievably complex.

Much better to be as whales. Momma calves, the child weighs a mere tonne, it swims beside mother and for a few days swigs at the teats. Before long, it's *tata, mater, I'm off to Kuchino Shima, me and the gang are having a little get-together.* And the mother simply bellows goodbye, perhaps cautions her lad to be careful in those Japanese waters, and that's it. They may pass each other in a decade or so. They will surface, blow off a delighted hail, and then go their separate ways.

Yowzer, that stings! I've been playing tuba for the past little while (long while?) and it has torn hell out of the old chops. My chubby cheeks are woefully flaccid, I don't think I could speak a word that didn't sound like shit sliding down a brick wall. I

55

lean back, stretch my arms behind my head and yawn like a
sea-elephant. Time for bed, then — Call Dr. Tockette! — time
for beddy-bye, indeed. I wander out into the backyard in hopes
of a brief but spiritually rewarding gaze at the heavenly
firmament. Wrong again. It's daylight out here, sunny with a
vengeance, Claire is reclining in the chaise-longe reading a
book. Well, I'm adaptable. If it's not time for bed, then it's time
for something else. I plod over, allowing my flat, ugly-toed feet
to fall loudly, because I don't want to alarm the little creature.
They are skittish up on Toronto. "Hi," I give out, the traditional
Earth greeting.

"Desmeroony," she smiles. "What's doing, hon?"

"Oh, you know. I've been working on the Whale Music.
What have you been doing?"

"Reading. Eating. I cleaned up around the place some. Des, I
found a cheque for like twelve thousand bucks. You think
maybe you ought to put it in the bank or something?"

"I don't know." How did my mother miss that one? She is
distressed by Maurice's health, I suppose. I momentarily feel
remorseful, but I have had plenty of practice at hardening the
heart. I sit down on the ground beside the chaise-longe. "Did
you crash into the sea?"

"Huh?"

"Let me guess. Your craft started sputtering in the
exosphere, the air being too rich for your carburetor. Happens
all the time. Then the ship plummeted into the ocean. Dolphins
ferried you to the shore."

"Desmond," says Claire, "sometimes you get just a little bit
too snaky. I mean, I'm used to weird people, but you push it."

"I thought you'd come here for a purpose."

"Oh, yeah. I came here because back home they're after me
with butterfly nets."

"A renegade, a refugee! How exciting."

"I guess I should tell you, Desmond, you'd probably be in a
lot of trouble if they found me here."

"They won't find you. And if they do, we fight. Er, just how sophisticated is their weaponry?"

"Pretty fucking sophisticated. They use electricity."

"Aha! Then we repulse them into the water."

Claire laughs lightly, but she is not cheered.

"Why are they after you? What did you do?"

"I didn't do fucking anything. They did stuff to me. It doesn't matter." She waves her small hand in the air, dispersing her speech like stale cigarette smoke. Speaking of which, I think I'll have a butt. I extract a crumpled package from one of the bathrobe pockets, pull out a bent Salem Menthol. Claire *tsks* her tongue. "Cancer-stick," she says. "You ought to quit."

"I mean to," I lie. "Just as soon as the Whale Music is completed. Perhaps the morning after the party."

"Party?"

"I'm inviting the whales. They can sit in the ocean there, at the bottom of the cliff. We can wave and smile at each other as we listen to the music. You're going to stay for that, aren't you?"

"I wouldn't miss it for the world, Des."

"Yours or mine?"

"Huh?"

"Tell me about Toronto."

"Well, it's a lot like it is down here. It's got some nice parts, some shitty parts." Claire turns over on her side, leaning close to me, and excitement sparks in her eyes. "I'll tell you the best and the worst thing about Toronto, Des. The best thing is that it's got more seagulls than anywhere in the universe. We got billions and billions of the little dudes. There's this place called the Leslie Street Spit, and you can walk down there and see nothing but gulls. And I like to do that, don't ask me why. And the very *worst* thing about it is that everybody thinks this is a big problem. They say that seagulls are stinky, smelly birds, and people want to poison all the gull eggs and turn snakes and mongeese and hawks loose on the Spit. And when I hear people talk like this, I get mad. I think, hey, slime-bucket, if these seagulls are so bad, why did God make so fucking many of them? Don't you think He knows what He's doing?"

"He makes a lot of everything," I point out. "That may be His way of compensating for engineering and design flaws."

"Weird Desmond," laughs Claire. "He only made the one of you, babe."

"Torque Torque" was a local hit. It was a hit because the father shoved it down the throat of every disc jockey he could find. It was a hit because, as Kenny Sexstone noted, the youthful record-buying public was very much concerned with automobiles. It was a hit because the young Danny took a good picture, because he looked like a greaseball that would be polite to your mother. It was a hit, in part, because it was a good tune.

We were the Howl Brothers, the names Des and Danny bracketed underneath on the forty-five. The triumvirate — the father, Maurice Mantle and Kenny Sexstone — decided that we needed a band, that the Howl Brothers had to play live in order to promote the record. They decided to accent our youth, auditioning only people between the ages of fifteen and eighteen.

The drummer they found was a small, dark-skinned boy named Sal Goneau. His hair-do was something to see, a shiny and intricate sculpture that always looked like it was about to slide off Sally's head. Sal had a face like a bird, a nose that could be used as a letter-opener. He wore his shirt open to the navel as if proud of the fact that a swarthy Latin type like himself could have not a single solitary hair growing anywhere on his person (except for the precarious bouffant perched atop his noggin). Sal wasn't a very technically competent drummer, but he was awesomely mechanical. Once he got into a groove there was no stopping the lad. I'd pit Sal against a metronome any day of the week and bet good money that the machine broke time before Sally did.

On bass we had Dewey Moore. Dewey is doing well these days, isn't he, I believe he was recently voted Country and Western Artist of the Year. And I likewise believe he's in the Guinness Book of World Records for most marriages. When I first saw him he hadn't any of this silver-haired dignity for which he is so widely regarded. He was a scrawny, leather-jacketed man with his four-day beard doing a re-enactment of the Civil War. Dewey's eyes were red and ringed like Saturn. He walked into the auditioning room dragging his bass dolefully. A cigarette dangled from the corner of his mouth, little flecks of what looked like vomit spotted his filthy jeans. The triumvirate regarded him sceptically. Finally Maurice asked, "How old are you?"

Dewey removed the cigarette from his mouth and spoke. His voice sounded like someone was making mud pies in Hell. "Sixteen," Dewey croaked, and then he strapped on his instrument and commenced to play.

He got the job, mostly because not a lot of bass players showed up that day.

The guitarist was, as you probably know, Monty Mann, he of the quote-unquote Californian good looks. What was Californian about his good looks is beyond me. I think of California as ruggedly beautiful, redwoods, jagged coastlines, Big Sur, etc. Monty had a tiny nose, a tiny mouth, tiny ears. I couldn't look at him without imagining God creating Monty Mann, mincing around like a hairdresser and exclaiming, "Too cute for words!" Danny took a glance at Monty and hated him. I didn't hate Monty, but I did think he was a lousy guitar player, ruthlessly dragging slothful quarter notes out of his Telecaster, pulling and working at them like they were goobers stuck up some musical nostril.

The father attended the rehearsals regularly, but he didn't seem at all concerned with our musical progress. Instead, he'd show up with wardrobe ideas. Where he was getting these "costumes," I'll never know. We never had to make a firm veto on any of them because the father was quick to change his own mind. "Naw," he'd holler as soon as we were all uniformly attired. "No schnooze." The other thing the father had in abundance was ideas on hair. "You're all gonna dye your hair white!"

Sal Goneau shivered at this prospect. Dewey Moore's hair gave the impression that it would fight off tampering of its own volition. Monty's hair was close to being white anyhow, and replacing God-given bleach with a bottled brand was to him repugnant. This is the first true fight we had with the father, Danny leading the attack.

"No way," he said.

"I'm the boss!" screamed the father.

"No way," repeated Dan.

"I *made* you !" The father was perhaps referring to the two doggedly relentless bits of sperm that had produced my brother and myself. This was not the last time we would hear this peculiar claim.

"We are not dyeing our hair," Danny said with finality.

The father crossed quickly to Danny and slapped him twice on the face. Danny then reared back and caught the father with a roundhouse, laying him out on his duff. I picked the father up, whispered that I would be willing to dye my hair. He said, "Who cares?" and stormed out. The incident was never mentioned again.

Our first gig was in some swank nightclub high in the Hollywood Hills. The father had an unclear notion as to where the Howl Brothers' audience was, although we could have told him they weren't in this velvet and chrome emporium into which people pranced from the golf courses and tennis courts.

Setting up took twenty minutes. It's funny to think that in a few years we would be having to fly our equipment to a city two days in advance of a concert, that we would have no less than three road crews in our employ, three complete sets of sound systems. Back then, we just had tiny tube amplifiers, little boxes that hummed discordantly.

The patrons eyed us with suspicion. They winced as we tested our instruments. I played a sweet little major C triad and they winced. Sal patted out an inoffensive paradiddle and they winced. Monty strummed G, the chord of the singing cowboys, and they winced. So Dewey dropped a note in their laps that sounded like an elephant voiding last night's dinner. Their faces froze in rictuses of terror. Danny grabbed the microphone, pulled it out of its holder and said, "We're the Howl Brothers." He gave the count and we launched into "Torque Torque".

Until then, rock and roll songs had threatened only that the young people would dance a lot. The worst that might happen, according to the tunes, is that the young people might stay up all night. We were different. Our songs threatened *mobilization*, we were going to climb into powerful machines and actually go out on search-and-destroy missions! No wonder the older people fished the fruit out of their cocktails and hurled it in our direction. Likewise that their children made for the stage like it was Valhalla. Danny was doing his thing, his hands twisted in the air, his head shyly buried into his chest. The kids started doing this too, it became quite the rage, you know, this dance of awkwardness and crippled emotions.

The triumvirate were there, of course. The father was sure we were ruining our chances, he hollered at us to break out the schnoozy tunes. He wrote requests on cocktail napkins and had waitresses ferry them up to the stage, and although he changed his handwriting on every one, I had him spotted. Not many other people were likely to request "Vivian in Velvet." Maurice Mantle was there, wearing a three-piece pin-stripe that looked like he'd borrowed it from God, who was exactly the same size. Kenny Sexstone grinned like the Vienna Boys Choir had gone co-ed and was gathered under the table, chewing him up from the waist down.

Girls stood slack-jawed, mesmerized by either Monty or Danny. The ones who would worry about wrinkling their clothes tended to favour Monty, who looked like his shit came out pressed and folded. Girls without such concerns gazed upwards at Danny, they twisted their bodies in concert with his, they attempted to commingle on some spiritual plane, they made no secret of the fact that immediately after the show things were going to get down and dirty. Dewey Moore grinned from ear to ear, a hound dog who knew that he could feast forever on little scraps from the dinner table.

Among the young girls danced my mother. She didn't stand out, particularly, her hair was as blonde as theirs, her skin as perfect. Her clothes were sedate — at least the designers had aimed for sedateness — but my mother could shake the booty. *Agh*. Her fanny would bob like helium balloons through the clouds. *Agh. Agh.* Buttons were always working themselves undone, glimpses given of lace brassieres. My mother would kick out, arms aloft, thrust her pelvis, *come and get me soldier and slap some jelly on it!*

A photograph exists of that night. It's in a cookie jar which I deep-sixed in the mighty Pacific several years ago. It shows the dancing crowd, my mother among them, my mother frozen in a position that, whew, merely looking at it would turn you into a pillar of salt, at least throw your back out for a week. My brother Daniel is in essentially the same posture. I'm standing behind my keyboard, looking baffled and bewildered, a visitor from the Dogstar Sirius.

And then, right before we were supposed to play "Jaguar June", Dan announced, "Hey, everybody, we got a special guest artist tonight." News to me, news to me. I would grow used to this, why, one night (a few years to come) Jimi Hendrix got up on stage with us and, for reasons of his own, immolated

by flame not only his own guitar but Monty Mann's as well.
"The composer of 'Vivian in Velvet'..." (I clearly recall
thinking, *what a coincidence, someone else has written a song with that
same silly name,* and then the horrible truth struck home.) "Mr.
Hank Howell!"

The father came prancing on stage with the tenor guitar. Do
you know the tenor guitar, the thyroidal ukulele? *Nelson Eddy
played the tenor guitar!* The father began, his right hand slapped
the contraption's belly, his left grabbed ahold of the fretboard
and throttled. A D-chord, worse, a D-sixth. A D-sixth sounds
like a Sunday School teacher farting and then giggling with
embarrassment. The chord was strummed limply. Apparently
this was a ballad. *All right, all right,* thought I, disdainfully
playing the whiny notes. Down to a B-minor, yes, yes, E-minor,
oh no, don't tell me, *ah!,* the A-seventh, the father has
plagiarized whatever finned quadruped first emerged from the
ooze with a Sears & Roebuck six-string. And then came the
lyrics.

> *You dream, you incredible dream,*
> *I dream of the following scheme,*
> *That one day, we will float down the stream,*
> *You dream, I dream, we dream.*

The youngsters sat down. The dance floor was empty, save
for my mother, who stood staring up at the stage, expression-
less. The father attempted to aim a soulful gaze at her, but he
ended up squinting like Popeye. And then Maurice Mantle
appeared beside her and — with no exchange of word or
gesture — they fell into each other's arms. Mantle placed one of
his elegant hands on the small of my mother's back, the plateau
before the valleying of her buttocks.

You dream, crowed the father, *you indelible dream.*

(Had the thesaurus out again, have we?)

I dream until I think I might scream.
That one night, we will ride on a moonbeam,
You dream, I dream, we dream.

Danny jumped off the stage and tapped Maurice Mantle on the shoulder. Mantle stepped back gallantly, Danny took his spot, the father broke out into a rancid sweat. I did what I could. I added some ninths, anything to soup up the stodgy stew of his progression, I improvised a little counter-melody, I even added some vocals, harmonizing on the snivelling *you dream, I dream, we dream.* But, as we like to say here in the War Zone, damage had been done.

I am voyaging down the gold and platinum record hallway. In this hallway are also many Grammy Award plaques, which Danny and I often used as coke mirrors. Many things in the popular music industry can be utilized as coke mirrors, no mere coincidence. At any rate, there used to be more of these gold and platinum records and such, but one night Danny was in an extremely drunken bad mood because he'd caught his wife Lee in bed with another woman. Lee was by far the most beautiful of Dan's wives. Danny called Lee many filthy names and then, following a logic that eludes me still, he started pitching our gold and platinum records to the fishes. I was worried more about depleting our supply of potential coke mirrors. Those were the days when I did quite a bit of that stuff, although I've cut down recently, mostly because no one will sell me any. Let's face it, I can't purchase No-Doze. I don't really see what the problem is, it's not like I'm going to go out in public and shame myself. I'll stay home and shame myself.

I must be on my way somewhere, although I seem to have stalled in this hallway. From another room I can hear music, Claire is listening to a Van Morrison record. If she really wants to file an accurate report on our planet she should listen to Perry Como. My best guess is that I was headed for the kitchen. It seems like I haven't eaten in days, I've actually lost a bit of weight. But I'm bogged down in the hallway, which means something unpleasant is about to happen.

Knock-knock.

Front door.

I should hire a butler to drive these people away, but then who would protect me from the butler? I press myself against the wall, hoping to bury myself in a shadow.

"Desmond?" comes a voice. "I know you're there."

It's one of the Dr. Tockette impersonators.

"Desmond! Let me in."

"If you're really Dr. Tockette, use the secret password!"

"Desmond. For your treatment to be successful, it's imperative that you allow me to enter without this password nonsense."

"Do you think the president of the United States just allows anyone to come in? No, sir. I'll bet he has a highly complex system of passwords. And yet no one calls it nonsense or accuses him of mental imbalance."

"Certainly they do!"

"A bad example."

"If I say the password, will you let me in?"

"I most certainly won't if you don't."

"This once then, and never again. *Garuda.*"

"Garuda?"

"Open the door."

"No. You've alarmed me. You conjure in my mind this

65

terrifying image of some mythical beast, half-bird, half-human, and then you ask that I open the door?"

"Play fair, Desmond. I'll tell your mother on you."

"By the way, Columbia University will not admit to ever hearing of you, let alone awarding the Doctorate of Psychiatry that you lay claim to."

"Not that Columbia. Colombia the country. "

"You studied psychiatry in the country of Colombia?"

"A very reputable school."

"Dr. Bolivar's School of Advanced Torture Techniques?"

"Your mother says you have a girl in there."

"There is a visitor here."

"Don't you wish to discuss your sexual hang-ups?"

"Don't *sexual hang-up* me, you mountebank."

"Garuda! Garuda!"

Claire is beside me in the hallway. She says, "Fuck off!"

"Who's that?"

"It's the person telling you to fuck off," answers Claire.

"Young woman, I am Mr. Howl's personal doctor. I insist that you open the door."

"Well, I don't believe you're his personal doctor, because you know dick on a stick about him."

"I know everything about him! I have one entire filing cabinet devoted to him."

"So then," says Claire, winking at me, "what's with this sexual hang-ups business?"

"Sexually speaking, Mr. Howl is retarded at about the level of a three-year-old."

"Yeah, well, that don't sound like the Desmond I know."

"Oh," snorts Dr. Tockette, "I suppose you and he have had intimate relations?"

"Absolutely. He's great."

"What, you manually stimulated his little apparati?"

Claire shoots me a look, rolls her eyes towards the door. "Nope. We do it all."

"All?"

"We fuck, we suck, usual stuff."

"Desmond? Is this true?"

"Well . . ." We fuck? We suck?

"He's modest. Take my word for it. He gave me head for about eight hours straight yesterday."

"Are we talking about Desmond Howl?"

"Yeppers."

"Desmond? Is this true?"

"Eight hours seems like an awfully long time," I say.

"Sure is," agrees Claire. "Dr. Fockette out there would have creamed his jeans in about three minutes."

"Young lady, I demand that you open the door. You could be doing severe damage to my patient's psyche."

"*You* could be doing the fucking damage, buster. It's his house, and he doesn't want you in it, so fuck off."

"Desmond, I'm telling your mother."

"And tell that douche-bag to stay away, too."

Ooh, what nasty language they have up on Toronto.

"He's insane, young lady."

"So the fuck what?" shouts Claire. Suddenly she is crying. She reaches out, touches my fat arm, and then runs away.

I follow the alien, alarmed by her weeping. She should not be crying on my behalf. I am the Whale-man, I live in an ivy-encrusted manse with my tiny bag of shadowy memories. I am not worthy of so many vicious tears.

And here, in the living room, the alien is destroying things. Vases are pitched against walls, the shrivelled husks of flowers rendered to dust. Empty glasses and crumby plates are dashed to the ground. An automatic card shuffler is mangled. Record albums sail through the air. This gives me an idea.

"Wait!" I shout.

The alien does wait, her breathing heavy, her face twisted.

"Watch!"

I disappear into the gold and platinum hallway, select one at random. "*Catch a Ride.*" A biggy, crates to Crete. The back of the mounting is cheap cardboard (the popular music industry is all gloss), I poke my fingers through and tear out the argental disc. I waddle into the backyard with the thing. This must be satisfying when your innards are on the boil, because Danny did it. I cock my wrist and let fly. Look at it go! The sixties weren't a waste of time after all, everyone learned how to toss a Frisbee. The thing climbs regally into the sky. The platinum catches the sun and sends it splashing. The record lilts to the right, it loses its loft and slices through the air, there is a very satisfying noise as it is dashed upon the rocks below.

"Say," I comment, "that *is* fun."

The alien is right behind me, a golden platter in her hands. She elects to use the two-handed delivery, which adds distance but takes away from the graceful flight. Each to its own. The record clears the rocks at the bottom of the cliff. It bounces among the foamy waves and disappears.

Claire and I run back into the house, we gather up gold and platinum records.

The alien's tears turn to laughter. I, on the other hand, am reminded of my brother Daniel, and my eyes begin to sting.

When Danny was fifteen years old, he fell in love with a girl named Brenda Mackey. This was a bit odd, because Brenda was no beauty. She was a big girl, a bit pot-bellied, large-breasted in a doleful fashion. She had a tattoo on her left forearm, one of those faint blue institutional jobs. It was merely a crudely drawn cross — it might have been of a religious nature, it may have been a dagger. Both arms were covered with scars. Fine, straight scars. Orderly, arithmetical rows of scars. Brenda's face was pleasant enough, except she had a repertoire of about twenty-two frowns and sneers, from which she made her selection of facial expression.

The thing about Brenda Mackey was, she was the owner of a reputation. Her reputation was like a huge slobbering St. Bernard that followed along behind her, occasionally woofing its cookies. I have no desire to be cruel, especially to someone

who owns a reputation (I mean, just look at the monster I have),
but the truth of the matter is, Brenda was a slut. She certainly
educated Danny in these matters sexual. He would relate this
education to me at night as we lay in bed. I was baffled, I was
confounded. At the same time, there was something chivalrous
about Danny's behaviour. This became apparent when
Brenda's reputation, that hairy behemoth, was sullied.

The sullying was done by Phil O'Kell, who periodically got
released from some institution or another, usually for the day.
He never committed a crime that was particularly dastardly —
uttering false documents, fraud, petty theft, acts more of
muddle than malice. And I will say this, that when Phil O'Kell
sullied Brenda Mackey's reputation — he accused Brenda of
the one or two sexual acts that even she might find
distasteful — it was because his heart was mangled. Phil was an
aggrieved suitor. Squalor doesn't negate everything. So, Phil
O'Kell got released from prison one day, thought he might
spend time with Brenda, discovered instead that she was
cavorting with my young brother. O'Kell stood on street
corners and ragged her.

You'd have thought Danny would be petrified, instead he
seemed exhilarated. "O'Kell is horse meat," he screamed. His
energy knew no bounds, he grabbed me by the shoulders and
shook hard. "O'Kell is a dead man!" Did I mention that O'Kell
was a massive specimen, that he spent his time in prison lifting
weights? Danny needed some advantage, any edge, and with
that in mind he created Stud E. Baker.

Stud E. Baker was a rancid and mealy greaseball. He wore
bluejeans coated with crankshaft oil, a torn T-shirt. Stud wore
cowboy boots that might have been stolen from the Dalton
gang as their dead bodies were lined up to be photographed.
Stud E. Baker's hair was worried into an elaborate do,
duck-tailed, a surf running down the middle, but then this
intricate creation was destroyed by a rumpled Confederate
Army cap. Stud E. Baker smoked continuously, his body was
fuelled by high-test Mexican beer. He swallowed ampheta-

mines. Stud had a gimpy leg and a sexual disease he'd caught in a tropical clime. This disease made his crotch endlessly itchy, and Stud E. Baker usually had one hand in his pants, scratching with vigour.

Stud E. Baker hit the streets in an old ragtop, the engine souped up till it howled, it bombinated, it shook public buildings.

The call went forth. Stud wanted to play chicken with Philly O'Kell.

Palomountain had a perfect place for the playing of chicken. Just to the south of town, in a small forest, the government had once thought to build an airforce base. They mowed a wide swath, five hundred yards long and a hundred feet across, and then abandoned the idea, I assume because someone realized it was stupid to be taking off and landing airplanes in a forest. At any rate, they'd burned that strip to the nubble, there was little subsequent vegetation.

Danny set the time: midnight. I was recruited as his second. Phil O'Kell was waiting when we arrived. He had three or four thugees with him. They threw beer bottles and belched. Maybe fifty or sixty town kids (Brenda Mackey among them) showed up to watch. Danny — Stud E. Baker — roared up, slammed on the brakes, the two cars sat facing each other at either end of the aborted landing strip.

The thing could not be done without preliminaries. Stud E. Baker opened the car door, grabbed ahold of the roof and pulled himself up. His eyes were red, his ears were steaming, he gave off tequila effluvia. "Take it back!" he screamed.

Phil O'Kell reared himself likewise. "Er, nope."

Danny reseated himself, started building up the revs. The animals in the forest fled.

I was the starter, which is to say I stood in the middle of the aborted landing strip waving a handkerchief over my head. When I judged the howls to be sufficiently loud, I let the thing fall. Then I hustled my fat ass off to the sidelines as fast as I could.

The cars headed for each other, Danny quickly getting up to about sixty, O'Kell contenting himself with about thirty, as if obeying a posted speed limit. At the last possible moment — really, several moments before the last possible moment — O'Kell veered to the right.

Stud E. Baker never let up on the gas. Danny claimed that the accelerator stuck, that the brakes failed, but I'm inclined not to believe him. He flew the length of that aborted landing strip and hit the trees spectacularly. The hood crumpled, exploded into flame. From the wreckage emerged Stud E. Baker, and local legend has it that he lit a smoke from the flames before limping away.

Stud E. Baker, having defended his woman's honour, walked by Brenda Mackey and gave her a disdainful glance. He spit in the direction of Phil O'Kell and muttered, "If you'd suck him, you'd suck ripe shit." He kept going, waving a hand at me. "Come on, Desmo. Let's get drunk." I trotted to keep up, panting like an overheated dog.

The strangest part may be this: two or three days later, Danny handed me a sheet of paper. Written on it, in a cramped and arduous script, was:

Brenda, you give me peace of mind.
Brenda, like a jewel I find
In a dark place where nobody goes
In a strange place where the wind blows
In a cruel place where nobody knows
Brenda.

Danny grinned. "Fucking poetry."

Brenda, you give me reason to
Brenda, live my life for you
In this dark place, where the rains fall
In this strange place, where the night calls

71

(Already I was singing in my head, lush harmonies, dense chords, sevenths, ninths — my god, a Neopolitan sixth!)

In this cruel place, I will give my all
To Brenda.

Danny gave me a little jab to the belly. "Hey, brother," he whispered, "we are on our way."

We went into a real studio this time, state-of-the-art machines, separate cubicles for bass, drums and vocals. The father knew that to get good product, you had to spend good money. Freaky Fred Head thought he'd died and gone to Heaven. The song "Brenda" was recorded, the five voices laid down on individual tracks, but as we listened to the playback, I was dissatisfied. "It's not big enough," I complained.

"Do it again," said Fred Head.

"Well, there's nothing wrong with the way we did it."

"No, do it again. Sing everything twice."

Kenneth Sexstone shook his head. "His elevator doesn't go all the way to the top floor." Kenny Sexstone liked to hang around the studio when we worked, and I will say that he never tried to force his will. I didn't know that if anything had gone wrong, Kenny likely would have ordered bombers to destroy the building.

"Watch." Freddy directed us back to the vocal booth. He set up the echo machine, a separate loop of tape that adds depth.

We redid our vocal parts — *doubling* it's called these days, as common as tuning-up, unheard-of back then — and then Freaky Fred pressed down on the echo-tape flange ever so lightly. There was a slight, ethereal *wow*, and suddenly the music opened up like the Pearly Gates.

"Freaky Fred strikes again!" shouted Danny.

"Nyuk-nyuk," chortled Freddy. He continued this manual manipulation of the echo-tape for the rest of the song.

"What are you doing?" demanded the father. The father was still nominally our producer, although on that session he spent most of the day figuring out how to operate the intercom.

"Disturbing the phases," Freaky Fred answered cryptically.

"Weirdness and abnormality," noted Kenny Sexstone, not unhappily. "The ferry doesn't quite make it to the other side."

This wasn't Fred's only innovation, although it certainly is by way of being his most famous. He went home that night and designed a box to do what his finger was doing. He called his invention the "out-of-phaser," and sold the idea to an electronics company for three hundred dollars. Nowadays the phaser is used all the time, whoever owns the patent is a multimillionaire, but Fred Head, I guess, has the satisfaction of knowing he invented the thing. (Except, you know, it's a bit of an iffy question as to whether or not Freddy actually *knows* anything these days.)

His other noteworthy contribution that session was on the flip-side, the raucous number "Jaguar June." This is the first recording where Danny lets down his hair. We're talking Rapunzel time. Daniel entered the vocal booth stripped to his scivvies, his teeth clenched with amphetamine grit. A drunken lion with its balls in a bear trap. At any rate, there is a guitar solo overdub on this tune, and Monty worked out an effete series of licks that implied that uppermost on Monty's mind was not mussing his hair. As Dewey Moore put it, "Sucks like my daddy's boot in a cowflop." Freaky Fred Head reached forward and picked up a screwdriver that was lying on the recording console.

"Freaky Fred prepares to strike again," whispered Danny.

Fred Head walked into the studio and savagely stuck the screwdriver into Monty's amplifier. Monty was stunned. Freddy dug the metal into the speaker and ripped the paper. Then he stood back and nodded at the guitar player. "Go," said Freaky Fred. And of course the sucky little licks screamed out of the ruined speaker like banshees having their nosehairs tweezered.

"A classic," muttered my brother Danny.

And it is. Ask anybody, ask a critic, ask the verminous rodent Geddy Cole if you must! Maybe five of our tunes are bona fide rock and roll classics: "Jaguar June", "Brenda", "Kiss Me, Karen", perhaps "Slow Sundown" (the critics are divided), "Big House" for certain. Mind you, we had a special guest artist on that last tune, the Killer himself. Jerry Lee Lewis came into the studio, drunk and tormented. Jerry Lee banged away at the piano keyboard, each chord another step towards eternal hellfire and damnation.

Danny was very taken by this.

By the way, I am not speaking to Geddy Cole. Oh, I know, I am not speaking to anybody, if you want to get technical. But Geddy Cole is high-lighted, underscored, capitalized, and has been ever since the release of his libelous little tract, *Howl! An Unauthorized Biography of the Howl Brothers.*

I first encountered the scabrous lout in those early days. The Howl Brothers Band had packed our equipment into an old station wagon and lit out for parts unknown. We were playing a town in Oregon, and after the first set this kid approached us. He wore huge glasses, like his mother had bought black horn-rims four sizes too big in the hopes that the child would grow into them. This kid was also afflicted with the worst case of acne I'd ever seen. I was usually sporting a whitehead or two, but this kid looked like the pimples were battling over possession of his very soul. The kid selected me as the likeliest target for his purposes, which, I admit, was simply to make friends. He sidled and angled over, leaned against the wall beside me. "Hi," he said.

"Hello."

"It's real cool stuff you cats are playing."

"Oh, thank you very much."

"You want to blow some reefer?"

"Oh, I think not." I didn't know what he was talking about, but the phrase rang with illicitness.

He removed the scrawny and bent cigarette from his shirt pocket. "It's good stuff," he said.

"I smoke Salem Menthols myself," I said, taking out my pack by way of illustration.

This weird kid laughed, sucking on the intake, one of those mulish guffaws. "Hey, pretty funny. Come on, let's smoke this." He took my arm and led me outside. The kid fired up the little cigarette with a lighter that flamed like an acetylene torch. He inhaled deeply and held the smoke in his lungs for a long time. He passed the thing over to me. I followed his example. "Strange-tasting stuff, not exactly pleasant, reminiscent of fetid jungle underneath trampled by smelly feet." This kid then grabbed the thing back, I had never shared a smoke in such an urgently formalized fashion before. When we were through I turned to re-enter the club and promptly walked into a wall.

That, then, was my indoctrination to the world of Better Living through Pharmaceuticals. Very impressive. Much more impressive, in fact, than my indoctrination to Sex. That transpired in Little Rock, Arkansas. I wandered into Danny's motel room in search of a light for my cigarette, a scrawny home-made with a taste recalling bogs in Mesopotamia. There I found three girls, in various states of undress, and Stud E. Baker.

"Big Desmond!" shouted Stud, standing on his bed in stained underwear. "What's cooking, Daddy-o?"

"I'm watching television next door. Dewey and Monty are out somewhere."

"Right." Stud E. Baker bounced off the bed, caught my head in the crook of his arm and ran with me into the bathroom. He slammed the door behind us and fished two beer out of the sink. The sink and the bathtub were loaded with ice cubes and beer. Stud tossed a beer in my direction, bouncing it off my forehead. (Those scrawny cigarettes mess up your reaction time.) Finding himself in the bathroom anyway, Danny/Stud E. Baker decided to have a pee. He pulled his thing out of his underwear and blasted. Stud E. Baker had an overhand holding technique. I tried to adopt it myself, except it obscured my line of vision and usually made me spray all over the wall. "Desmo, baby," he said, "pick your choose."

"Huh?"

"I can't figure three women all at once. I *know* there's a way, dig, but right now I can't figure it. So pick your choose and take her away."

"Take her out for a soda or something?"

"Desmo!" shouted Stud. "Take her to your room and get your horn scraped, for God's sake. Get a bee-jay, get reamed! Do whatever you like to do."

"I don't know."

"How about the big one? The one with garbonzas?"

"Well . . ." My stomach tied itself in complicated Boy Scout knots.

"Her name is Lois. You just say, like, hello Lois, would you like to come next door and watch a little television?"

"She wants to stay with you."

"Who can blame her? I am Stud E. Baker! I wear the wang that makes the women whimper! I own the dork that pops their cork! But I'll say, like, you want to go with my brother, that's cool, I'll dig you later. Get it?"

"Umm . . ."

"Come on." We re-entered the main room. Stud E. Baker removed the Confederate Army cap and became, for a moment, Daniel. "My brother Desmond," said Dan, "is lonely. I think the world of my brother Desmond, and it makes me sad that he's lonely. Now, if any one of you wants to keep my brother company" — he singled out this girl Lois with a stab of his hawklike eyes — "then I'll be very, very grateful."

"Grateful enough to give me a solo shot tomorrow night?" asked Lois.

"Absolutely, Lois. Tomorrow night, it's me, you, the Stud and the stars."

She bounced off the bed. "Let's go, Desmond."

"Don't you want to get dressed?"

"I sort of assumed you wanted me this way."

"Sure he does," said Danny. "And Des, for god's sake, take it easy on this one. Don't break her heart. Don't show her Paradise and then say baby, you can only glimpse it."

"Danny —"

"Go!" Danny gesticulated grandly, he rammed the Union cap back on his head and became his alter ego, Stud E. Baker. "Present those backsides!" he bellowed at the two remaining girls. "Let's do it jackal style, like laughing hyenas!" Lois and I ran next door to my room. I sat down on the bed and watched the television. Lois sat down beside me, laid a hand on my hip. "What's your favourite thing?" she whispered in my ear.

"Music," I whispered back.

"What's your favourite pleasure?"

"Mu —" I started, but she placed a finger to my lips, shutting me up.

"How about a bee-jay?"

I shrugged. Lois worked at my zipper, she extruded the pale thing. "Hmm!" she said. I concentrated on the television. Lois placed one of my hands on one of her large garbonzas. She lowered herself, took me into her mouth.

I needn't go on. It was less than satisfactory, and it was less than educational, as for a long while I thought that sex consisted solely of bee-jays. Eventually I grew to appreciate

77

the bee-jays, and then I married Fay, who refused to give me one.

Up the stairs, up the stairs, a feeble ascension towards the Land of Beulah. This means I'm going to bed, I suppose, at least into my bedroom. What prompted this course of action, I'll never know. I've been working on the "Song of Congregation". It's not going especially well, there is an undercurrent of menace, subtle, yet more than enough to drive the whales away. I think I might be depressed. Watch out.

Down the hallway, then.

Here is a photograph on the wall, one not likely to cheer me any, a picture of Fay and me vacationing in the Bahamas. She is wearing a string bikini, her breasts tumbling out of the top. I am dressed in a suit, complete with watch-fob. Fay is quite an attractive woman, I'll give her that much. Actually, with the divorce settlement, I'll give her a lot more, and for the rest of my life. I only glance at this photograph. (Lurking in the background is Farley O'Keefe, my erstwhile probationer and nursemaid. He is wearing a bikini swimsuit, his thick and pugnacious prong all but peeking over the top. I would mention that he is as hairy as an ape were it not for a desire never to offend apes. Look at his big muscles, look at his tiny head. I hate Farley O'Keefe.)

I pass the bathroom. Claire is in there applying makeup to her face. It looks like war paint, heavy black lines across her eyes. Claire's body is no longer pale, it is quite a rich gold, every square inch of her. I thought I had grown used to it, but Claire's nudity is somewhat unsettling today. I pull the door shut. And into my bedroom. There is a white grand piano. I sit down on the bench, and, because my nerves are ruffled, I draw out a major ninth. A major ninth is a lot like a major seventh, except it not only makes the soles of your feet itch, it makes the hairs in your ears tingle. Then it's up to the second, the minor, adding a flattened seventh for lushness. The door opens and Claire bounces into the bedroom. "Sounds good," she tells me. Her hair is piled atop her head, contained there by an ingenious arrangement of bobby pins. Claire goes to the closet. I watch her buttocks, the muscles working hard. She swings open the door and appraises her small collection of clothes. First she draws on a pair of black panties, then she puts on a frilly and feminine undershirt. Up to the third, again a minor, I'm gearing up for the next chord, which is going to be the fourth, a major seventh, except I'm going to cluster all the intervals tightly together. It will sound like God gobbing on the sidewalk. Claire pulls on a pair of leather pants, then a satin shirt, a silver one that reminds me of metal. Here comes the chord, are you ready for this, ooh, I'm horripilated, I'm . . . my goodness. Do you see what I see? Is that not a bulge underneath my bathrobe? Call Dr. Tockette!

Before I can stop her, Claire sits down beside me on the piano bench. She plucks out a couple of high notes — real beauties, too, the very ones I would have played had my enormous fanny been perched up at that end — and then she glances at me with a smile. I guess I have a peculiar expression on my face, she realizes something is not as it should be. "Well, well," she says.

"There's likely some simple medical explanation."

"I guess."

"You look very pretty."

"Thanks, man." She continues to dabble with the high notes, it sounds like a little girl playing by the side of the ocean, Saturday morning in your pee-jays, Clarabelle on the boob-tube. "You see, Des," she begins, "I got this real problem. My dad, he used to, like, come into my room. You know?"

"To kiss you goodnight?"

"Des, fucking grow up."

"Oh." When in doubt, go back to the tonic.

"I mean, he used to come into my room and get into the bed with me and do it to me. Okay?"

"It's not okay," I mumble.

"No, it's not okay. And the thing of it is, like, I can't help you with that." She nods towards my bathrobe. "I even want to, in a way, but I just can't."

"Is that sort of thing common up on Toronto?"

"I don't know. Probably. It's not like my dad's a real prick or anything, either. In a lot of ways he's a pretty nice guy. But . . ." Claire shrugs. "I guess being a nice guy's not what it used to be."

"Oh, say," I point out, "no need to worry. It has died. Wormy once more." I curl my fingers and pound the keyboard hard, searching for ethereal polyphony, that place where logic and beauty intersect and the world makes a wonderful sense. I miss. "Why are you dressed so nicely?" I ask the alien Claire. "Are you going out?"

"Des."

This is something new, this little undertone of annoyance that has bled into her voice.

"Yes?"

"Don't you remember yesterday, there was a phone call? And it was your old friend Dewey Moore? And don't you remember inviting him over for dinner tonight?"

"Company?"

"Absolutely."

"Agh!" I blunder up from the piano bench and scurry under the covers. "Tell him I'm sick. Tell him I have trichomoniasis."

"Desmond. He's going to be here any time."

"You can entertain him."

"So now, we're going to get dressed."

"In clothes?"

"Yes, in clothes. Nice clothes."

"None of them fit. Those are vestiges from the days when I approached normalcy, both physically and mentally."

"I let these babies out." She removes a pair of pants from the closet. "And," she says, pulling out a shirt, "I figure you could get into this."

"I don't want to see Dewey Moore. He's a born-again Christian and he wants to convert me."

"Well, you're the guy that invited him, Des. He just got married —"

"Again?"

"And you said, come on over for dinner. Which, by the way, I have cooked, and it took me a fuck of a long time, and it's Bouillabaisse for god's sake, and it's not as if you can buy Bouillabaisse Helper in the grocery store. So are you getting dressed or are you pissing me off? Them's the choices, babe."

"Agh."

"Quit going *agh*."

"It's a sound I make when deeply distressed."

"Where do you keep your gotchies?"

"How should I know?"

Claire buckles her hands on her hips, she glares at me. Then she marches over to the chest of drawers and bangs around for a bit. She finally comes up with a pair of underwear which has seen better days.

"Are you gonna put these on?" she demands.

"All right, all right. Give them to me."

She tosses them hard, they hit my face. I drag my legs over the side of the bed and slowly draw on the underpants.

"Satisfied?" I ask.

"For fuck's sake." She tosses me my trousers. "Jump in."

I pull them on. Amazingly, they fit. Claire flings a shirt at me. I stick my arms through and do up the buttons. Claire marches over and tucks the tail into my trousers.

"You look good," she announces, appraising me.

"You lie, alien."

Then the doorbell rings. Claire sticks a little finger at my face. "You say *agh*, Des, and so help me I'll scream."

"Company!"

"That's right. We got company."

"Say, though. I've just had an idea for the Whale Music. If you would excuse me for no more than twenty minutes — "

"Sure. And then four days later you'll show up again." Claire grabs a hairbrush, scrapes my scalp and beard. "Let's go." She turns. Perhaps one small and soothing major seventh chord. I spread my hand like an eagle's talon, poise it over the keyboard. "Desmond!" Claire hollers before it can alight.

"Coming."

As I descend the staircase, Dewey Moore is entering. Look at Dewey, his silver hair and beard perfectly sculpted. He has a pot-belly, but he seems proud of it, like it was a bowling trophy. Dewey is dressed entirely in black, in his hands he is holding a dark Stetson bordered with huge pieces of silver. Dewey wears a lot of jewellery, more than I've seen on anyone, even Fay. He turns, watches me come down the stairs. He smiles, and for a second he's a shit-kicker again.

"Desmond," he says.

"Dewey."

Dewey opens his arms, I realize with horror that he means to hug me. I would stop, but heft like mine produces a certain amount of momentum. I have no choice but to waddle into his embrace. Dewey squeezes tightly, kisses the nape of my neck. "You are looking okay," he says. His voice is so low these days that it is almost infrasonic. (Infrasonic? I'm getting ideas.) Dewey releases me, turns and says, "And now I want you to meet Bobby Sue. My wife."

Bobby Sue is a small woman. Before I can stop her she has rushed forward and put her arms around me as far as they can go. She is chesty, there are large firm globes pressing into my belly. I gaze down on her red hair. "Desmond," she says, "God bless you."

"Yes, well, He's the man for the job, all right." I manage to tear her off like a three-day-old Band-aid. "Have you met Claire?"

"Yo," says Claire. "We been through it."

"So, Des," says Dewey, "what have you been up to?"

"Oh, you wouldn't be interested."

"I wouldn't be interested in what my favourite musical genius has been up to?"

"Well . . ." I grab him by the arm, I haul Dewey towards the music room.

"Desmond," says Claire, "we're eating in half an hour."

"Absolutely. I'm merely being sociable. Dewey expressed an interest in the Whale Music. You and Bobby Sue get acquainted."

"Claire," asks Bobby Sue, "have you accepted Jesus Christ as your personal Saviour?"

"Half an hour!" shouts Claire as I disappear.

"I'm just saying," says Dewey, "there's gonna be litigious hell to pay if I don't get a big credit here, likely as not on the front of the album cover."

I nod, I am running a microphone cord into the echo chamber, I'm not really paying much attention to Dewey Moore and his little worriments.

"I mean, Des, I am big news right now. Everybody wants me on their records. *Every*body. Willie, Waylon, Crystal, Dolly. And I won't do it. But for you, old buddy, I'd go to Hell and get a pizza. Lookee-here, I haven't even mentioned money."

"Mention money, Dewey, it's all right." I am using a special German microphone, very sensitive, I'm going to be able to pick up the sound of Dewey's nostril hairs waving in the breeze.

"I ain't mentioning money."

"I've got some. Just ask Claire where it is and help yourself."

"Now that Claire, she's a fine-looking young girl. Where'd you find that Claire?"

"I didn't find her. She found me. She crash-landed on the sofa in my living room. From Toronto."

"I was up there," says Dewey. "Got so cold I could use my balls for ice cubes."

"I had no idea you were so well travelled."

"I been everywhere, boy. I'd been practically everywhere before I met you. And where'd we get to? Australia, England, India. Hey, man. Remember India?" Dewey laughs, he has a laugh like a coyote that owns a meat freezer. "Babboo Nass Fazoo talking about peace and shit, I'm laying the pud to all them hippy girls. Excuse me." Now that Dewey is a born-again Christian, he always says "excuse me" after talking filthy.

"Are you sure you know the lyrics?" I ask Dewey.

"Shit, everyone knows this old chestnut. My daddy used to sing it whilst straining over his stools."

"I want it *low.*"

"So you keep saying. You want low, you got low. This will be down to where you got to reach way up to scratch your foot."

"And slow."

"Slow as molasses over on the soft shoulder, Des."

I power-on the Yamaha 666. It screams — for a moment I imagine licks of flame shooting from it — but I pull a few levers, press some buttons, feed the Beast a handful of microchips, it eventually calms down to where I can touch the keyboard. I invert the chords, odd intervals in the bass. The music boils and bubbles volcanically. I complete the chord progression, nod at Dewey Moore. He reaches up and pulls his headset just slightly off his ears, the better to hear his actual voice, and then he begins to sing. I am recording all this at double speed, so when I play it back this song will plummet like rocks from the sky. The whales should like it, unless I've missed my guess.

"*The pipes, the pipes . . .*" sings Dewey.

I slap the Yamaha 666, it begrudgingly does a flawless string section imitation. I add some soft lines, wisps of mist around mossy tree trunks.

"*For I'll be there,*" sings Dewey, up to the high note, which in this case means that the floorboards stop vibrating. The Beast yawps, I bring a fist heavily down on its top.

"*I love you so,*" concludes Dewey, and I try to soothe the Yamaha 666, to stop it without resorting to the tranq-gun. Gently I release my fingers from the keyboard, and a final chord skitters around the floor before racing out the door and into the universe.

"I don't think it's a hit, man," says Dewey Moore. "People like a bit of pep these days."

"People would," say I.

"Des," says Dewey, "I just want you to know that Danny is a lot happier now."

"Say, you don't have any heavy-duty dope, do you?"

"He's with his Saviour right now. Nestled in His bosom."

"I've just got a slight hankering for, say, nineteen lines of snow and fourteen speedballs."

"That's what I wanted to come over and tell you. Because just a week before his accident, Dan-Dan came to see me. And he was born again."

"Please, Dewey . . ."

"We knelt and held hands. The tears came to your brother's eyes. First he asked for forgiveness . . ."

I play upon the Beast, hoping for a roar, but it is strangely quiet and emits only a tiny sweet sound.

"The Lord forgave him. And then he was filled with the Spirit. So don't you worry about him anymore. Well, my man . . ." Dewey slaps his belly. "What do you say we go chow-down?"

"Yes, yes. You go on ahead, Dewey. I'm just going to rewind this tape." That was pretty cagey. That's one thing you learn in mental hospitals, how to fake these sensible moments so that people will leave you alone. Dewey nods and slips out the door.

I know all about this Jesus fellow. You are dealing with a man who is constantly on the prowl for salvation, a stupid fat tomcat climbing into holy trashbins. One night, I was seated in front of the TV, the drugs had conspired to keep my eyeballs popped open, and suddenly there was Tammy Faye Bakker exhorting me to invite Jesus into my heart. It seemed like a good idea at the time. I dropped to my knees, weeping every bit as profusely as Tammy Faye, and I invited Jesus into my heart. He peered into my heart from the stoop, decided that the place was too messy. That's the last I heard from Him.

So I don't believe Dewey, because Danny's heart was hurricane-hit. Nothing but debris.

The night, the night, Danny's home. I am prowling outside my own house, peering through windows, making sure that the guests have gone away. There is only gloom in there, so I think I am safe. I slide my body through the sliding doors.

Look. A bottle of wine that is still half-full, or half-empty depending on how you look at things, a philosophical nicety that I don't really bother with, seeing as in about two seconds it's going to be neither. (Any signs of you-know-who, Farley fucking O'Keefe?)

"Some friggy-diggy half hour, Des." The alien Claire is sitting on the sofa. She is bristling.

"I was working."

"Whoopee-shit."

"I just had to do a few over-dubs. A cretinous tambourine. A pump organ, as played by Mrs. Peabody. She is very pious. Worried about her husband's drinking. She suspects he may be a latent homosexual and therefore puts her money on the Man Upstairs."

"Shut the fuck up."

"Yes. Er. Um. I'm sorry if I missed dinner."

"Well, don't worry your gnarly little head about it, okay, because dinner sucked sewer water through party straws. We ate some of that Bouillabaisse stuff and just about gagged."

"Let me try it."

"It's no good now, it's all cold and shit."

"We could heat it up."

" 'Cause the thing of it is, Des, I said half an hour, and you were gone for four. You ignored your house guests — "

"I lose track of the time . . ."

"Couldn't you just take some portion of your mind and make it hang chicky, you know, keep an eye out for things taking place in the real world?"

"I'm going to go reheat the Bouillabaisse."

"I'll reheat the stuff for you, goofus. I don't think you know how to work a stove."

"I have tamed the Yamaha 666. I am not daunted by mere kitchen appliances."

Claire huffs into the kitchen, she starts banging pots and pans around.

I follow meekly. "Is all this noise really necessary?" I sit down at the kitchen table, play with an automatic card shuffler. It chews up the deck and spits little pieces of cardboard at me. Optimistically, I gather together the remnants and stuff them back into the machine. You must never assume the nonexistence of magic.

"If this stuff stinks, just say so. I don't think we should lie to each other."

It's a no-go here on the automatic card shuffler front, I have created a small pile of mulch.

Claire sticks a bowl of food on the table, hands me a spoon. She takes a napkin, unfolds it and stuffs it down the neckhole of my shirt. I lift a spoonful, hover it beneath my nostrils. *Fish.* Ironically, the Whale-man loathes fish. Claire watches me, she tilts her head quizzically at my hesitation. "What's wrong?"

"I thought it might be too hot." I ram the spoon into my mouth. This is some sort of fish stew, the various nuances of fishiness are intermingled, it takes all my self-control not to vault this food all over the far wall. "Very good."

Claire stares at me and slowly starts to grin. "You fucker," she says. "You hate fish, don't you?"

I nod meekly.

Claire laughs. "*Quelle flaque.*" She reaches forward, messes my hair. "I'm tired," she announces. "I'm going to bed."

"An excellent notion."

"You know, Des, we could sleep in the same bed. I got no particular objection to that scenario."

"Except for I, you know, am rather irregular in my habits."

"That's what I'm thinking. Like, if we slept together, then I could say, hey, it's time for bed, and hey, it's time to get up."

"Do you think it would work?"

Claire shrugs. "It's worth a try."

We are trying. I have the whole of my carcass teetering on the left side, about a sixteenth of the mattress. The alien occupies the rest of the bed, all flayed limbs and waterfalling golden hair. Suddenly, though, with a small muffled cry, Claire scrunches up into a tiny ball. She draws her knees into her chest, she wraps her arms around herself. A kind of evil electricity affects her, she twitches and gnashes her teeth. I touch her shoulder with my fat fingers — the resulting scream is short but terrifying. Claire climbs out of the bed, she stands in the darkness and tries to remember where she is. She stares at me without tenderness. "Gotta piss," she says, and disappears.

Seems to me it's rise-and-shine time. I'll just check the old bedside clock here — 3:14 A.M. Perfect. I stretch, yawn, slap my gums contently. I certainly enjoy domestic life.

I was eighteen when I met Fay Ginzburg. She was seventeen, in
the company of her best friend, Karen Hoffman, the pair of
them standing directly beneath me during a concert in
Sausalito. This was surprising. I looked and saw that there was
a bit of space available beneath both Monty Mann and my
brother, ample room under Dewey Moore, so why these two
girls should be right there was baffling. I was so shocked I
misplaced my hand on the organ keyboard. I made some
clammy notes and threw them into the engine of "Torque
Torque".

Karen Hoffman was a tall girl, flat-chested, she closed her
eyes and weaved back and forth, a creature in search of a
Svengali. Her lips were thick and very red, and she always
looked to be pouting (always was, in fact, pouting). I took one
look at those lips and was covered with goosebumps. My hands
tossed fishy black notes all over the music. Even Monty Mann
noticed, that's how rank my playing suddenly became. Beside
this tall and amply lipped person was Fay Ginzburg. She
danced like a prizefighter, a masculine bob-and-weave,
left-hooks and uppercuts whistling through the air. The other
patrons gave her a wide berth. Fay Ginzburg's breasts were like
a division of Panzer tanks crushing the border at dawn. And
she was similarly endowed at the other end, a very serious
keester indeed, a huge battering ball of flesh. Fay Ginzburg's
hair was red, when I first saw her it was a pile on top of her head
like autumn leaves about to be torched. Her eyes were grey or

black, depending on her mood, and the most conspicuous thing about her was a large, birdlike nose. (Later a doctor whittled away at the beak until it was a button.)

Not that I was at the time fascinated by Fay Ginzburg. No, all my attention — all my heart, so I fancied — was given over to the tall, gorgeously lipped creature with dreamily vacant eyes. I felt nauseated, my throat got tight, I was suddenly made aware of my elephantine awkwardness. After the set I went backstage and had a sip from Dewey Moore's flask, I filched two beers out of a sink and popped them back. Bolstered, I walked into the larger dressing room, found it to be full of people as it always was, and discovered the object of my love (and her shorter, frightening friend) in conversation with my brother Danny.

I fired up a cigarette, a scrawny, ill-made affair, a taste like medieval peatmoss.

"Desmond!" Danny hailed me. "Come here and meet these womens. This here is — "

"Fay," said the same, even though Danny's finger had been aimed at the taller girl. "Fay Ginzburg. And this is my friend Karen Hoffman. You know Hoffman's Drugs?"

Already my field of expertise, but I could only shrug uncertainly.

"That's her uncle," said Fay.

"Ah," said I. I tried to think of something to say to Karen, to tell her, for example, what a noble line of work I felt her uncle was in, but Fay was sticking her finger into my chest. "What are you doing after the show?"

Danny answered, "Probably going for something to eat."

"You want to come back to my place?"

"Hey," said Danny. He looked at Karen. "Are you going back there?"

Karen produced an elaborate shrug, one full of philosophy and world-weariness. She did this quite a bit, and the effect would have been striking except that she usually did it in response to simple yes/no questions.

"So—" The girl Fay Ginzburg was poking me in the stomach. Throughout our brief interview she prodded me constantly, checking for weak spots. "We'll see you after the show."

"Absolutely," said Dan. "My brother and I are looking forward to it."

The two girls walked away.

"Well, well," marvelled Danny.

"Daniel," I spoke quite earnestly, "I want Karen."

"You do, do you?" Danny lit up a cigarette, pretended to be reflecting seriously, but as he did so he stuffed the butt up his nostril.

"Desmo," asked Daniel, "did you dig the lips?"

"The lips," I agreed.

"Think of the things you could do with those lips."

I nodded lasciviously, although I could only think of kisses, and rather chaste ones at that. (A melody popped into my mind, an airy gossamer affair, a spider's web.)

"But hey, you're my bro'!" said Danny. "We are issue of the same flesh, the same loins." He kissed me on the cheek. "Make her happy, Desmo. Go get your nuts cracked."

So after the show Danny and I got into the back seat of a huge red Edsel and we screamed off (Fay behind the wheel, tires squealing, red lights treated as a Joe Gutts Brake Test). I was silent, sullen, having smoked too much peatmoss, ingested perhaps a beer or two in excess. Danny was quite talkative, he beat out rhythms on the shiny vinyl seats, he concentrated on Fay Ginzburg and left me to speak to she of the Lips, except that it was like we came from different planets, her and me, orbital paths that in a million or two years might come within a hundred yards of each other.

Suddenly a mansion appeared, a huge, oddly built thing sitting on top of a hill. "That your house?" demanded Danny.

"My parents' house," nodded Fay.

"It's kind of," said Dan, "Transylvanian."

The Edsel doggedly climbed the hill. (By the way, I was

always fond of Edsels. I even wrote a song about them, it's on the *Highway* album, which is not one of our better albums, I'll grant you.) And then we went through the front door and were introduced to Fay's parents, Professor and Mrs. Ginzburg.

Mrs. Ginzburg had something wrong with her back, she was always bent over as though searching for lost change on the sidewalk, but she was a cheery sort, full of jokes, usually of a practical nature. One of her favourites was, whenever she should catch her husband off-guard, to shove him into some piece of furniture. These would usually be soft pieces of furniture, sofas and so forth, but I saw the professor shoved into the credenza a time or two. If it should seem odd that a humpbacked woman should be able to do this shoving at will, I should tell you that Professor Ginzburg was the slightest man that ever walked the face of this planet. If he topped seventy-five pounds it was only soaking wet, the day after Thanksgiving. The professor and his good lady were both survivors of a Nazi death camp, they both had a furious need to enjoy life, and I guess that accounts for much of what Fay was.

Mrs. Ginzburg's main concern in life was food. She liked me from the instant she saw me, for although I was then relatively slim, she detected star potential. "Eat!" shouted Mrs. Ginzburg.

Professor Ginzburg was anti-food. "Talk!" he protested. "You don't bring guests into the house and drag them into the kitchen. You sit down and talk like civilized people."

"Who can talk with an empty stomach? You want to listen to growling stomachs all night?"

"So who's growling?"

"One bowl of soup couldn't hurt!" screamed Mrs. Ginzburg. This was her credo.

"One bowl of soup," conceded Professor Ginzburg. "Then I want to discuss music with the boys. Beethoven, Mozart, all them bubbies."

Fay scowled. "Daddy, they don't know about that stuff. They play rock '*n*' roll."

"Rock 'n' roll? What, you're so busy you don't have time to say *and?*"

Danny said, "Desmond knows about those guys."

Fay looked at me, very surprised by this news.

"Desmond!" shouted Professor Ginzburg. "Who's your favourite?"

"Debussy," I supposed.

"He's good," agreed the Professor. "No slouch."

"Soup!" battled back Mrs. Ginzburg. "Feed the stomach, then the soul."

"So go eat soup," sighed Professor G. wearily.

"Then I thought we might go down to the basement and listen to records," said Fay.

"Right," said the professor. "Just don't get pregnant."

"Daddy," said Fay, "you're disgusting."

"What's disgusting? Sex is all of a sudden disgusting?"

"First feed the stomach, then the soul, then the . . ." This train of thought was getting Mrs. G. into a bit of trouble. "Soup!" she announced grandly, herding us into the kitchen.

We were given borscht, which I hadn't had before and took a powerful liking to. Professor Ginzburg hovered in the doorway — it was as if he didn't even want to set foot in the kitchen — and he and I discussed serious composers. His highest praise was that the artist in question was no slouch. Except for Mr. Mozart, who's name Professor G. could not speak except as a kind of herald, hardening the *z* until it cut like a saw.

"I can play the fiddle," Professor Ginzburg told us. "I should say the *violin*, but if you heard me, you'd know. The fiddle. I had a string quartet once. The Commandant — who, as monsters go, was all right — he liked music. So he gave us these instruments, allowed us half an hour a day for practice. Once a week we would play for him. While he ate meat and tickled the tootsies of this milkmaid."

"Don't," cautioned his wife. "They're eating."

Professor Ginzburg, however, had disappeared.

After soup we went downstairs. Karen and Danny immediately fell onto a sofa and commenced kissing. I stood there with a hole in my heart until tackled by Fay Ginzburg. She mowed me down, propelled me into an easy chair and jumped on my lap. "Kiss me, Desmond," she demanded. I did so, first with reluctance, eventually with eagerness. Her body, so frightening and energetic, was delightful to contain, warm bits of flesh surfacing at the oddest times. The kissing was fun, too. Fay's tongue was an eager adventurer, it examined my mouth like a faculty of dentistry. We necked for quite a while — I noticed out of the corner of my eye that Karen and Danny did little more than neck as well — until Professor Ginzburg came racing downstairs, screaming, "Meteor shower! Meteor shower!"

"Daddy!" screamed Fay.

"Radiant points colliding in the empyrean!" The professor disappeared back up the stairs. My brother was quick to follow. "Come on," said Fay wearily. She grabbed my hand and pulled me after her father.

We stood in the backyard, all of us bathed in starlight. Above us, the sky was streaking with silver.

Danny couldn't help himself. He tilted his head back and howled.

"That's it, Dan-Dan!" shouted the professor. "And put in a good word for me."

I stood there flat-footed and slack-jawed, my head canted awkwardly. Professor Ginzburg elbowed me in the side. "Know what slays me?" he asked. "Some people see something like this, a celestial phenomenon, they say, *it makes me feel so small.* Putzes. It makes me feel so big. Like God did this just for me. So I watch, I give it a little, hmmmm. . . ." Professor G. reached out his hand and waggled it judgementally. "*Not too shabby.*"

The stars are stagnant tonight. The Great and Little Bears are hibernating. Orion has taken off his belt, laid down his sword, he's eating a TV dinner and watching "I Love Lucy." I've popped outside for a breath of fresh air because I do not feel well. I am having some kind of a reaction. Hot flashes, chills, convulsions, nausea.

I need drugs.

Let's check the music room. You look over there, I'll poke around the control room. I must calm down if I mean to do any serious Whale Work. I'm going to work on the Song of Congregation. I have a plan; it requires intoxicants and plenty of 'em. The control room, however, is clean as a bone, it looks like Farley O'Keefe might have preceded me.

The mention of that name is not likely to help me in my particular state. Indeed, it adds a certain urgency to this stimulant-finding mission. Check behind the speakers, check inside the speaker cones. Farley O'Keefe, former college football hero. Hero, that is, until he bit off an opposing player's ear. That's not even the first time that's happened, but Farley walked back to the line of scrimmage *chewing.* A scurrilous knave, Farley O'Keefe. A real fucking prick. (Do you see the trumpet and horn cases? Check inside the velvet pockets, check inside the flaps meant for concealing mouthpieces.) A huge man, increasing amplitudes of muscle ultimately adorned by a tiny head. Farley sported a handlebar moustache, he wore spectacles when he wasn't beating someone (usually me) to a pulp. Somewhere along the way (the drums, the drums, pick up each separate unit and rattle it, please) Farley O'Keefe acquired the knack of sounding both intelligent and hip (he was neither), he was forever brandishing some book in your face, Hermann Hesse or Ayn Rand, and saying, "Simplistic, but all right in its way." When he dies I mean to drive a wooden stake through his heart.

Did you just burp? What was that chilling sound, extremely unhealthy effluvium? I don't think it was me, it seemed to come from over there.

Over by the Yamaha 666.

I think they may have gotten in over their heads when they invented this particular beast. There's a rumour that Stevie Wonder is having trouble with his machine, which probably means the Yamaha 666 is chasing him around the house. We are the only two people, as far as I know, who own a Yamaha 666 (they cost many hundreds of thousands), except for a studio in Glendale, which purchased one and burned down that same night.

The Yamaha 666 gives forth another reboant snarl. That it isn't plugged in means nothing to the Yamaha 666. The keyboards, seven of them, are curved and cantilevered, they produce an enormous pool of shadow, but as I take a cautious step forward a light flashes from within the darkness. The Yamaha 666 emits another sound, gentler this time, almost a purr. The light flashes again, a reflection off glass. I stumble quickly towards it and find, perched on the middle keyboard, one entire bottle of bourbon. As I pick it up a little tube of paper rolls forward, waterfalling down the keyboards, and before it has hit the ground I've recognized it as a joint, a number, a bomber.

Now we're set. I mean to wash the humanness out of my system, then I can work on the "Song of Congregation" and get it right.

I think the Yamaha 666 likes me, that's what I think. It's too bad I didn't own it when Farley O'Keefe was around (in the employ of my wife Fay) because I could have locked Farley in the music room overnight, and I'm pretty sure that in the morning he would have been disappeared, perhaps all but his curly moustache.

This bourbon is good stuff, it makes me feel a bit better. I can't even recall precisely why I felt poorly to begin with. Liquor has a bad reputation around these parts (I am in large part responsible); but it can have a very beneficial effect. And it was Farley O'Keefe's ignominious task to keep me and booze forever separated. He was also paid to maintain distance between me and pharmaceuticals. This is, you'll agree, not fit employment for a grown man, but at least it's better than his sideline.

You see where humanness gets you? I have just roared, a scream originated deep within my belly and came rushing out. I am decidedly miserable now. If Farley were here he would *tsk* his tongue, he would fold those thick arms across his chest and sigh, "Des, what are you doing to yourself?" Easy for him to say, O'Keefe never drank. What would be the use? The liquor would travel around his endless miles of bloodstream searching uselessly for the little brain. Even if I could come up with a good answer, such as *eradicating humanness*, Farley O'Keefe would remain unimpressed. "You don't want me to get physical, do you, Des? I detest violence, Des. It would hurt me more than you." So why aren't you walking around with contusions all over your body, Farley? "Life is beautiful, Des. Wake up and look at it." When did this happen, this beautification of life? The most one can do is try to produce some pitiful piece of prettiness, a song, and send it out into the world, a cripple dressed in rags. *Agh, agh.* I should be working. The "Song of Congregation", the remaining movement of the Whale Music. But I am immobile, I am cataleptic. An image pops into my mind, it's time for the daily Memory Matinee.

Up the stairs, down the hallway, into what is jokingly referred to as the master bedroom.

You see, Farley was successful for a while. I got clean, I even took to donning a suit and going to the Galaxy building every morning at nine o'clock. I had my own office there, the door had a sign that said DESMOND HOWL, PRIVATE, and I would enter and tinker on the piano. I wrote "Sunset" under those circumstances, a mega-hit, number one for seven months. That one charted in Kotzebue. At five o'clock I would repack my briefcase, leave the office building, nodding at all the executives and secretaries. "Afternoon, Mr. Howl." "Good day, Mr. Howl." I would bestow a smile and a nod upon these lackies. It was not a bad life. It was boring, but excitement is highly overrated. I likely would have kept it up indefinitely. Except one day I became very tired at two in the afternoon. There was no music within me, which happens sometimes. The ringing in my ears moved front and centre, it vibrated until it worked up a headache of heroic proportions. I decided that I must go home. Which I did. I entered my house, wandered upstairs, only to find Fay and Farley O'Keefe naked in the master bedroom. Very grim. Worse, Fay was humped over and administering a bee-jay, something she was ever unwilling to do to me. Farley O'Keefe's member was a gruesome thing, ribbed with purple veins. *Bing, bing,* went the heartstrings, *boing* went the tenuous grasp on reality. I flew down to the kitchen and located the cooking sherry.

Since then I have known only confusion. Farley was fired, Fay was given the boot. Lawyers chewed through the woodwork. Dr. Tockette appeared with appalling regularity. Danny drove his new silver Porsche through a guardrail. The car burst into flame as it smacked the surface of the Pacific Ocean. The whales gathered to watch the pyrotechnical display. It seems like years that I have been labouring on the Whale Music, but great care has been given to get it exactly right. There have been no bright spots in my life. Except, I guess, for the strange creature from Toronto.

Agh, agh. I must summon the wherewithal to work. I wonder

how this eradication-of-humanness process is doing. Half of the bourbon is gone, the scrawny ill-made cigarette has been rendered into clouds. I would judge that the process is working, except that I seem to be weeping. A very bad sign. Whales do not weep. They make outraged bellows, which is what I should be doing. Wait though. Here's a thought. I have been working on the "Song of Congregation", and the call has been *come on over, whales.* Surely the whales can only think, why bother, if they've had a better offer (if a school of baitfish is travelling nearby, a huge shimmering cloud of munchables) at best the whales might ask for a raincheck. If, however, I incorporate the outraged bellow, if I howl at the vagaries of fate, the whales might figure, hey, he's playing our tune. What do you think? It's certainly worth a try. Given the way I feel right now, the outraged bellow should be no problem.

A final sip of the bourbon, I struggle to my feet.

I'm going to use the Yamaha 666. This is going to be a Beast solo. No drums, rhythms are manmade, they have nothing to do with the world. No guitars, they are too mathematical, too much the division of frequencies. Only the Beast. If I survive, I shall be the world's greatest Yamaha 666 player. I take off my bathrobe, toss it into the corner. Man against Beast. Pure and elemental. I wipe my palms free of moisture. I crack the knuckles, I do digital exercises. The Yamaha 666 is already humming, it is taunting me, daring me to plug it in, to feed it juice. The Yamaha 666 can sense fear, so I move without hesitation, tossing in the wallplug nonchalantly. The Beast lets out an ungodly ululation. I pretend not to notice. Electrical cross-currents swim in the gloom. I throw switches, I slap buttons, I slide faders. The Beast is cowed for a moment, but as I'm about to put my fingers down it roars defiantly. I kick it in its underbelly! There is silence. Then, closing my eyes, I begin to play.

I thought she was the only girl for me . . .
(Awoo-oo-oo, cry the halt and the lame.)
When she left I was as lonesome as could be . . .
(Awoo-oo-oo, even Freaky Freddy joining in.)
But then in my rearview I saw your lips
I could have pulled my U-ie on a poker chip
You gave a little wave with your fingertips
And then I got a look at your pouting lips

(And Dewey stomps up from his vocal basement,
a-pow-pow-pow, you got to . . .)

Kiss me, Karen,
kiss, kiss, me Karen
(Awoo-oo, pow-pow)

Let's face it, ladies and gentlemen, the chorus to perhaps my most famous songs does nothing but go "Kiss me, Karen" over and over again. It is the popular song equivalent of a circle jerk in the shower room, but it does possess a certain urgency. The father hated the song, between takes he'd lean back and roar, "Kiss him, Karen, for Christ's sake!" Even Dan disliked the song, he pulled me aside and said, "Desmo, I got to tell you, kissing this girl was like sucking a sponge." He didn't know we'd passed into the realm of art. All *I* knew is that it made a lot of sense rhythmically if five young men chanted "Kiss me,

Karen" over and over again, but great care had to be taken not to get boring. So what did I do? I got positively baroque. Freaky Freddy couldn't feed me empty tracks fast enough. There's as many as fifty separate voices on that chorus, they weave in and out, collide like bumper cars. Freddy set up Sal Goneau's drum kit in an adjunctive garage, he ladled on heaps of echo and phasing, the result sounded like someone taking out their trash in the Twilight Zone. Dewey's bass was fine-tuned electronically until it achieved awesome purity. Monty still had his special screwdriver-altered amplifier (he dared not bring another, lest Fred Head pull a similar stunt), and I was by this time much enamoured of electronics myself, I'd rigged up a special pre-amp that functioned as a sort of overdrive, forcing too much juice into the speakers, so that what finally trickled out was high-octane white gold.

Yes sir, I don't believe the Howl Brothers ever functioned as well again as we did that day. It was magic, it was a time we'd spend years trying to rediscover. Magic is a hard thing to hold on to.

But we had it that day. When we were finished recording "Kiss Me, Karen" b/w "My Baby Burnt Out My Clutch," Kenneth Sexstone pranced to the middle of the room and said,"Thank you, boys. You have just made me filthy rich." We all started to grin. Even the father grinned, despite what was happening to him in the outside world, where the piece of granite he used for a heart was getting shattered. The father grinned because he knew what was about to happen. Within two weeks of its release, the record was number one in the United States of America.

Success, success, it's time for all hell to break loose!

You can take my word for it, it certainly is fun, at least for a while, being one of the more famous people in the world. For one thing, people notice you. Complete strangers stop dead in their tracks and gawk, people who under other circumstances wouldn't give you the time of day. Do you know that feeling, when you're buying shoes, and the clerk is racing here and there, up to nothing more, it seems, than ignoring you? Well, become famous and those guys will race out onto the sidewalk with all sizes and colours balanced on their heads. And as for girls, my my. Formerly my interaction with the opposite sex was largely stammered inanities. It didn't take long before I was talking to them like Danny: "Oh, hi, Caroline. You're looking very sweet today. Say, Caroline, do you think that if we were to step into that bus shelter over there you could give me a little bee-jay?"

We were on the cover of magazines, the five of us grinning like idiots from newsstands across the nation. We had to do countless interviews, and it was at one such interview that I made the reacquaintance of the strange kid with the too-big glasses, Geddy Cole. His spectacles were no longer oversized, his acne was clearing a bit, but he was still a startlingly odd chap. He worked for a rag called *Rockin' Rods* a music/car journal, a genre that flourished at the same time we did (no coincidence), and Geddy Cole demanded to know my preferences in clothes, food and automobiles. I had stock answers for all these, citing Monty Mann's taste in clothes, Danny's in automobiles, my own in food. When the interview was done, Geddy asked if I wanted to go "catch some tunes." Geddy and I had shared some scrawny cigarettes, zombie reefer it was, and the notion of "catching tunes" appealed to me, so the strange kid and I went out. Before we went, though, Geddy reached into his pocket and removed some pills. Oblong pills, bright yellow.

"Take a few of these, Des," said Geddy.

Another pharmaceutical adventure for Desmond Howl. These magic pills seemed to put me on equal footing with the universe.

Geddy took me to a cavernous nightclub, the band and most of the patronage black. The group was The Lamont Brothers, three men of such disparate aspect that, if they were not lying about their relationship, Mrs. Lamont's character would have to be questioned. The most memorable of the back-up musicians was the sax player, an overly tall boy of about seventeen. He was dressed in a pink tuxedo and ruffled shirt, as though he expected at any moment to be pressed into marriage.

This was the first player who I had ever heard go outside. Do you know what I'm talking about? A solo is like a little door in the song, and most instrumentalists step over the stoop, see what the weather's like and duck back in. This young fellow, he ran out that door, sprinted around the block, he took the cross-town bus and hired a cab back. Granted, I was so zombied at the time perhaps Lawrence Welk would have sounded as good, but it was a critical experience for me.

After the set, Geddy Cole waved some members of the band over to the table, and they joined us, because Geddy had a reputation for holding good dope and was more than willing to spring for drinks. The sax player joined us, he brought his horn with him and throughout the break he toyed silently with the levers and buttons, his long fingers popping pads. He was introduced as Mooky Saunders. When he heard my name he raised his eyebrows. "You write that 'Kiss Me, Karen' thing?"

I nodded.

"Shee-yut," said Mooky Saunders, grinning at me. "When you gonna fawk that woman, Desmond?"

When, indeed? Fay Ginzburg and I had kept up a correspondence throughout my ascension. Our letters were little more than basic rundowns on the weather and such, but I did notice something interesting happen to her sign-offs. They began with "Your friend," then they gained this long-lasting character, "Ever your friend," then those cute little *x*'s and *o*'s started mushrooming, then *the word* appeared, "Love, Fay," then "Lots o' love, Fay," and finally she was writing "All my love, Fay." We had a big concert scheduled for Sausalito. Fay

103

and I agreed we would see each other afterwards and, in her almost illegibly scrawled words, "talk seriously."

So though it might seem that all was right with the world, such was not the case. It was Daniel who pointed out that something was very odd. "Desmo," he asked me one night, "are you rich?"

"Rich?"

"Yeah, rich. Do you have a lot of money?"

I took some out of my pocket, thinking that he was soliciting a loan. "I got maybe forty bucks, Dan-Dan. You need it?"

"Desmo, you wrote 'Kiss Me, Karen'?"

"Yes."

"It sold a million or three?"

"Yes."

"Desmo, why ain't you a milly-un-aire?"

The father seemed to be prepared for us. He was standing at the top of the stairway in his dressing-gown, smoke from a cigarette curling around his head. The father hadn't shaved for weeks, but his whiskers were (like him) feckless things, they fuzzed up the soft lines of his face but stopped quite a distance short of becoming a beard. The father's eyes raged. He pointed a finger at Dan and myself, riveting us in the foyer. "I *made* you!" the father screamed. "Just don't forget that. Without me there is no Howl Brothers!"

"Daddy —" I began.

Danny cut me short. "What have you been up to, old man?"

"You boys." The father shook his head wistfully. "So young, so carefree. You don't know nothing about the way the world works. You don't know business. You don't even know how to copyright your own tunes. So, because I'm your father, I'm doing it for you."

"Copyright them how?"

"Copyright them under Howell Music, Inc., what did you expect?"

"Who do you list as the writer?" shouted Danny.

"I *made* you!"

"He's screwing us, Des."

"You boys were underage, you couldn't sign no contracts. What does it matter what it says on a piece of paper? It might say that I wrote a song, what does it matter?"

"I can't believe this," muttered Danny. "This is unreal."

"Don't worry, I'm setting aside money for you boys. You're my sons. Besides, what do you need money for? Beer money, poontang money, that you got. What else do you need?"

This was certainly a kick in the head. The man at the top of the stairs suddenly weaved like a blade of grass blown by wind. I realized that he had been drinking.

"Besides, the stuff is *shit*," said the father. "Think about my reputation."

Danny suddenly said, "Is Maurice Mantle in on this little scam?"

"Maurice," said my father. "Moe-fucking-reese? Moe-reese don't know shit from sushi."

"So you're screwing us, and you're screwing him."

"I am *not* screwing you boys," said the father. He sat down on the top stair. "Now, Maurice," mused the father, "Maurice I'm screwing." He had softened suddenly. "You see," he said calmly, for the billionth time in his puny existence, "when a song hits big, then you'll be sitting on Easy Street."

"Where's Mom?" I asked.

"Just never mind where your bimbo mother is. You boys are like your mother, do you know that, you got no consideration for my feelings, you just think you can do whatever you want and never mind if someone should get hurt."

"Mommy is with Mr. Mantle?" I asked, or realized and spoke unwittingly.

"Affirmative, Desmond. You're pretty smart for a jagoff."

"Well, that's too bad —" said Dan.

"Don't give me *too bad*, Daniel. Do not stand there and give me *too bad*." The father stood up wearily. "We're a bunch of flies on a shitpile and it's got nothing to do with *too bad* because it's all . . ." He lost his train of thought, the father grabbed ahold of the bannister. "So what do I get out of it? I get all the fucking money, boys. That's not much to ask. I get all the fucking money. I'm headed for Easy Street." The father turned, headed for his den. "*I made you!*" he hollered.

The father was a victim of limited imagination, that's what Daniel said. Immediately after this encounter, Dan and I made for the bars, the scuz palaces. My brother and I pounded boilermakers in the company of lepers. Naked women paraded before us. Humanity's last-ditch attempt to keep a lid on things.

"What," said my brother, "a dipshit."

"Why did he do it?" I wondered aloud.

"Why? 'Cause he had to."

"Had to?"

"Man, he fed her all these stories. How great everything was gonna be. When a song fucking hits big. The way I see it, he had no choice."

"So mom wanted money . . ."

"Desmond, you're the same as the old man. You got a limited imagination. Mom never wanted money. She wanted fairy tales." Danny took a moment to whistle a nearly-naked woman over to the curtain of the stage. He stuck a fifty-dollar bill into her g-string. "There's more than one kind of goddam story. Didn't the old man ever hear of *love stories*?"

I wake up in the music room. My mouth is fuzzy and my head aches. I have a hangover, how quaint. This hangover doesn't know what it's up against, trying to inhabit the body of Desmond Howl.

I dreamt I was a whale. I swam in the ocean contentedly, occasionally rising to the surface for a little blow. I ingested huge quantities of plankton. Some dolphins told me that a silver star had fallen out of the sky and burst into flame upon the waters. Those crazy dolphins.

Fay was a great believer in dreams and was always after me to write down my dreams immediately upon rising. Then my dreams could be examined, my inner thoughts and feelings discerned. This dream, wherein I dreamt I was a whale, means that I want to be a whale. There, what's the big deal?

The Yamaha 666 is asleep, perhaps dreaming machine dreams, producing a soft purr. I gently reach up and press its power button. The Beast lets out a sigh, the energy collapses.

The Whale-man is tired, these hours of drug-induced stupor do not really rest one, you know, they lay one out in a coma, allowing the various humours to conspire to more deviltry. The Whale-man is jangly, though, energetic and exhausted at the same time, my hands shake and there is a ball of gas about to go nova in my belly. Let's face it, people, I have ended badly. Why couldn't I have been a baseball player, why couldn't my worst problem be that after four beers I like to arm-wrestle with guys named Sparky and Lynn?

I pull myself up gripping the Yamaha 666, the Stradivarius of emulators. I took the Beast so far outside that we started spotting igloos, and there was never a peep of rebellion. The Beast knows no fear.

Let us listen to the "Song of Congregation". I wander into the control room, power-on, switch switches, the music pumps out octaphonically, the mouth of the Beast filling the world. This is okay. This sounds like Venusian footsoldiers, this says *whales, get the fuck over here STAT!!*

107

Now the real work begins. Mixing.

Even with the computers, the digitalizers, even with the sound enhancers and graphic equalizers, mixing is a tough game. What wouldn't I give to havé Freaky Fred sitting beside me, looking off into vacant space, staring almost *at* the music, suddenly reaching out towards a pod, panning a sound half a degree to the right, and *kerpow*, it's like da Vinci getting the Mona Lisa's smile just right: "Dattsa da teeket!"

Did you hear that? That sudden loud noise buried in the music? Oh my goodness, I hope there isn't some imperfection on the tape. I throw it into reverse and listen again. Yes, there is a loud noise, but — I swack the power-off. A loud noise, but it's coming from the studio itself, someone is stumbling around in the gloom, uncertain of their footing. I crouch behind the console and peer out. My eyes are used to it, night vision is my most acute sense, and I can see that it's — *agh* — none other than Kenneth Sexstone, president of Galaxy Records.

Kenneth does not seem to have aged over the past many years. He claims that this is due to science. He has had his skin stretched, he has had pockets of fat liposuctioned away, he injects himself with megavitamins and is on some kind of meat-free, mucus-free, food-free diet, but I believe that he has bartered with Lucifer. He still looks about fifteen, he still resembles Howdy Doody. "Desmond?" he hails me in the gloom. "I know you're here."

I press the in-studio speaker button, I push up the levels until they make everything shake, I boom out, "Go away."

"We have to communicate," he calls back. He has figured my location, he stumbles towards the control room. "We must make speaks, Desmond."

"Desmond Howl is not here," I respond. "This is an automatic sentry system. In fifteen seconds strategically mounted Howitzers will commence firing. Consider this your final warning."

"Desmond, toy not. Your ass is in a very serious legal sling."

"Ten seconds. Mr. Howl covets his privacy."

"Tremendously serious trouble. Contractual chicanery. Stab in the back. *Et tu* and all that. I mean only to help."

"Mr. Howl doesn't know what you're talking about. This is your last chance. If you do not leave, you have chosen death."

"Mr. Howl knows what I'm talking about. I talk of music. I talk of a song named 'Claire'. A haunting though dirgelike ditty. But, Desmond, from what I understand, you gave the mastertape of this song to your mother. She and her husband have released it under the aegis of something called Mantlepiece Records. What do I feel, Desmond? I feel hurt. I feel pain. Stung by duplicity. After all we've been through, Desmond, after all our years of friendship, surely you know that you can't record a fart without it being *mine*."

I think I'll try the Yaqui Indian trick. Hold my breath, make myself invisible.

"DESMOND!!!"

New scientific research indicates that whales often bark to stun little fish. They produce a roar of such magnitude that the anchovy's innards are busted all to pieces. Kenneth seems to have acquired this knack. Stupefied, I open the door, although it seems to me that for a recluse, a virtual locust-devouring hermit, I am seeing an awful lot of people lately.

Kenneth skips into the control room, the monkey-gland robustness of his face shines in the half-light. "Desmond," he says, spotting me. "Good to see you, Desmond."

"Kenneth. We missed you at the funeral."

"The obsequies for young Daniel?"

"I played the accordion. 'Jesu, Joy of Man's Desiring' on the titty-tickler. Many people came. They wept. Women wailed and keened for seven days and seven nights. Men became drunken and fought in the meadhalls. The country reeled with chaos, ruination."

"I'm sorry I missed it."

"You are a very busy man."

"So, Desmond," he says, "would you care to explain to me what goes on?"

"I gave my mother a tape?" This sounds vaguely familiar.

"Of the song 'Claire', a beautiful if threnodic avowal of passion. It is receiving airplay, Desmond. It *might* — note the uncertainty with which my voice is freighted — it might be a hit. Nothing mega, we're not talking moving units to the Bozon tribe or anything, but this song might represent a respectable little piece of fruit on the tree of musical money. This I do not know for certain. What I do know is, the song should not be on Mantlepiece Records. Your contract clearly states that your next work is the property of Galaxy Records."

"The song is a mere piece of dross and frippery. A novelty tune, somewhat akin to 'Vivian in Velvet.' I have not forgotten my legal, my *Mephistophelean*, obligations to your company. Here, listen." I power-on the machines, we hear the majestic "Song of Congregation".

"Turn it off," says Kenny.

I do so. When Kenneth tells me to do something, I do it.

"When I hear this music, Desmond, I hear magnificence. Munificence and majesty. I don't hear money, Desmond. I strain my ears, I can't hear two nickels scraping together. You were a young man, Desmond, a boy, when you came to me. I listened to the music, I decided to invest heavily. We are speaking great big gobby greenbacks here. This policy has been maintained at Galaxy Records. Over the past years, we have financed albums which, in the argot of this business, stiffed. Dogs, Desmond. Howling mastiffs. Not that our faith has been shaken, no, nay, never even think it. We *know* that Desmond Howl is a genius, we *know* he can get that money back. But the vehicle for this reclamation is a commercially viable song. Not this masterwork, not this astounding display of moral courage, not this art with an *A* as big as a mountain, *no*. What we want is a little song. Such as 'Claire'."

"Now," my volley, "the situation as I see it: Galaxy Records invested money in me — money that I earned it in the first place — and then released a series of albums. These albums, I believe, averaged sales of seven hundred thousand units per — hardly doglike, Kenneth, very respectable, I believe the Rolling Stones have rarely sold more than that. Also, two of those albums are considered classics, doesn't *Grin* turn up on every writer's top-ten list of all-time great records? Furthermore, my contract gives me complete artistic control, which to my mind implies some measure of responsibility over what I do or do not deem acceptable for release."

"Be that as it may, my friend," Kenny neatly sidesteps, " 'Claire' is out as a record."

"Hmm. Well, Maurice is very ill, they no doubt needed the money."

Kenneth Sexstone jumps onto the Revox, if he weren't such a scrawny little human being I'd worry about my machinery. Kenneth crosses his legs and braids his arms. *Agh.* I'm about to get a dose of the famous Sexstone earnestness. "Maurice and I, we're close. His illness, do you know what it's doing to me? It's like someone has taken my heart and put it in a Cuisinart." Kenneth rips open his shirt, his preternaturally hairy chest stares at me. This is the Sexstone earnestness at its highest pitch. "A broken heart lies here." The effect is undone by the nancy manner in which he rebuttons. "But money, Desmond, for all that I love it, cannot buy back the man's health. A sad truth. We should have read the fine print, Des, but that's the deal we signed. So, I don't see how I can sit back and allow myself to be reamed in this outrageously royal fashion."

"What do you want me to do, Kenneth? Sue my own mother and her dying husband?"

"Of course not. Don't be absurd. But if you threaten to, maybe we could work something out."

"Kenny, you jest."

"You sued your father, didn't you?"

"I did not."

"Well, I attended the court proceedings. It seemed to me that you were suing him."

111

"That was Danny's idea. I just happened to be there. Anyway, how fast is the record climbing? Are we charting in the small towns, in the metropoli, or what? Did we grab the chains right away?"

"Mantlepiece Records put the rink in the dink, Desmond. It's a scuzzy-looking label, they just sent it out to a few stations, it's a miracle it's doing as well as it is. If Galaxy had it, we'd do it right."

"If the record is out, it can't be recalled like a car with faulty brakes. You win some, you lose some, Kenneth."

"Ah, yes, I see your point. However, Desmond, if we can't manage to clear this thing up somehow, then, I hate to say it, the legal arm of Galaxy Records shall flex its impressive bicep and come out pointing at you. Do you know what that means, Desmond? It means court appearances. Subpoenas and special discoveries. Newspaper and magazine people. *Unpleasantness.* It means getting dressed and leaving the house, battling through the press people into the federal building and then being attacked — let's not pretend it isn't so — by people who have a very clear idea of how you lead your life. And, if it comes down to it, Desmond, it means an assessment of your mental capability, and I don't want even to speculate on where that might lead."

"Agh."

"Just so."

"Double agh."

"Your mother wouldn't want to subject you to that. So here's what I suggest. Talk to your mother. The mere mention of legality should do the trick. Then, because Galaxy Records are basically kind-hearted folk, we shall buy Mantlepiece Records at a very reasonable price. Extremely fair. Philanthropic. Enough to ensure Moe his medical needs, for all the good it will do the poor man. We take over supervision of the record, and *poof*, you have another hit, you have made a comeback! Your star burns bright in the firmament once more. I sit in my counting house counting all my money. Everybody is happy."

"Oh, Kenneth. Are you not already fabulously wealthy? Do you not own a mansion and several cars? At what point do you say, maybe I just close my eyes and let the tilted earth spin?"

"At no point do I say this, Desmond."

"Currency, Kenneth. Mere currency. At the Pearly Gates they do not ask after your material wealth. They make inquiries about such things as charity. You shall be tongue-tied, Kenneth, you shall hem and haw and mention that you once tipped a whore in Venice."

"I was a weird little boy, Desmond. Empathize. I was teased and taunted. The bigger boys would hoist me into the air holding the back of my underpants. But like you, I was a prodigy. At the age of four I could beat my father, my uncles, at chess. I was a grandmaster at seventeen. There exists the Sexstone Response to the Queen's Pawn Gambit, a rare thing, but when played it is often accompanied in the notation with a series of exclamation points. It is a bit complex, but basically the response is this — take the pawn and then fuck him in the heart, screw him three ways from Sunday, leave nothing but carnage and mayhem in the middle game. Do you see where I'm coming from, Desmond?"

"Whales have no money, and yet they are happy."

"Whales are ungainly, Desmond. Whales swim around going ga-ga."

"You're serious, then, in this threat you have made?"

"Absolutely. One hundred percent."

"Is there no one playing the game for the love of music?"

"There's you."

I knew there'd be a catch.

"By the way," says Kenneth Sexstone, "I detect the distinctive odour of alcohol. As your friend, I advise you not to indulge."

"As my friend. I see. I suppose you are considering rehiring Farley O'Keefe?"

"And just who," asks Kenneth Sexstone, "is he?"

I must speak with Claire. I check poolside, she is not there. I go to the living room, she is not there. I check the kitchen, she is not there. I hope that she hasn't fixed her starcraft and zoomed back to the planet Toronto.

I am howling. How could I, the fat phantom, have gotten myself involved in another legal imbroglio?

I climb the stairs, huffing and puffing, and hope that Claire might be in the bathroom or bedroom. She is in neither one, she has disappeared. Perhaps she never even existed, did you ever think of that?

I will go to bed. Bed-going can be rather radical with me, you know. At one point I climbed into the sack and didn't emerge for close to a year, other than hurried and furtive trips into the bathroom. Mind you, I was indulged in my egocentricities back then. There were people who would bring me food, for example. Judging from my weight, there was a whole army of the little ants. Still, I can probably live off my subcutaneous fatty tissue for a month or two, which might be enough to do the trick. You have no idea, really, how big a deal bed-going is in our society. It's a sad thing when a person's normalcy is established upon the regularity with which he/she scurries under the blankies and launches into never-never-land, but sad things abound. If you eat three squares a day and clock in the requisite eight hours nightly, why then, you could collect shrunken heads and no one would bat an eye.

Yes, it's true. Take it from me, a veteran. The indicators of mental health in this fair land are sleeping habits, hair length and beards. Those doctors hate to see beards, especially long ones, it makes them antsy. A beard and long hair, they reach for the constraining garments. If you have a beard, long hair and stay up late, why then, they shoot the drugs into you, not the fun drugs but the dark lugubrious ones, the drugs that make you go "Blah-blah-blah." Of course, if you walk around going "Blah-blah-blah," you're mentally ill. Checkmate.

I take a few steps, I lift off and deposit the girth on the mattress.

This is not good, and I'll tell you why. There is a scent, an odour, there is a sweetness here that certainly has nothing to do with me. Claire was no apparition, then. She existed, and now she is lost to me. I toss the pillows angrily across the room. There was a sect of monks who bedded down on nothing but dirt floors and they achieved spiritual enlightenment. I'm not willing to go quite that far, but I can do without pillows.

Loss, loss. Is that what life is, an accumulation of things that must then be lost? Bingo. Some people become inured to it, that's how they survive. Danny, for instance, took loss in stride, and he lost a lot. He lost money, girlfriends, wives, control of the silver Porsche.

What are the chances, do you figure, of me falling asleep? I'm talking actual slumber here, the restful variety. Las Vegas odds-makers would give you a long line on me going to sleep, but I'm here to tell you, go put down two dollars at a thousand to one, because I think it might actually take place.

Yes, quickly, two dollars at a thousand to one . . .

So here we are in Dreamland once more.

You likely won't notice any big difference. Whales occasionally happen by, the furniture is strewn with seaweed, otherwise it's situation normal. Which is to say, I get locked in a Memory Room from which there is no escape. The irony of the situation is not lost upon me, I mean, I can't remember what happened seven minutes ago, but when there is no music in my head, the Anamnesis Association holds a convention, there is drunkenness, cavorting and mayhem.

I'm seeing Fay Ginzburg for the second time. She has undergone a metamorphosis. Her hair is no longer red and piled like autumn leaves; it's black and industriously straight. A great bolt of it covers most of her face. One grey/black eye burns beside this hank, the tip of her nose pushes through, otherwise Fay Ginzburg's aspect is one of midnight, witchy blackness. She's lost weight, is more than slender. Her body has trouble coping with the bombastic breasts and buttocks. Fay wears a turtleneck sweater and a skirt that shows off her dimpled knees. I've just come off stage. I've sweated profusely, I smell rank. Fay has pushed her way backstage, she seeks me out and kisses me soundly upon the lips. "Desmond," she whispers. "Coming back to my place?"

"Um . . ."

Fay grabs my arm, we march out of the dressing room and into the night. I see Karen out of the corner of my eye — she is standing in a corner looking like an addled kitten staring at sunbeams. Danny will ignore her for the rest of the evening. If he's in an especially sensitive, kind-hearted mood he might try to slip out without Karen noticing, otherwise he'll treat the girl like so much odourless gas.

(Such reflections are big danger in Dreamland, because now we have Danny appearing, water-logged and puffy. Danny wants us to know that he was never as bad as all that. Nod politely, smile like an idiot and wait until he goes away.

(He was, you know. He was every bit as bad as that, and here in Dreamland we see him at his worst. Open up that door, sneak a peek inside, what do you see?!)

I'm certainly pleased to see the Professor and Mrs. Ginzburg again. Mrs. Ginzburg has become a rabid Howl Brothers fan. The mansion is decorated with posters and buttons and eight-by-ten glossies. She even has an autographed picture of Fred Head, can you believe it? Mrs. Ginzburg greets me with a hug, she pats my ballooning belly appreciatively. "Good, Desmond," she says. "I've been worried. Fay has given up eating."

"Mom," says Fay sternly.

"Let's go to the kitchen and eat soup," whispers Mrs. Ginzburg conspiratorially, perhaps not conspiratorially enough.

"You don't bring a person into the house — especially not so famous a person as Mr. Desmond Howl — and drag him into the kitchen to eat soup. You sit him down in the living room, we get cozy, we cross our legs, we hem and haw, maybe have a little fruit juice, then you say, Desmond, *how's 'bout soup?*" The professor seems to have lost a little weight, he's hard to pick out against the white of the carpet. He's saddled with a lethal-looking oaken cane, and he uses this to tap my leg affectionately. "Desmond, where'd you get them ears? That chorus in 'Kiss Me, Karen,' boy oh boy, I think that would have confused Mr. Johann Sebastian Bach!" The professor grabs me by the arm, hauls me towards the living room. "I bet you play chess," he says.

Mrs. Ginzburg gets ahold of the other arm and makes for the kitchen. "Who could play chess on an empty stomach?"

"What, you need strength to pick up the pieces?"

"Brain work is hard work!" returns Mrs. Ginzburg.

Fay stands back and watches the battle. Part of her new image involves a stinginess as regards energy and emotion.

"We'll play chess, you keep an eye on us. Just when it looks like we're about to keel over from exhaustion, rush in with the refreshing soup, save our lives, my darling. Desmond, follow me."

Mrs. Ginzburg lets go of my arm, retreats into her kitchen. The professor and I sit down on either side of an elaborate board, the pieces intricately carved ivory. "You be white," says the professor. "I fight best when I'm fighting back."

(But this is Dreamland, don't forget, the pieces resemble the father, the mother, Maurice Mantle and Kenny Sexstone, the

117

pawns are all tiny replicas of Dr. Tockette, him and his legion of impersonators.)

I can play chess, you know, rather well. Many weird people can play chess (although I don't for a minute buy this Sexstone Response to the Queen's Pawn Gambit business). Freddy Head was a keen player, he and I had quite a few memorable games, we would even play in the truck as we journeyed from bad hotel to bad hotel in the early days. Fred Head and I would imagine the board, we had no need of the actual pieces. We would call out moves to each other and chortle appreciatively. The other lads were mystified by the process. Danny often pretended to be mystified, although if one of us should make a bad move, Danny would blow a raspberry. Then he'd catch himself and pretend to be mystified once more.

Professor Ginzburg's opening moves are crude and clumsy. He has no concept of the subtleties, the intricacies of the game. He's tough, though, I'll say that for him, he plays like a Mama Grizzly, ferocious in his protection of even the lowliest pieces. It takes me more than an hour to do away with Professor Ginzburg, an hour in which we speak of composers, an hour in which Mrs. Ginzburg ferries out any number of vittles.

Fay and I descend into the basement, ostensibly to listen to records. Fay puts an album on the phonograph, and then she removes her sweater and bra and bounces on my lap. Her breasts are rather impressive, more than enough for a boy to fool around with for an hour or two. There is much kissing, Fay is a great one for kissing. In fact, if sex consisted solely of French kissing and breast caressing you'd get no argument from Fay Ginzburg. I blame Dr. Tockette for changing her mind. I think he convinced Fay to get into more sophisticated satisfactions as a political move.

(Don't forget we're in Dreamland, though, which explains the presence of the alien Claire, who just slipped through a doorway and started pulling off a pair of bluejeans.)

As content as I am with Fay's breasts in my hot little hands, our tongues duelling as in a Saturday matinee, I find myself growing distracted by the music coming from the phonograph. It features two voices, one sweetly resonant, the other strident and nasal. This combination shouldn't work, the voices should repel each other, but instead they come together like swans in love. The music is odd, twangy guitars (a twelve-string here and there?), a bass that is not content to lurk in the bottom registers but romps up whenever it feels like it, a huge and friendly sheepdog, and in the background the most cretinous sort of drumming, a persistent hammering at the wash cymbal, covering the music in metallic clouds. Even as I toy with Fay I listen to the music, my efforts on the breast front become somewhat desultory.

"Play with my tits, Des," whispers Fay.

"Who," I ask, "is playing this music?"

"Who?" This is apparently a funny question, because Fay laughs, which adds a bit of sport and spice to the breast fondling. "It's the *Beatles*," she says.

And I say, "Oh."

You've likely heard stories that what drove me to my present state was the weirdest kind of jealousy as regards the Beatles, that I was embittered by the *Sergeant Pepper* album, which predated the release of my so-called concept album, *Grin*, by a scant two weeks. People like to claim that I was tinkering with the mixes too long, throwing out perfectly good tracks only to start again, that my eccentricity was my undoing, and there is a tiny grain of truth somewhere in there. There is even more truth, though, to the assertion that it was Kenneth Sexstone's fault, that man has all the artistic courage of a football, he delayed release for months on end.

Things are getting interesting here in Dreamland because, if you'll recall, the alien Claire is pulling off her jeans. Underneath she wears no panties. Her buttocks are firm. Don't mind me, this is what dreams are for. And now she pulls off her number twenty-one Maple Leafs sweater. She has small breasts, sporty models as opposed to Fay's Sherman tanks. The alien Claire is brushing her hair now. I study her body, her flesh bounces with animation, with life. Look what happens in Dreamland! The loins stir, the penis rears its head, a grinning little brute. Only in Dreamland. Dr. Tockette can tell you that I have certain quote-unquote hang-ups, that erections do not happen my way under the normal course of events. But in Dreamland I appear to be unafflicted, this boner is a biggie. The alien Claire bounces this way, over to the bed. Do you think I should attempt a spiritual, astral-type coupling? Claire jumps onto the bed, and, my, how lifelike, the little vibrations, the aftershock of her landing reverberates in the mattress. I appear to be fully sensate here in Dreamland, good news indeed.

"Hey, babe. You finally went to bed, eh?"

Peachy, a naked dream figment that wishes to converse. Such is my lot in life. Let's see how I do. "Yes." That was easy enough.

"I went out, bought some food and stuff."

Food. Again we are reduced to physical tediums. I can only take so much. "Excuse me," I say, "but here in Dreamland I seem to be possessed of an erection, a veritable chub. I'd appreciate it if we could elevate the level of our concerns."

"A hard-on? Let's take a gander." The blanket is peeled back, a sudden rush of cooling air, aha, I see you've figured it out long before the befuddled Whale-man. I have drifted back to the realm of Wakey-wakey without realizing it.

"Yo!" exclaims Claire.

I smile sheepishly. "I was sleeping," I explain.

"Well, you ain't sleeping now."

"So I see."

"Oh, Desmond." What she means by this, I've no idea.

"This often happens to men upon waking," I explain. It doesn't to me, but there's no reason to mention that. Danny was often roused from slumber by his own member tapping him on the chest. Danny would grab hold of the thing and it would lead him into the washroom.

"Well, man, I think I can help you out."

"It will wither and die."

"Too many things wither and die, Des."

"You speak truth."

"You want me to, you know, give you a blow-job?"

A bee-jay! If memory serves, a truly delightful experience.

"Well, yes, please."

"Okay. But don't, you know, touch me. Just lie there. And don't say anything."

"May I grunt inarticulately?"

Claire giggles. "Yeah." She lowers her head. Her hair spills onto my belly.

The Howl memory, so faithless in the past, has this time served me well.

How does this sound to you? I'm going to put in eight hours down in the music room, then Claire is going to prepare me some spicy Mexican food, which I shall eat with all the grace I can muster, then perhaps we shall sit around and watch television (I hope things are still basically all right up on "Love Mountain"), and then it's back to bed, where, with any kind of luck, I can inspirit Wee Willy. And you know what else I just realized? A whale, for all his majestic insouciance, has never had a bee-jay! This may not be a lot — I mean, it hardly balances the scales — but it's nice to know that God didn't put all the picture cards into the cetacean deck.

Why, if it didn't involve going *outside*, I believe I might even go for a walk on a day such as today. However, I've too much to do.

Down to the music room.

Ignore the face pressed against the glass doors leading to the flagstone patio. It is ghastly sight, a swarthy visage gutted by the most savage of diseases. No self-respecting ghoul would dress so foolishly, a satin smock, leather pants, gaudy jewellery the length of the withered body. Have no fear, this is merely residual pharmaceutical after-burn, quite common in a brain such as mine.

Mind you, this vision is banging against the glass door — weakly, barely audibly — and also seems to know my name.

"Desmond," it says.

It might be the ghost of Post-Holocaust Christmas.

"Desmond . . ."

"I'll change my ways, I'll change my ways. Watch. Here, lad, do you know the turkey in the shop around the corner? Yes, that's right, the one as big as you. What a remarkable lad, what an intelligent lad!"

Agh. The creature is demanding that I let it in, and I suppose I must, if only because it bears a very slight resemblance to Sally Goneau. I slide the glass door open. The sun is bright today, it tweaks my cheeks and I feel like a favourite nephew.

"Um, I'm sorry, I'm extremely busy today."

"Too busy to talk to me?" The creature puts on an enfeebled display of happiness, it stretches a loose mouth into a clownish grin, it opens grey eyes widely.

"Is this a vision of things as they must be? Is it too late to change?"

The ghost walks by me, thankfully without the accompaniment of chain-rattling, although the jewellery sends up quite a racket. "Too late to change, Gertie. It was always too late to change."

"Your hair finally tumbled off your head."

"Well, you know, I've had wigs, but Christ, are they ghastly.

And I don't wish to discuss my appearance, thank you very much, because it's out of my hands. But *you*, my dear, you are looking more than a little porcine. Excuse me for saying so, but your Aunt Sally cares. Aren't you going to offer me something? A coffee, maybe?"

"Coffee?" ·

"Yes, thank you. And don't bother. Just show me the kitchen."

"This way." I lead the creature — it is my friend Sal Goneau undergone some hideous transformation — down the gold and platinum record hallway.

"I'm sorry I missed the funeral," Sal says. "I was in the hospital at the time."

"The mourners wailed for seven days and seven nights. The golden hills rang with jeremiads."

"I read the article in *Personality* magazine. Really. That bitch Lee saying how much she still loved Danny. Give me a holiday, Lee-baby, buy me a ticket on the bus out of town. And if you don't mind me saying, you looked horrid at the funeral. You have got to take pride in your personal appearance, Desmo. Your Aunt Sally cares."

"The towns became empty places, no flowers bloomed. There has been naught but desolation since."

We are in the kitchen. Sal putters around the coffee pot, putting grounds into a filter.

"So," he says, "what's new, Petunia?"

"Nothing much. I've been working on the Whale Music."

"Kenneth told me. That man, I swear, he's been varnished or something. I mean, is he well preserved or what, not that he was ever anything worth preserving."

"You talk to Kenneth Sexstone?"

"I work for Galaxy Records. I'm the head A and R man. You remember that, don't you?"

"Are you here to talk to me about the Whale Music?"

Sal merely grins. "What's this I hear about a female in the house?"

I suppose I blush.

Sally lets out a squeal. "Tell me *everything*."

"She's from Toronto, which is a planet in the Alpha Centauri galaxy—"

"Hold it right there, Minerva."

"I could be wrong about the galaxy."

"Toronto is a city in Canada. It's even kind of a nice city, very modern and fashionable, although every few blocks they have these fur-traders and hockey players who like to beat you up."

"Canada?"

"We played there, some time in the seventies, a concert in some soccer stadium. There was us, let me see, Sly and the Family Stone, The Band, Van Morrison—"

"And Stevie Wonder."

"That's right."

"Is Stevie all right these days?"

"As far as I know."

"Good." I should talk to him one of these days, give him a few pointers on Yamaha 666 training. The fact that he's blind leaves him particularly vunerable to surprise attacks.

"So. Toronto is a city in Canada, this we know. What else can you tell me about this female?"

"She's pretty."

"That's good."

"She can be very sad, sometimes, but when she laughs I feel a bit better."

"What do you take in your coffee?"

"Drugs and liquor, thank you, Sal."

"Uh-uh. Not while Aunt Sally's here, you don't."

If Aunt Sally wasn't here I probably wouldn't have this longing for intoxicants. This is one of God's crueler jokes, what He's done to Sal Goneau. I think I should take it lying down. "Who do you think you are?" I demand a bit petulantly. "Farley O'Keefe?"

"What the *what* is a Farley O'Keefe?" A cup of coffee is set down in front of me. I empty the sugar bowl into it, anything for a little buzz.

"Well, that's watching your diet," says Sally. "Are you in love with her?"

"I don't think love is an option, Sally."

"Nonsense, child."

"Do you want to hear the Whale Music?"

"That's what we're here for."

In the music room I crank up all the knobs, I shove the faders, I pan the pods, there is horripilant zizz and cackle leaking out of the speakers as we wait for the music to begin. I have spliced the tunes together, put them in the right order, done a very rough mix, and first out into the world is the "Song of Congregation". The Yamaha 666 howls into the abyss. I busy myself making minute adjustments, I've really no time to waste on simply listening to the Whale Music. I tentatively alter the sounds, shading, adding nuances, programming morsels of information into the computer. The "Song of Congregation" ends. I let the last chord ring, I extend its life electronically, I milk that baby for everything it's worth before I slide down the fader and allow the sound to escape. The next movement begins. It is odd, I'll admit that, Dewey Moore's voice buried in there like an old gold watch under a pile of manure. I have added some horns, trumpets and things, and I even overdubbed a small bit of accordion music. This piece has a strange kind of beauty, fragile and doomed. If I wasn't busy making these minute changes—pan the echo-send four degrees to the left!—I think I might weep. It ends, though, the music ends. I certainly don't milk this last chord, though it seems like whole minutes pass by before Mooky Saunders's dolphins start leaping through the crest of waves. The "Song of Flight" is exhilarating, even Sally Goneau feels better. The next movement starts. I cannot remember creating this. I was in radical shape. I'd seen something very bad. It is the "Song of Sadness". Whales are capable of the most enormous grief, are

125

you aware of this? What do you think drives whole pods to beach themselves, to commit suicide upon our public beaches? Do you believe, as some so-called scientists do, that they simply lose their sense of direction? This does not sound very reasonable to me. If a human being suddenly turned tail and lumbered into the ocean, would you say he'd lost his sense of direction? No, whales off themselves, they do away with life in this hugely pathetic manner, their great carcasses shivering and twitching in our fouled air. That is what this song is about. It is about the sadness that breaks even the greatest of hearts.

When the music ends I brace myself. "All right, Sal," I sigh wearily. He is head A and R man at Galaxy, how could I have forgotten that, he is the Joseph Goebbels of popular music. He will tell me how wonderful this music is, then he will evoke the name of the great god Mammon, he will speak of demographics and marketing strategems, if you don't want to hang around to hear it I can certainly sympathize.

First of all, though, like any good record executive, he has to pull at his chin and pretend to be deep in thought.

"It's even better than I thought it would be," Sal announces, a novel prelude, not that I'm fooled. Beware the high praise of A and R men, it means more savage damning. A tear is rolling over Sal's sallow face. He seems to be at a loss for words.

"*But*," I remind him.

"But?"

"*But* it's not commercial, *but* the kids won't like it, *but* it won't get airplay, *but* record stores wouldn't stock it if it came with a free gram of cocaine. Don't make me do your job for you, Sally."

Sal nods, stand up, wanders a bit aimlessly in the gloom of the control room. I check my computer, make sure that it has glommed all the information I've fed it recently. It is a long while before Sal's voice ventures hesitantly into the air. "Desmond. I'm dying."

"I know."

"You likewise know that I haven't done anything particularly worthwhile in my forty-three years upon the earth."

"I don't know that. You were a very good drummer. Steady as a rock."

"I'm not leaving anything behind. Nothing that says Sal Goneau was here, which is a damn good thing."

This ploy is unnerving.

"But here's my chance, Desmo. They're going to try to kill this music. I won't let them. I can press half a million units, I can package it so that it gets into the stores, I can come up with some sort of promotional gimmick that will get the radio programmers to spin the thing *once*. If it dies, it dies, Desmond, but I won't let it be killed."

"Half a million units? Are you crazy, Sal?"

"Maybe a million, what the hell. Do not go gentle and all that poop."

"And you're not going to want to add back-up vocals or strings or something? Are you sure your courage won't desert you when the blood begins to flow?"

"Mix it. I'll master it, no questions asked."

"Hot dog."

"How long will it take?"

"Mixing is an awesome task. It could be weeks. Even months."

"I don't have months. I don't even have weeks. Isn't there any way to speed things up?"

"No. Yes. But they won't let him out."

"Fred?"

"Freaky Fred."

"Leave it to Aunt Sally."

Claire comes into the living room. Sal and I are talking, and you'll never guess what, I'm rather enjoying it. Sal is a huge gossip, and he's telling me about some of our erstwhile cohorts. Do you know, I'm not as bad as I thought I was! Fancy that. At the very least, I'm still alive, which is more than some people can say. I don't like to brag, but facts are facts. Claire sits beside me on the couch, puts a hand on my leg. She powers-on the television, flips through the channels, rubs my thigh with her soft fingertips.

"See if you can find," I suggest, " 'The Ed Sullivan Show'."

Claire and Sally explode into laughter.

Guess where I was when the Beatles did that historic telecast away back when, just see if you can guess where I was, who I was with. I was with Danny, I'll tell you that much, but I was often with Danny in those days (no points for that!), so guess where I further was. At Graceland, absolutely, give the man a cigar. (Someone out there knew, a short-circuited, pimpled wormboy, one of those bespectacled geeks who would have no joy in life if not for the tiny tinny pleasures of rock'n'roll.) Yes, Graceland, visiting with Elvis Presley, the former King. You see, I believe we had tallied six number one hits in a row, we were the biggest thing that had ever hit except for a meteorite in Africa and Mr. Presley himself.

(Behind the scenes, much trouble. Danny and I — although I was responsible for none of the machinations, I held no command over the horde of lawyers that crawled out of the woodwork — had brought a suit upon the father. The father was sequestered in the house on Whitman like a drunken Texan defending the Alamo. I was not talking to my mother, which brought daily telephone calls full of tearbursts and shrieking. The band was receiving our first little snippets of bad press. Compared to what was to come they were mere bagatelles, but enough to alarm Kenneth Sexstone. For example, Dewey Moore threw up onstage someplace in Oregon. Paternity suits flew at Danny and Monty. Sal Goneau was often spotted with beautiful blonde women hanging off his arm, but these women were so beautiful and blonde that suspicion was immediately aroused. And Fred Head, well, poor Freddy, he was arrested in Des Moines. It wasn't a very serious thing, he was just acting suspiciously in a schoolyard. For one thing, Fred was an odd, a startling, nay, a disgusting sight. He'd bloated obscenely. He had found velour of colours never before seen on our planet, he wore sunglasses and smoked cigarettes in long ivory holders. Freddy was talking to the schoolgirls mostly because he only felt comfortable talking with people four and five years old. Who could blame a policeman for scraping that mess off the sidewalk? Kenny Sexstone flew to Des Moines and pulled his Moses act, the Red Sea of Justice opened and the Israelites walked to freedom. As for my personal life, Fay and I had consummated our relationship, it was an unsatisfactory thing, especially for Fay.)

I had written a song called "You and the Dog", a whimsical little ditty. It had no inspiration, other than the sighting, through a hotel window, of a tall woman with an Afghan hound, both precious and regal, looking as though their brittle existences could be shattered if you informed them of beerfarts and toejam. So I wrote "You and the Dog", it was the flip-side of "Hunger in the Moonlight" (Danny's great angst-ridden vocal, the song he is most identified with) — and we thought nothing more of it, until word was received that Elvis Presley was interested in recording the thing. Further to this

129

was an invitation extended to Dan and myself to visit Graceland whenever we wanted. We happened to have two or three days off, and although I had intended to use them to visit the Ginzburgs, Dan persuaded me to board a plane and fly to Memphis, Tenn. The limousine that met us at the airport needed three or four sideburned goons to operate it. Mind you, Danny and I were packing a couple of sideburned goons ourselves, so the stretch limo was packed full as a sardine can. No one said a word for the duration of the drive.

At Graceland we were hustled inside like a couple of serial killers under guard and deposited in a large room full of fun things, televisions and pinball machines. One or two goons assumed lounging position on the sofas and tried to look inconspicuous. The rest retired to a special goon room. Then nothing happened for a long time. Danny played the pinball machines. I flicked on the television set and gazed at the dots of light. It was maybe an hour before Elvis was escorted into the room.

Presley was still in good shape back then, thankfully I don't have to bore you with stories of his sad deterioration. (I hate such stories, they are the stock and trade of rodents like Geddy Cole, journalists apparently ignorant of the fact that deterioration is the normal course of events in this vale of tears. Besides which, it seems to me that Elvis did nothing more than grow a little plump, allowing his insides to go fatty and soft.) The Presley organism was not complete without five or six goons clustered around him. "Gemme a Fresca, please," he'd intone to one. "Let's go sit down over there, please." The multi-limbed Hindu god would move across the room ceremoniously.

Elvis caught sight of Danny playing on the pinball machine. "Hey," he said softly — all his words were soft — "hey, you're pretty good at that there."

Dan was a hustler at heart, he bit his tongue and said nothing, he launched a silver ball with too much force.

"I used to be good at that," said Presley. The goons nodded

half-heartedly. "You want to go up against me?"

"Sure," said Dan.

"You want to play for quarters?" asked Elvis.

Dan nodded, bashed at a flipper button, caught the ball off the end and sent it spinning.

"Y'all let go of me now," Elvis advised his entourage. "Me and this gemmin gone play on the pinball machine."

What the goons feared was any show of autonomy. They backed off reluctantly. Presley shifted like a newborn colt, unsure on his pegs after having been so long supported. Danny allowed the ball to drain through the flippers, then he turned and grinned at Elvis. He held out his hand. "Danny Howl," he said.

"Nice to meet you, Dan," said Elvis. He pointed at me. "That your brother there?"

"Des," acknowledged Danny.

"I don't have no brothers nor sisters neither," said Presley. "I was the onliest one. Tell you what, though, I had a brother, Jesse Garon. He was my twin brother but he died when he got borned. Now, lemme see if I remember how to play on this machine." He placed his hands on the contraption. "Yes," he said. "I believe I do. Y'all spit and go first, Dan."

Danny launched a ball and set the machine ringing. He racked up a sizable number of points before sewering.

Presley grinned broadly. "Man oh man," he said. "You is a humdinger." Elvis moved forward, pulled out the plunger and let a silver ball fly. Behind him, the goons murmured uneasily. I don't know what they were afraid of. Presley was easily a match for Dan. Before long his hips were going, he was kicking out with his legs, Presley was filled with the most natural kind of grace. "Hey, hey!" he'd sing. "Keep it going, mama, the baby needs new shoes!"

The goons settled in beside me on the sofa. They needed to be beside someone, even a slug like Desmond Howl.

"Okay, Presley," said Danny, taking over on the machine. "Your lawn's about to get mowed."

"My, my," chuckled Presley. "Now don't be letting your mouth write no cheques your ass can't cash."

Danny slammed his loins against the machine, setting off the TILT light. Presley laughed heartily, he slapped Danny on the back. "You done premature ejaculated, sonny-jim."

"Ed Sullivan," muttered the goon beside me, identifying the man on the television.

"Yes, I know."

Presley wrapped his elegant hands over the flipper buttons. "Start polishing up that quarter, Dan-boy."

"Ed Sullivan!" said the goon a bit louder.

"You tell Eddie to put a holt on that tee-vee show," said Elvis as he worked the machine. "I'm augmenting my personal fortune here."

"They're on," said the goon.

"Shit." Elvis Presley· abruptly abandoned the game. He slapped the flipper buttons uselessly and let the ball run between them. Then Elvis looked apologetically at Dan. "I got to watch these girly-boys here. The Colonel done said so."

"Who's that?" asked Danny.

"Them watch-you-call-it *Beatles*." Elvis wandered over to the sofa, where the goons opened wide enough to allow him to sit down. "I sent a telegram wishing them luck. Eddie gone read it after they done playing. Sit down here, Danny, let's watch these boys."

It was quite a snug little sofa, my brother and me, Elvis Presley, goons. On the television screen four uniformed men appeared. They wore their hair in Buster Brown style, bangs dangling over their foreheads. The screaming started before they even touched their instruments.

"Shit," marvelled Presley. "I have to give 'em a little of this here before they commence to screaming." Even sitting on the sofa Presley managed a licentious wriggling of his crotch. "These boys just stand there looking pretty."

As the camera isolated each member of the group, lettering identified them. PAUL, said the screen. Paul *oo*'ed and shook his bangs. "Hot-damn!" said Presley. "You damn right she loves *him*, Paulie. You look like you keep your dick in your back pocket." GEORGE, said the screen. "Hey, Georgie-porgie," cackled Elvis. "Whyn't you get a hair cut, son?" RINGO. "Well, what in the name of Heaven is that there?" JOHN. "He looks like he might could be all right. Looks a little bit mean, that one there." Additional writing: SORRY, GIRLS, HE'S MARRIED. "Well, that's your answer right there," said Elvis. "Speaking of which, where is that Priscilla at?"

"Shopping," answered the goons in unison.

"Well, what you think, Dan?" asked Elvis. "You think these Beatle-boys got anything there?"

Danny shrugged. "I guess so, Elvis."

Elvis turned to me. "Desmond?"

"I guess so, Elvis."

Elvis nodded glumly. "Reckon you're right."

"We've just received a telegram," said Ed Sullivan, "and I'd like to read it to you now. It says 'Best of luck here in America,' and it's signed Elvis Presley."

The televised crowd applauded enthusiastically, but Presley seemed to neither notice nor care. "Daniel, my son," he said quietly. "Y'all want to get hooched up and play pinball?"

"Absolutely."

"Yeah." Elvis climbed to his feet. "Tell you what. It hurts to all the time be doing this shit" — Presley set his leg atwitching, he rotated his loins in huge, hormone-infested circles — "and them Beatle-boys just stand there like they's waiting for an elevator."

Danny wandered over to the machine. "You're still the King."

Elvis chuckled lightly. "Well, I don't know about that, Daniel. But it's right nice of you to say so. And now, as my daddy Vern likes to say, I'm gonna cork my asshole and set to drinking."

In the music room I pull down all the faders. When you mix, you know, you start with silence. Slowly I push up tracks four and six. The Beast begins to howl, only its lowest frequencies. A lioness warning away buzzards from the carcass of the kill.

My mother appears. She stands perfectly still, and in the shadows she is young again. She is the seventeen-year-old Claire Graham, modelling a Kirby sweater. In fifteen minutes, big blustery Hank Howell will storm through the doors like a Hun, and in a moment of absent-mindedness he will pat what he thinks is a plastic fanny. When I look at it that way, my mother is as much a victim as anybody else.

I power-off my machines, speak through the intercom. "Hi, Mom."

She jumps. My mother clutches her perfect small bosom. "Desmond?"

"In the booth."

She enters the small room. My mother runs her fingers along the machines, although she takes care not to disturb any of the sliders. She is fascinated and frightened by the technology.

"Des," she asks quietly, "has Kenny Sexstone been to see you?"

"Everyone has been to see me lately," I answer.

"And he told you?"

"Yes."

"Are you mad?"

"No. How . . ." I need something to do with my hands, so I pry open an effect box and clean the dust away with a tiny brush. "How is Maurice?"

"Oh, you know." Her hands flutter about in the air like crippled birds.

The train of misery must make some stops along the way. "Mom, I'm going to sue you."

"Des, I didn't mean to hurt you, I just — "

I wave her silent. "I just threatened to sue you, correct?"

"Y-yes."

"Okay. That should satisfy the evil creature Kenneth. Now, Mom, let's eat some lunch."

The alien Claire — whoops, I mean, the Canadian Claire, which in some ways is even weirder — makes cucumber sandwiches. She quarters the bread and slices off the crusts. My mother appreciates this. She holds the tiny things twixt thumb and middle finger, she nibbles at them gingerly. A mouse could consume them at a quicker pace. I myself eat some soup, which is nourishing. Imagine that. Claire — wearing a dress today — putters about the kitchen. She makes tea, she makes more sandwiches, she pours me a glass of milk.

And the two Claires talk. About nothing, seemingly. About the weather. They discuss the savage sun, they discuss protection against its power. They compare notes as to a storm that passed through Los Angeles. The conversation puts on weight as they become more comfortable. They discuss Maurice Mantle. His disease has a mind-boggling scientific name. The Canadian Claire mentions how several of her forefathers died. My mother mentions that my own grandfather died falling out of an apple tree. He was peckish, he was eighty years old, he climbed up a tree to fetch the fruit and tumbled out on his conk. There is a moment of silence, and then Claire laughs, like buttered popcorn. My mother laughs too, and so do I. My mother turns to stare at me, at first aghast at the sound that has blasted out of me. My mother reaches over and massages my fat hand. Then she and Claire are talking again, women's talk, which involves the dust in the corner and the heavenly firmament.

The father, the father, the great unruly man.

I mean, surely it is better to be like me, an eccentric recluse, than to do what the father did, that is, put on a public display of such embarrassing emotionality that Tammy Faye Bakker would have cringed. The father sat in the courtroom and wept, and when he wasn't weeping he was making a big production out of not doing so. The father didn't weep on the few occasions that my mother attended the proceedings. At that point, my mother's goal in life seemed to be to see just how tightly she could stretch the material of her dresses across her backside. When she entered the courtroom there was an audible intake of air. Reporters trampled each other to death. She declined to speak, her sole comment being this silent one, the material stretched tight as a drumhead across her buttocks.

My father was charged with what in legalese was called copyright fraud, but was really *cheating*. He sat next to his lawyer — a very fat man named Jeb Lajoie — looking like a five-year-old who'd been up to pettifoggery in Go Fish ("Naw, I ain't got no threes," all the time clutching a pair beneath the table) only to find himself rounded up by the Gestapo, thrown into a cage and tortured. Jeb Lajoie was the perfect lawyer for the father, Lajoie's main strategy being obstructionism. He wouldn't allow three words to be spoken aloud without rolling on to his feet like one of those Popeye punching bags, sticking a tiny stump of a finger into the air and bellowing. Our lawyers were cool and dispassionate. They milled about like carpenter ants, each responsible for various small bits of paper.

I had to take the stand. *Agh*. My own lawyers were relatively kind, they merely had me recount the circumstances under which I composed the tunes. They asked if the father had had any input. I replied that the father was a great influence upon me but had not actually contributed words or music to the songs in question. Very diplomatic if I do say so myself.

Then Jeb Lajoie rolly-pollied up to the stand. "Desmond," he said, "do you know what marijuana is?"

"Er," I replied, "yes, I suppose I do."

"A drug."

"Just so."

"Desmond, have you ever taken marijuana?"

I expected one of our tiny lawyer ants to bound to his feet, but they sat there and examined the contents of their briefcases. Daniel, typically, seemed to find the whole thing amusing.

"Could you please repeat the question?" I stalled.

"Do you know what amphetamines are?"

"God's gift to the slothful."

"I beg your pardon?"

Surely my lawyers had watched Perry Mason, didn't they know how to stand up, breathe in heavily and say, *Your Honour, I fail to see what relevance this has to the proceedings.* No, not these yobbos.

"Likewise a drug," I responded to the question.

"Have you ever taken an amphetamine?"

"Only as part of a diet plan regulated by my personal physician." I was rather proud of that one.

"And he further prescribed cannabis?"

"For glaucoma."

"Mr. Howell, do you in fact suffer from glaucoma?"

"I take no chances."

"I put it to you, sir, that you are drug-dependant."

This at the tender age of twenty! The man should have seen me in my prime.

"I deny the allegation. I defy the allegator."

"I put it to you that you have no idea of the circumstances under which these songs were composed, that you were flying high on beans and lulu!"

"Beans and lulu?"

"I put it to you that your father assisted you, that you then conveniently forgot his contribution, ingrate that you are!"

"I think not. Daddy hates my music, he wouldn't stay in the same room with it unless he had to. Furthermore, your allusion to my usage of drugs — which I am not at this time admitting to — is a mere canard, for it is surely not at odds with the creative process."

"Just respond to the question."

"Coleridge was smoking opium just before his composition of Kubla Khan and yet this did not prompt Mr. Coleridge *père* to step forward and claim to have written the thing."

"Shut up, Desmond."

"Your Honour, surely he is not allowed to say 'Shut up, Desmond.'"

The judge said, "Shut up, Desmond."

The father picked that moment to break into the most torrential sort of tears. "My own son!" he cried, if he could have rent his double-breasted worsted double-knit he would have. And then, as if all that wasn't quite bad enough, my brother Daniel got up, crossed the courtroom, and gathered the father's balding head into his arms. Danny pressed his lips to the father, the judicial hall became radiant with flashbulbous light, and the judge threw everyone out until the next day.

I got extremely drunk that night. The sort of drunk whereby I woke up in the morning with only the vaguest notion of what I'd done the night before. I declined to get out of bed. Sometime during that long afternoon I resolved to marry Fay Ginzburg. Even here she beat me to the punch, because as I lay sprawled upon my sweaty sheets trying to think of romantic proposals, the door to my room burst open and Fay bounded in. She stripped naked in such a fashion as to suggest that she was a competitor in a rodeo. Fay spit in her palms and leapt upon me, and for the first time in our sexual relationship she got on top, and I groaned and toyed with the pendulous breasts. Even Fay seemed to enjoy it, she breathed heavily and said my name over and over. I screamed "Marry me!" sometime near the finish. She stopped her gyrations long enough to say, "Sure."

And in case you're wondering, on the following day the jury decided that the father had absolutely nothing to do with the composition of the tunes, that his copyright was fraudulent, and the judge ordered him to turn everything over to me, which he obediently did. In a sense, the father even did me a favour — because he'd stolen both writers' and publishers' credits, the whole of the music was given into my care. Maurice Mantle cornered me outside the courtroom and asked that I reassign the publishing as per the previous, though unhonoured, agreement. Beside him my mother wriggled in her too-tight skirt, a butterfly trying to emerge from a cocoon.

"By the way," I told my mother, "I'm getting married."

She only nodded. She didn't even ask the girl's name, let alone make any inquiries as to my personal happiness.

"We could do a fifty-fifty split," said Maurice Mantle. "You can still keep some of the publishing."

Maurice Mantle looked like he had been sculpted by Madame Tussaud. My brain began to gnarl.

"I can still keep *all* of the publishing, Mr. Mantle."

"Look —" he protested.

"Everyone likes to play these business games, well, I can play this game as well as the next chap. Split publishing? Fuck you. I got it, I keep it, bend down and kiss my rumperoony. Ta-ta, Mother."

The father suddenly appeared. In a period of ten minutes he

had become a bum. His clothes were old and tattered, he stank of Bay Rum. He was a spectacle of awesome, biblical misery, he wept, he gnashed his teeth, he smote him his grievous breast.

"Daddy," I announced, "I'm getting married."

"Good. You deserve it!" The father swayed in the quiet halls of justice. "Hey! Here's Dan. Let's have a frigging family reunion."

Danny merely took a bent cigarette out of his pocket and lit it. A photographer drifted by, circling like a vulture, his camera raised menacingly. Danny shook his head. "Private family matter," he said. The photographer worked his finger, a flashbulb exploded, Danny was on top of the guy in a second. I suppose Danny learnt to fight in reform school, but I had no idea he was so practised and vicious. The photographer's face was bloody pulp within seconds. Mind you, if you're going to severely beat someone, there are better places to do it than a Federal Courthouse, which typically has hallways lined with peace officers. Danny was carried off, arrested, the case would drag on for months, seeing as the photographer would later claim that one of Danny's punches had affected his eyesight, therefore his career.

What a colourful family I have.

Fay and I got married about a month after that. It was a small affair. Daniel was my best man. Karen Hoffman the maid of honour, the Professor and Mrs. Ginzburg the sole witnesses to our union. Then we went on our honeymoon.

I should tell you, a month was how long it took for the royalties to be redirected my way. You likely have no idea how lucrative song-writing can be. Even a small hit, even the flip-side to a modest little number that never even grabbed A-rotation, even a downright flop can rake in the dough. Fay sat on my bed naked as a jaybird, tearing open the envelopes like a shark on a solo feeding frenzy. "Thirty-three thousand for 'Stranger'?"

"Covered by Johnny Mathis. Used as the theme song to a soft-core pornographic movie, 'How to Love a Stranger'. I believe also it pulled down some airplay in the midwestern states, don't ask me why."

"This is great!" she shrieked.

I could only nod vaguely.

We banked much of this money, but it seemed that the leftover nickels and coppers still totalled several tens of thousands, and Fay and I went on the Grand Tour. That is to say, Fay did. I myself went on the Great Wine Tasting, the most exorbitant binge ever. Spiritually it was no different than sitting in a parking lot and drinking Ripple with an old woman named Sasha, but materialistically I set some sort of record. The whole thing remains cloudy in the memory banks. I remember Portuguese wine. I remember that somewhere in England Fay informed me that she would under no circumstances give me a bee-jay. She cited reasons of hygiene. As far as any power struggle within my marriage was concerned, I was a lost puppy, a dead duck. I was sent out for cigarettes in the Sahara, dispatched for diet soft drinks in the Himalayas. It worked out fine for a while, I had a ready supply of yellow pills, Fay was nightly sating my physical needs, and then suddenly — on one of the Greek islands — my pills ran out, Fay decided that we were over-sexed, she cut us back to once a week but never told me which day!

And when we returned I discovered that in my absence a song called "The Great Blue," which I thought was mere filler on the *Drive* album, had been released as a single and was racing up

141

the charts, grappling with the Beatles' "Help!" for the number one position. Yes sir, those were the good old days, grappling with the Beatles.

We met the Beatles when we did that big concert at the Coliseum, the famous one, the only time the two biggest bands in the world shared a stage.

The dressing rooms were side by side, inner sanctums, tables laden with cold cuts and salads, vats filled with chilled beer and champagne. Our dressing room was packed with hangers-on, groupies, four or five sideburnt goonies and various family members, for example my mother and my wife. (Fay and my mother did not get along, from the very beginning it was like dropping two toms with chewed ears into the same trashbin and throwing on the lid. What they found to argue about is beyond me. They certainly weren't bickering over which were my most sterling qualities, neither one had much of a kind word to say in that regard.) Professor and Mrs. Ginzburg were there. The good lady, although not personally responsible for all the food, still took it upon herself to get people to eat, she had special praise for the potato salad. Fred Head obligingly ate about a mountain's worth. Fred had pushed his heft up to the three-hundred-pound mark, he was a mass of Jello wrapped in strange velours. He wore mirrored sunglasses and had a tiny ruby imbedded in the larger of his two front teeth. Professor Ginzburg talked to Daniel over in a corner, the old man gesticulating grandly, his arms waving like he was going fifteen rounds with hefty sprites, Daniel nodding, occasionally laughing. Kenneth Sexstone was there, imperturbable. He sat on one of the food tables in an elfin fashion, his ankles crossed and swinging back and forth. I never saw Kenneth get angry or excited in all our days together, when catastrophe fell he simply nodded, as if possessed of a sorceror's foreknowledge.

At any rate, we were all having quite a good time — Monty Mann in pursuit of some high-breasted, bubble-bunned blonde, Sal Goneau dressing (tearing off one outfit, stripping down to his skivvies in full view of us all, climbing into another, though essentially identical, costume), Dewey Moore consuming beer, leering at the woman who, if memory serves, became the first of his many wives — when the door to the adjoining dressing room opened and there stood Ringo Starr. He held a complicated and ambitious sandwich in his hands, something like the edible monuments created by Dagwood Bumstead in the Sunday funnies. Ringo had a look in his doleful eyes that suggested all was not right with the world. This look changed as soon as he saw that our food table held a huge tureen of mustard. He rushed in and slathered yellow goop all over the crown of his creation. Meanwhile, of course, our room had all but silenced, only Professor Ginzburg was unaware of Starr's presence, he was busy explaining some aspect of physics to Daniel.

John Lennon poked his head through the doorway. "Ringo," he said, "don't bother these nice Howl people."

You should have seen our groupies scatter! They are a fickle lot, those young girls, they scurried through to the Beatles' side in a twinkling. I believe we were even deserted by a couple of sideburnt goonies and one or two family members. John gave us an apologetic grin. He singled me out with his dark eyes. "Hullo," he said lowly. "How's yer belly fer blackheads, mate?"

"The farbulous How Brossers," said Paul McCartney, entering behind his partner. "Doosmin and Dinny." McCartney chuckled at his strange little joke and shook my hand enthusiastically. "So vahry plissed," he said. "So vahry, vahry plissed."

"Here," said Lennon, his hawklike eyes flying around our dressing room. "They have nicer digs than us."

"Let's trade," suggested George Harrison, likewise entering behind Lennon.

"Yeh," agreed John, and he turned back to his own side. "You lot! Come over here."

Ringo, meanwhile, was contentedly munching his sandwich.

143

The Beatle entourage began to file into our side, soon the place was shoulder-to-shoulder.

"All right," screamed Lennon, "the Howl people are not leaving! Come now, Howl people, let's play fair! There's a perfectly nice dressing room next door, pop along now!"

Paul got up on a table. "This is Pewl McCartley spikking. We must evarcuate immidzatly this rheum!"

"*Eeee*-vacuate!" hollered Lennon.

"*Eeee*-mediately!" responded Harrison.

Ringo Starr finished his sandwich and began to construct a new one. Mrs. Ginzburg watched him. I knew that look in her eyes, it meant that she was considering adoption.

One of the Beatles party, someone associated with their record company or publishing house (not Lennon himself, as Geddy Cole giddily scribbles on page 119 of his snotty little book *Howl! An Unauthorized Biography of the Howl Brothers*), wandered over, plonk held high, to where my brother and Professor Ginzburg were talking. The professor was still oblivious to the pandemonium, busily disambiguating one of the universe's little mysteries, stabbing at the heavens for emphasis. The Beatles' hanger-on confronted these two, plonk sloshing over the side of his plastic cup, and exclaimed, "I say! The fabulous Howl Brothers. You must be Danny," he said, pressing a finger into my brother's shoulder, "and you must be Desmond," pressing his bony finger into the good doctor's shoulder. The buffoon misjudged, of course, how insubstantial Professor Ginzburg was. His one slight shove sent the old man careening backwards into a table full of cold cuts. The professor turned quickly to grab ahold of the table's edge, and his face landed in a mound of potato salad.

Daniel executed one of his most brutal hoodlum moves. He grabbed the idiot's collar and gave one short turn. At the same time he fashioned his hand into a fist — not your everyday pugilistic John L. Sullivan-type fist, a vicious hoodlum fist, the knuckle of the third finger protruding — and brought it up into the clod's face. Danny knew how to fight in crowded places, he made no attempt to get a wide arc on the punch, he used physics, turning his hand over as it came so that when it arrived at the dickwad's nose it was as full of energy as an Englished billiard ball. There was a crunch, there was blood, there were screams from around the room.

" 'Ere," said Lennon quietly, coming through the crowd. "What's this all about?"

"Fuck off," said Daniel, who had gone to assist Professor Ginzburg. The little man, blinded by potato salad, held his hands in front of him and moaned like King Lear.

"This man has blood all over his face," Lennon pointed out, picking up his associate.

"That man has shit in his brains," remarked Danny.

"Oooo. Yer very nasty."

"Fuck off outta here. Nobody asked you to come in here."

McCartney screamed, "Just being ferndly!" Paul could be a real asshole.

Lennon stared at Dan for a long while. Finally he said, "Sorry."

No one ever said Danny Howl was eloquent. "Fuck off."

What we had was a hawk fighting with its mirror image, a drunken yahoo exchanging insults with his echo. "I said we were sorry," said Lennon, stropping up the edge on his voice.

"And I said fuck off."

Lennon turned away, supporting his associate, and mumbled something.

"*What?*" roared Daniel.

"I said," muttered Lennon, "that you're likely in such a pisser because yer drummer's a poof."

"Right," nodded Dan. "At least he leaves his own band alone. Not like your manager."

This was a sore point with Lennon, this thing with him and Brian Epstein. If you don't know the story, you won't hear it from me. It's in numerous Geddy Cole books, the rancid seedpicker always finds a way to work it in, I believe that Geddy wrote a bio of Pyng-Pong, an all-girl trio from Norway, and still managed to work in this thing about John Lennon and Brian Epstein. At any rate, so sore a point was it with the Beatles' rhythm guitarist that he raced at Danny and, being somewhat of a punk himself, managed to lay a fist near Dan's mouth. Dan pummeled him in the stomach, Lennon's air raced out and he sagged. Danny brought his shoulder up underneath Lennon's chin and sent him flying. Naturally, our sideburnt goonies and their sideburnt goonies rushed each other, there was a sound like a thunderclap. In a matter of seconds the scene had degenerated into a donnybrook. Dewey Moore was doing the most serious brawling. Dewey had taken on the extra goonies from the Beatles' team, when he finally hit the stage he was glowing purple-blue. Even I, by nature pacifistic, got involved to a certain extent. What I did was, I grabbed plates from the table and brought them down on people's heads. I was rather indiscriminate in this, I'll admit that, I believe I coldcocked Sal Goneau, but I did manage to aid our team, I K.O.'d the lout who'd started the ruckus in the first place, smashing a piece of china over his crown even as he stumbled about, still not fully recovered from Dan's punch.

Kenneth Sexstone calmly picked his way to the door and opened it. No less than eight burly sentries stood there, diligently making sure that no one came into our dressing room. They were rather surprised to see a riot going on behind their backs. The guards came in and settled things down.

Claire is getting ready for bed. She has many ointments and unguents. I don't understand half of what she does when she prepares for bed, but it doesn't frighten me. Fay was another story. Sometimes when I watched Fay getting ready for slumber, a cold clammy fear started rotting in my inner tum.

"My aunt was there," says Claire.

"Where?"

"At that concert."

"People like to claim they were there."

"No, she was. She told me. She blew somebody in one of the

bands. It wasn't any of you guys though. The group had a genorky name, The Fantastic Sounds or something."

"The Sounds Fantastic. I remember them. They stunk. Instrumental band. They turned good music into Gerber Baby Food."

"Yeah. My aunt Fiona blew the sax player."

"And this was something she related to you? Perhaps at Christmas, the fire burning brightly in the hearth, the turkey basting in the oven, your aunt sat you on her knee and recalled fondly how she blew this sax player?"

"I got a weird family. What can I tell you?" Claire bounces towards the bed. "Shove over, Whale-man."

I move my carcass to the side, Claire climbs under the blankets. "We never had a Christmas like that, anyways."

"No. We didn't either."

She flicks off the bedside lamp, and starlight spills into the room.

"Des?"

"Yes?"

"I think maybe it might be all right if you touched me."

Well, all right. Maybe I am a genius. When I listen to the Whale Music, something happens. I horripilate, the elflocks dance upon my head. My scrotum contracts, my stomach becomes acrobatic. Good stuff, very good stuff.

It is now — wait for it — three o'clock in the afternoon! Furthermore, I think it's Thursday. Very well, I'll confess, the

Thursday is just a wild guess, but it very definitely is 3:00 P.M. I shall work for a couple of hours more, then go up for dinner. *What, macaroni and cheese again?*

This mixing is a sticky business. Working with echo is like working with quicksilver. It's impossible to keep hold of the stuff, it slips through your fingers, it spills onto the floor, it's messy and sloppy and generally a pain in the butt. However, it has to be done. Echo is a little piece of galactic space, it's God-wrought and beautific, it shades the higher frequencies of the Yamaha 666's unearthly caw.

"Desmond?" Claire is always hesitant about entering the music room, frightened by the technology.

"Oh-oh. It's not three o'clock?"

"You got visitors, babe."

Mayday, mayday! I shut down all systems, the computer regurgitates its floppy disks, the Beast wheezes into silence. "I am an isolationist," I bellow. " I do not receive house guests!"

Claire enters the control booth, she is wearing her number twenty-one Maple Leafs sweater. "It's that guy used to be in your group. Monty Mann."

Bleak.

"And his daughter."

Gruesome.

"And some other chick."

"I assume you informed them that I was dead, at the very least dying."

"Baby, it's no big deal. Right? You just give out with a *hey, howya doin'?*"

"Monty Mann is a disciple of Babboo Nass Fazoo, the fuzzy little mountebank. You have never heard insipid until you've heard Babboo Nass Fazoo's philosophy secondhand through the mouth of Monty Mann. Beth Mann, if you can believe it, is my erstwhile sister-in-law, Monty's eighteen-year-old daughter is Danny's widow. She is currently contesting Daniel's will. She is a stupid girl, she has not yet grasped the basic notion: *Daniel had no fucking money!* And you inform me there is a mystery guest? What sort of woman would keep company with those people?"

"Why don't you go find out, Des? They're sitting in the living room."

"You let them in?"

"It's what people do, Desmond. We can be normal. Somebody knocks on the door, you say come on in, take a load off."

"You had no right to do that."

"No right?"

"Absolutely none."

"Well what the fuck have I been doing here all this time?"

"I don't know."

"I thought that you and I were sort of happening."

"I happened a long time ago, Claire."

"So what am I here for, blow-jobs and cooking?"

"And leaving me alone when I'm trying to work."

"Fuck you."

"The Whale Music is important."

"Oh, for sure. More important than practically anything."

"I need to concentrate."

"You're just a weirded-out fat man."

"Yes, yes, yes. Are you just now arriving at this realization? I believe Beth Mann may have found her intellectual match."

"Fuck you."

Oh, fine. An argument. Of the sort of bitterness, rancour and barely contained violence that distinguished my fights with Fay.

"And I'll tell you another thing, fat man. I only came here because groupie-wise I was scraping the bottom of the barrel. I hope you realize that. I was living with The Holy Goats, who are these out-of-their-heads Satan worshippers who do ritual animal sacrifices and are always too drugged-out to even talk, and those assholes threw me out. So when I heard about the weird Howl guy up on the hill, I thought, shit, it's either him or Barry Manilow. And another thing. I thought you were your fucking *brother*, man. I thought you were the cute one. Not the fucking . . . the fucking *genius*. I'm outta here, fat man. I'm history. I hope you and your whales are happy together."

Claire turns away, crying, her face instantly so wet that anyone would think she commenced weeping the day before yesterday. She flees the music room, in the gloom of the studio she bumps into the Yamaha 666, stubs her toe, a furious Claire kicks the Beast's underbelly. It wails, whimpers, and is silent. Claire has killed the Beast.

God, You there with the flowing beard and gown, might I just mention what a poor concept this two-sex business turned out to be? It's true that we have these interlocking bits, but that strikes me as rather simple-minded, especially from the fellow who makes every snowflake not the same! Because, You see, we aren't hacking it, Sir, men and women do not appear to be getting along. The pistils and stamens are all well and good, God, they do fit nicely, but You do realize that You have square-pegged us, round-holed us, in the heart department. There appears to be no way to get those frail organs to mesh.

I personally have dealt with the situation. I have rendered my own inner bosom into a little lump of flesh about the size of a piece of coal, just enough to keep various drugs coursing throughout the body on a river of whiskey. Whiskey, that's what I need, I must mourn the death of the Beast, I must hold a Celtic wake for the Yamaha 666. Whiskey, or, if whiskey is not available, any kind of methylated liquid solvent. If memory serves — and I'm going to have to trust it on this one — there is a bottle of wine in the kitchen. The kitchen, of course, lies beyond the living room, wherein lurk the intruders. Fortunately, I am an old hand at dealing with trespassers. I mean, being psychotic and wigged-out has certain advantages, the main one being it's easy to alarm people. Monty Mann and his little entourage shall suffer, hmm, oh, *clamorous whale ejaculations*, as performed by Mr. Desmond Howell. That should frighten them away. Then, it's on to the kitchen where I bolt back the grape and pop into oblivion.

And you thought I wasn't on top of things.

I draw in my cheeks, cup my fat hands around my mouth, and let loose a beauty. The Whale-man storms through the sliding glass doors.

"Hi, Des," says Monty Mann.

"The bull and cow have been separated," I explain. "She was exploring a little fjord — you know how women are — when suddenly the tide went out, the water hauled away by the moon."

They don't seem especially alarmed. Monty is used to me, I suppose, Beth is a little dim-witted, and the third party, a woman who is attractive enough in a real estate agent sort of way, seems positively interested. I up the intensity.

"The rocky promontory breaks through the water. Bull sees cow on the other side and gives forth with this sound." I fill my chest and let loose. Beth covers her ears and giggles, but there is no stampede for the door. Monty Mann nods appreciatively, and the other woman stares at me. In some moments I abandon the call. There is no negotiating the rocky promontory.

"Hey, Des," says Monty, "this is Mandy."

"Monty and Mandy, is it?" Monty can't do anything without its being cute, not even select a short-term partner.

Mandy reaches out and shakes my hand. "Glad to know you," she says. She is a very matter-of-fact sort for one of Monty's companions. He usually likes them confused to the extent that they carry crib sheets marked *walking* and *breathing.*

"So," says Monty, "what's this about a reunion?"

"A reunion? Danny's dead."

Beth begins to weep. Does this mean she'd forgotten about Dan's demise until I reminded her?

Monty went bald, by the way, about seven years ago, and he had tufts of hair sewn right into his skull. His hair has a scientific aspect to it. "But the four of us," he says. "Me, Dewey, Sal and you. We could have a reunion." Monty has been playing the Holiday Inn circuit, him and a rinky-dink rhythm machine. MONTY MANN, the posters read, STAR OF THE HOWL BROTHERS. Monty plays a few of the old hits, between numbers he extols the philosophy of Babboo Nass Fazoo. Do you think this goes over big in Akron?

"Des," asks Mandy, "is it true that you have been seeing Dewey and Sal?"

"Well, yes. Dewey was over for dinner."

"And Sal Goneau?"

How do you figure this Jack Webb question-asking technique?

"Yes, Sally was here. He's very ill, Monty."

"Well, that's what you get."

"So," surmises Mandy, "the Howl Brothers are getting back together?"

"My brother is *dead*!! We cannot get back together. He drove his car through a guardrail at a very high speed. The force of impact rendered him mush. It particulated him! The car exploded, licks of flame touched the clouds. Whales crowded around."

"I loved Danny!" shrieks Beth. "How can you say those things?"

"Does this mean," says Monty Mann, "there isn't going to be a reunion?"

Mandy grins cannily. Aha! They have played me for a fool, but now I see what's up.

I stick a finger in Mandy's face. "Let me guess. *Personality?*"

"Bingo."

"Are you ready for an invasion of privacy suit?"

"Absolutely, Desmond. Are you ready to be locked up? Are you ready for them to throw away the key? Bellowing and talking gibberish, I mean, really."

"A man can bellow and talk gibberish in his own home if he feels like it."

"I'll be fair. Your mental state is obviously due to your brother's death."

"All I know is," says Monty Mann, "Kenneth thought that maybe there was going to be a reunion."

"Kenneth? You've been talking to Kenneth?"

"He's, you know, phoned."

"I spy the hand of Kenneth Sexstone behind this. It all makes sense."

Beth Mann, young and pale, continues to weep.

I believe Danny married Beth Mann just to illustrate a point. The point being that life is such a complicated and gnarly thing that sometimes the only solution is to reduce it to a joke. Hoot and holler, kick up your heels, laugh until you shit your pants. At least, that was Daniel's philosophy. Monty Mann got Beth out of a drug-addled young woman who went by the name Starflower. They were married, briefly. When Beth was five, Starflower committed suicide, in tandem with the boy who was her lover. They left behind reams of bad poetry. Beth was sent away to be raised by her grandparents in Spokane.

When she reappeared, at age sixteen, the Howl Brothers had ceased to exist as a group. I was here, in the house. Danny had made a solo album, which had its moments, but he was too far gone with the booze and pharmaceuticals. Dr. Tockette got his hands on Danny. He slapped his face and threw him into a clinic. They kept Danny there for three weeks, and he emerged bright-eyed and rosy-cheeked.

And then, of course, Danny did the most outrageous thing he could think of. He upped his intoxicant intake and took as a bride the sixteen-year-old virgin daughter of one of his best friends. He had affairs with several well-known female singers and actresses at the same time. Indeed, no less than four of these women showed up at his wedding! Danny was denounced from every pulpit in the country. When reporters caught up to him, or found him passed out in some honky-tonk, engulfed in the fumes of cheap wine and cheaper women, they often asked just exactly what he was up to.

"Me?" Danny would mumble. "Working on new material."

"Where's Claire?" I demand.

"Who's Claire?" asks Mandy.

"Never mind who she is, just tell me where to find her."

Mandy lights a cigarette. "I think she ran out the front door about half an hour ago."

I'm giving the Beast a proper Celtic death knell.

I am Celtic by heritage. Indeed, the profession I am best suited to, according to many tests administered by psychiatrists and social workers, is that of Druid. Can't you see me wandering the hills, my sackcloth robe rustling, warm moonlight shining on my fat face? Can't you hear me singing to the ocean, can't you hear my lamentations for the lost souls of sailors, poor men misled by the errors of high priests and mathematicians?

But no, I had to be a rock star.

I am corked. I drank the entire bottle of nouvelle pap, then I found half a bottle of Irish whiskey secreted in a cookie cupboard. With the Irish whiskey I mourn the passing of the Beast. The Yamaha 666 was poleaxed, scuppered by a boot to the electronic giblets.

I am in the kitchen now. Claire apparently never heard of dish-doing, stacks of plates and bowls tower everywhere, the place is full of china skyscrapers. Good riddance to number twenty-one is what I say, although it's really the Irish whiskey that says it. That, after all, is the purpose of consuming Irish whiskey, so that those spurious words *good riddance* can vault through your lips.

Have I ever shown you this, an automatic card shuffler? We take the deck — Tarot cards and Swedish nudies — we put them in this little compartment here and flick this button. Zapparama, a new alignment. The top card is from the Tarot deck. I'm going to flip it over, see if it is an augury of any kind. The Fool. Bingo, first shot out of the box.

Do you think the argument we had could result in her actually moving out? It certainly didn't seem at the time to be that serious. Mind you, I accused her of stupidity, *thwack-thwack*, I drive the heel of my hand against my already lumpy brow. The ringing in my ears is overwhelming, a convention of Quasimodos has rented all the space available in my brain.

Ssh. Listen. That sound, I recognize that sound. The brain is not pulling its weight around here (it would require antlike strength and determination, an ant can move something five hundred times its own mass) but the brain finally does the job, that sound is a *telephone ringing!* And I'm so drunk that I'm going to answer it. The phone is near the couch, Claire sometimes spoke into it — Claire, never mind Claire, she is gone, she is a phantom. I haul up the receiver and bellow out a hello.

"Des?"

Now this is interesting. Guess what we have on the other end of the line here, are you ready for it, an *ex-wife.*

I say nothing. I breathe laboriously.

"Des?"

"I'm sorry, Mr. Howl passed away early this morning. It was a pitiful death. He was all alone. The angels came but could not lift his carcass."

"Des. It's me."

"Oh."

155

"How are you?"

"Other than dead, very well thankee."

"I'm not doing so good myself."

"Doesn't surprise me."

"I miss him," she says.

"What, did Farley O'Keefe fly the coop?"

"*Farley?* What has this got to do with Farley?"

You got to be a football hero! Go deep, go for the long one! I rip the telephone out of the wall, my man eludes a block, into the endzone, I rear back, pump, and let loose the throw of my career. The picture window breaks into a thousand little pieces. Touchdown! Touchdown!

One morning Fay was puttering back and forth between the bedroom and the bathroom. She was naked as she did this. Fay was putting on earrings, and it became one of life's mysteries to me, why the putting on of earrings should necessitate this roaming nudist behaviour. Isn't it theoretically possible to sit still, dressing-gowned or slipped, and put on earrings? The sight of my wife all in the buff-bare was a bit straining. We were very infrequent in our love-making, as infrequent as thunderstorms in the Sahara. I lay between the sheets, watching Fay Ginzburg-Howl putter in her birthday suit, I balled up my hammy fist and discreetly dug it into my groin.

"By the way," she said, fastening her brassiere — now that she had earrings on, she could put on her underwear — "there's a reporter coming over today to interview us."

I hadn't achieved my present status as Howard Hughes protégé, but this news unnerved me. "A reporter, my sweet?"

"From this new magazine, *Skylark.*"

Now Fay got into her underpants, but I couldn't see why she bothered, they were small and flimsy and served none of the functions of underpants as I understand them.

"I do not wish to speak to a reporter, honey-bunch."

"Des, we've been married almost a year, and they haven't mentioned me once in any newspaper or magazine."

"You *want* to be mentioned?"

"Sure." Fay put on tight black pants and a tight black turtleneck sweater. "Sure I want to be mentioned."

"Kenneth told me to avoid contact with the popular press unless he himself arranged it." ·

"You're not married to Kenneth Sexstone, Des. You're married to me."

I didn't mention it, but I think it would have been easier to get laid by Kenneth Sexstone.

"Hey," said Fay pre-emptively, "it's not like you have a choice."

Wearily I rose, pulled on my clothes. I was quite a spiffy dresser in those days, I wore madras shirts and clam diggers. I wandered into the kitchen, had coffee and ignored the ringing of the phone. For some reason I knew who each unanswered call was from. "That's Daddy," I'd say. The father was regrouping, he'd found four brothers and was trying to turn them into stars. The Pennylegion Brothers they were named, The Fabulous Pennylegions, and between the four of them they had enough talent to make one lousy crooner, the kind of guy who'd play the Stardust Lounge of the Biltmore Hotel in Cleveland. "That's Mommy," I'd say as the phone rang once again. My mother was not talking to me since my betrayal of her true love, Maurice, but that required constant phone calls. If I ever answered the phone (not likely) she'd scream, "I am not talking to you, Desmond!" and burst into tears. "That's Kenny Sexstone," up to more of his intrigues. Kenny phoned daily to tell me how we were charting, what sales were doing. Our so-called Battle with the Beatles had been huge news, it had forced the young people to take sides, and many had come over to the Howl Brothers camp, so sales were booming. Pallets to Pago Pago. "That's Danny," I'd sigh sadly. You wonder why I didn't feel like talking to my brother, the being I loved most on the planet? I'll tell you why, because the telephone would be ringing at 10:17 in the morning, and Danny would be pissed as a newt! Dan-Dan was pumping back J.D. at seven in the morning while I was just noticing my tendency to imbibe one or two beer over my limit.

That is what I was doing that morning, anyway, sipping coffee, smoking Salem Menthols, listening to the telephone ring. Fay was in the living room watching television when the doorbell rang.

"Could you get that, dorkums?" sang out Fay. I rose from the kitchen table, ambled down the hallway. Already it was adorned with gold records. (No platinum, though, they didn't have those until the seventies.) I pulled open the front door and saw Geddy Cole.

"Oh!" It was even a pleasant surprise. "Hi."

Geddy Cole was getting stranger. His greasy hair now spilled in gleaming little ringlets onto his shoulders. He wore spectacles, tiny ones this time, round and antique, as if he'd mugged his own grandmother. Geddy was still doing battle with heavy-duty acne, and trying to cultivate whiskers and a moustache. Approximately seventeen hairs, valiant and stalwart all, had broken through the pustules. Geddy Cole wore a white T-shirt and bluejeans. The T-shirt was painted with a crude representation of a Mercedes-Benz hood ornament, the jeans were patched and repatched until none of the original denim existed.

"Hi, man, how's it going?"

"Enter," I said. "Are you now working for *Skylark*?"

Geddy nodded.

"Honey-bunch! It's the man from the magazine!"

Fay bounded in and alarmed poor Geddy Cole. She grabbed his hand and pumped it up and down. "Let's go into the living room, which I decorated myself, and we'll have some Colombian coffee flavoured with cinnamon and talk." She pulled the man after her, and despite the hatred which courses through my bloodstream, I can't help but feel sorry for Geddy Cole. He was thrown onto a sofa, my wife bounced down beside him, and for the next three hours Fay talked, gibbered and jabbered, prated and prattled. Geddy Cole sat there, bug-eyed, like Lucifer was mooning him, spreading his fiery cheeks. No one noticed when I slipped away into my rudimentary music room (a small acoustic piano, a prehistoric Revox tape recording machine) and started work on a song called "Matinee."

> *Let's go to a matinee,*
> *Let's you and me while away the day*
> *at the matinee.*

Double entendre, you see. I was a horny fellow back then.

Geddy Cole slipped into the music room, he looked like a rabbit at a hound dog convention, he slammed the door shut and peered at me over the top of his spectacles. "Des," he said, "you want to do something really neat?"

Remember, this is the same man who introduced me to marijuana and speed. I'm sure my fat face lit up. "*Really* neat?"

"Really, really neat."

"Absolutely."

Geddy Cole reached into his pocket and withdrew what looked like a scrap of pale blue Kleenex that had gone through the wash cycle and then been dried into a hardened bit of lint. "Eat this," he told me.

He had never steered me wrong before. I popped it back.

"I got to go, man," said Geddy. "Your wife is like real zesty."

I knew what he meant.

Geddy Cole left, and I turned back to the piano and got to work on this tune, "Matinee."

Perhaps you know the song, it is the second cut on the first side of my classic *Grin.*

Indians painted like the sky
Cowboys with their guns on fire
Mr. Marlowe with his cigarette
Chalklines on the wet cement
Native girls in waterfalls
Following the bouncing ball, the bouncing ball . ...

Uh-huh, uh-huh, you guessed it. Meet the original Mr. Acid Head.

I may have been the original, but I was not the supreme.

Look at him sitting at my kitchen table. He is eating doughnuts, they're hard as rocks, but that doesn't bother him. He wears his hair long, grey and greasy. He wears sunglasses, earrings, every single tooth imbedded with a small jewel. The clothes . . . *tsk tsk* . . . the clothes are too small, but it's understandable, they are military garb, fatigues, there are few soldiers that weigh four hundred-plus pounds. He has painted orange and purple slogans all over his body. LOVE is crudely lettered across his vast back. This gives a good indication as to when Freaky Freddy Head short-circuited his brain.

Fred is not surprised to see me, he doesn't even slow his chewing. Fred has to concentrate on mastication, not that he's doing a good job. Fred is neglecting to close his mouth and is producing repulsive noises.

"Hi," I venture.

Fred waits until he swallows and then responds. "Hi."

"Good to see you." ·

Fred has no response to this, other than to grow suddenly tired of his doughnut. He carefully lays it down on the table, covers it with a napkin.

Talk about your awkward silences, I mean, I'm garrulous compared to Fred the Freak. Fred is making a big production out of lacing his fingers together, setting this glob of knuckles down in front of him.

MAKE LOVE, NOT WAR is scrawled across Freddy's breast. He took all that stuff seriously. I remember we played an outdoor concert somewhere near San Francisco. It took place in a huge cow-pattied field. Freddy Head (still veloured in those days, Brylcreeming his newly grown-out hair into a duck's ass, wearing shades and, to achieve an effect of breathtaking silliness, smoking his cigarettes in long ivory holders) thought he'd died and gone to Heaven. There were naked girls running about! That was when we first heard about Free Love, heralded by a group called Geist, an inept quartet fronted by two lead singers, a girl and a boy. The girl was the first seriously braless female I'd ever seen. The male singer was a Christlike figure, slender and bearded, he had a rapturous manner about him, closing his eyes and weaving back and forth, his hands extended, tweaking invisible buttocks. In between songs, this Messiah would announce the Era of Free Love.

Dewey Moore, sipping from a bottle of Old Crow, said, "Sounds okay. It's been costing me a fortune."

The singer from Geist exhorted the people to be as children, and many of them pulled off their shirts and bluejeans, couples even lay down in the grass, locked their bodies tightly together.

Monty Mann, erstwhile surfer-boy, pulled off his clothes too, lay down beside our trailer, cradled his head and smiled blissfully.

"Mann," muttered Danny, "we could do without seeing your dick."

"Get with it, Danny-boy," said Monty. Some semiclad

female wandered over, knelt beside Monty, laid a flower over his heart as if he were dead.

Danny ran his fingers through his pomaded hair. Danny was a greaseball through and through, he stared at the dawning of hippiedom and scowled.

Fred was a convert. I believe he washed the Brylcreem out of his hair that very day. For him, Free Love and Drugs went hand-in-hand. He started gobbling acid, then got into other things — mescaline, peyote, opium. His mind got trampled underfoot, but Freddy stuck to it, popping back illicit substances and revelling in the Era of Free Love. Fred never seemed to notice that, despite the numbers of frolicking females, he himself was not getting laid. That sort of thing is easy to overlook when your brain is on constant broil.

Then there came — it was inevitable — that sad day when the Drugs and the concept of Free Love mixed in a horrible fashion, and I'm afraid that a ten-year-old girl paid a very high price for Fred Head's confusion. Kenneth Sexstone worked his wonders, the story was kept off the front pages, Freddy was quietly led away. But when the next issue of *Skylark* came out, Fred's fat face — rouged and war-painted, I shudder to think of some of the things he got into — was on the cover.

The article concentrated on Fred Head's problems and his incarceration, but the rest of us didn't get off lightly. The story catalogued Danny's run-ins with the law, the article followed Sally Goneau from leather bar to leather bar, and, boy, the vulture of journalism feasted on me, the fat recluse in his mansion, the windows boarded-up, the door never opened. The only one who came off at all well was Monty Mann, who was too busy being a Babboo Nass Fazoovian to get into any trouble. Also, it has long been a suspicion of mine that it was Monty who fed all this information to that kite Geddy Cole.

Please don't get me wrong. I think all that Free Love stuff ultimately did some good. I mean, there are tax auditors out there who are a little less zealous to have people drawn-and-quartered, and this is because they were hippies, because they attended love-ins and sunburnt their dinkies. But there are also some casualties, as in any revolution, and one of them is currently sitting at my kitchen table, making a big production out of folding his hands together. I wish Claire was here. Claire, I think, could make this fellow relax, she would tap him on his flabby shoulder, say, "How's it going, man?" and I think Fred would unclench his teeth, I think he might even smile.

"Boy," I mutter, "do I have problems."

Fred makes no response. I expected none. He lifts up the napkin, seems surprised to see a half-eaten jelly-filled there.

"Yes," I persist. "I lacked foresight, recorded a melody line on one track, and now I want it to be stereo, and what am I to do?"

Fred lowers his head. He links his fingers together, he is very proud of this dexterous ability. I am starting to think this is a lost cause, but then Fred mutters, "Bounce."

"Ah! Well you may say bounce, but Fred, I have left myself no tracks."

"Nyuk."

"Freddy?" I start to get excited. "Did you just go *nyuk?*"

"Nyuk-nyuk."

"What is it?"

"Shunt frequencies."

"I beg your pardon?"

"Like at a train station. Reroute the frequencies. Eight hundred megahertz, track four. Sixteen hundred, track nine. Get another machine to use as a switcher. Choo-choo. Shunt frequencies, you get a free track. All the way to Alaska. One free track, bouncy-bounce, split the signal from the melody line, pan left, pan right, stereophonic. *Très facile.*"

"Now that's a very good —"

"Desmond!"

"Yes, Fred?"

163

"Why are you sad?" Freaky Fred says all this overloud, he is bellowing in the kitchen.

"I'm not sad, Freddy."

"Oh. Why are you unhappy?"

"I . . . I miss someone."

"Did you miss me?"

"Yes. Yes, I did."

"Do you want to go shunt frequencies now?"

And in the music room Fred Head calmly assumes the chair behind the console. It has been some years since he's done this sort of thing, and technology has advanced in leaps and bounds. The concept of digital recording, for example, was sci-fi stuff when Freddy went away. He doesn't seem at all daunted, though. Fred knows machines. The computer behaves towards Fred like a friendly puppy, it leaps up and licks his face. Fred spends a few minutes deciphering its language and then programs in some basic information about noise. He picks up the various black boxes, compressors, expanders, etc., he looks at their circuit board diagrams and nods. It is only a short while before Fred is ready. He rubs his hands together, glances at me (I think I see a small smile buried underneath his beard), Fred reaches over and pushes the PLAY button on the big machine.

He listens to the "Song of Congregation". Fred always did that, concentrating very hard on the first play-through, touching exactly nothing on the board, just hearing the sounds as they were recorded. The Yamaha 666 howls at highest pitch, the control room shakes with the Beast's fury.

When the song is finished, Freaky Fred Head turns his head. He takes off his sunglasses, stares at me and says something he's never said before, not in all the time the two of us recorded gold and platinum records, things that sold mega-units to the Hutterites. Fred says, "I think it's a hit."

Hits, hits, hits. We had an unprecedented string of the buggers. I was hugely famous, I was inconceivably wealthy, I upped the dosages, I drank mightily, I did some things I'd just as soon not mention.

One morning I woke up, crawled to the bathroom, had a sip of water and threw up. This is indicative of poor shape, when your body refuses to deal with H_2O. Sicker still was the old spirit, do you know the feeling, you can't walk within a mile of railway tracks or freeways for fear that your soul will summon its last reserves and hurl your carcass towards oblivion? Fay was God only knows where, even her icy glares and fierce recriminations would have comforted me somewhat.

Monty Mann entered the bathroom. Monty later claimed that he was drawn to my house, to the washroom, by some urgent psychic beckoning. *I* believe he was drawn by some urgent need to drain his bladder. At any rate, he knelt beside me, he was kind enough to hold me, after a while I began to feel semihuman, at which I point I dipped into the pharmaceuticals, and in no time I was feeling fairly well. Monty, sensing my general despondency, insisted that I accompany him and his girlfriend Starflower to a lecture that evening. By then I was feeling well enough to have started drinking again, but for some reason this didn't reinforce my normal need for aloneness. I agreed.

We picked up Starflower who, I have to tell you, eclipsed me in the weirded-out department. Starflower wore a chiffon dress and a baffled expression. This is what happened when the debs were given bad drugs — girls with names like Muffy Seton-Beaton dropped acid, adopted astronomical and/or botanical monikers and lost the faculty of intelligent speech.

We drove to a huge stadium. Talk about your drug casualties, the psychically damaged, there were tens of thousands of us; all there to hear our spiritual leader, the King of the Fritzed, Babboo Nass Fazoo.

Inside the stadium hung a huge representation of the Babboo's blissful visage. It was an idealized portrait, but it still made me shudder, which gives you some notion of how ugly the Babboo could be at close quarters. I'll tell you what to do, make one of those hand puppets, curl your fingers and stick your thumb through so it forms a mouth. If you own an old, wrinkled hand this will work particularly well. All right, now imagine hair on this hand, grey greasy hair of a length of two-plus feet (subtract a mangy baldspot) and you have some idea of the appearance of Babboo Nass Fazoo. He came onto the stage (riding a great satin pillow carried by eight henchmen) gesticulating wildly. People rushed forward to lay flowers at his gnarly feet.

The Babboo began to speak, in a voice like a chipmunk being throttled. "Life is a powl of zoob," he began, then he told us about breathing exercises, he identified a spot about the size of a dime on one's palm that was the site of "energedig imbulzes," he turned quite wiggy for a bit, seeming to imply that if we weren't having sexual intercourse for three days straight we weren't doing it right. That's the bit that hooked Monty, I'm sure of it. I have no such easy excuse. Babboo Nass Fazoo seemed to know where one could purchase peace of mind, and I dearly wanted some.

The next night I dragged Danny down to the stadium. I think what got him was the breathing exercises. The Babboo snapped his fingers and approximately twenty-three thousand, four hundred and sixty two pert breasts stiffened. Dan became quite the zealot, and was in large part responsible for the

Babboo's tremendous popularity. Danny was a good walking advertisement for it, he stopped drinking, his face acquired this robust rosiness, his dark eyes glistened with inner knowledge, a cherubic grin bloomed across his face.

Sal Goneau and Dewey Moore were persuaded. Dewey's first marriage had just failed, he was eager for any sort of distraction. Sal was, well for god's sake, how can I put this, Sal was *spiritual*. I know it's hard to believe in this day and age, but there you have it.

We all five flew to India to study with the Babboo. Our next record album, *At Play in the Fields of the Lord*, was dedicated to him, the songs all espoused the Babboo Nass Fazoovian philosophy.

The record was a whimpering dog, it sucked like piglets at the teat, I am well and truly ashamed.

The "Song of Congregation" is like a searchlight in an inky sky, forgive me my immodesty, it is largely the work of Freaky Fred Head at any rate, he has worked on the music like a masseur, he has loosened the little knots, he has toned and conditioned.

I would be happy, I would be blissfully happy, except that there is no sign of Claire.

How do you figure a guy like Danny? I mean, really. You must picture the scene. There we are in India, all of us, our wives and girlfriends. Even Fay came briefly, although she decided that the Indian sun was bad for her complexion. The Jamaican sun, the French Rivieran sun, those suns were acceptable, but the sun that hovered over India, it was all wrong. Also down in India were the Beatles. I was somewhat impressed with George Harrison because he persisted in his sitar studies even when the master Ravi Shankar stated publicly that it would be some years before George learned to *hold* the thing. A little-known bit of trivia: Monty Mann took up the sitar, Ravi Shankar said that he would *never* learn how to hold it.

It was an idyllic existence there in India. We meditated, made music, went on long walks. We dressed in robes when we dressed at all, what with the human body being like a bowl of soup.

So who would have thought that such Elysian surroundings would wake the slumbering Stud E. Baker?

I first became aware of Baker's re-emergence while being tutored by the Babboo Nass Fazoo. The Babboo would give you private tutelage if he thought you were (a) capable of true enlightenment and.(b) revoltingly moneyed. He would lead you down to a stagnant pond, point to the shade of a tree and giggle, his lackies would arrive with pillows, bare-breasted women would come bearing fans like garden rakes, children would rush forward with refreshment, dewy fruit and the Babboo's favourite beverage, Labatt's 50, a beer he had flown in by the Boeing 747–load. The Babboo would expound his philosophy and giggle, as if he himself could not believe that anyone was actually buying this drivel.

I had seen Daniel the day before, wandering around the site dressed in a snow-white robe. His face was ruddy from the sun but possessed of a tranquillity that I could scarcely credit. Beside him walked (floated, more like it) a naked woman. Her breasts were large, mother-of-pearl, traces of vein shining lightly. Daniel didn't seem to notice. He was holding a blade of grass in front of his face, concentrating on the symmetry. He was approaching true holiness, I'm sure that cow-patties would have jumped out of his way had he, in his contemplative state, come close to treading through them.

I felt happy for Danny and thoroughly ashamed of myself. For one thing, I wasn't buying any of the Babboo's malarky. I know, I know, I was won over by the lecture back in California, I admit that for a while I was quite boringly het-up about the whole thing, a rabid proselyte, but my enthusiasm waned. I was there with him only because I enjoyed the atmosphere, the tranquillity, I was there because we didn't tell Kenneth Sexstone where we were going, ha ha! Babboo Nass Fazoo was very down on the use of drugs ("drupping rappit-belledz indo the powl of zoob"), but I was ingesting them by the handful, me and (this is in Geddy Cole's mean-spirited little publication anyway, it's not like I'm divulging secrets) Johnny Lennon. John and I would also get into the booze a little bit, that fellow could put it away, if Fate had allowed John an old age, I'm sure he would have been one of those crimson-faced, blossomed-nosed gits who sits around the nobby all day picking fights with the publican. " 'Ere," he'd growl, "that weerent *us*. It weer the Dave Clahrk Foive!"

No, I was not in harmony with my surroundings, even to the extent of hobbling around with an all-day boner. It's hard to believe I have trouble popping a chub these days — in my youth I couldn't shake or slake them.

On this particular day, the Babboo was droning on, the bare-breasted women were wafting cool air over us, my mind was wandering, all of which was run of the mill for India, when suddenly I caught sight of Stud E. Baker.

He stood some fifty feet away, taking a leak into the pond. His hips (wrapped in filthy bluejeans, the denim stretched tight as could be) were thrust forward, the legs would often buckle in a muzzy, beery fashion. Stud was holding his pecker in an insouciant overhand fashion. His upper half was T-shirted, the T-shirt full of holes and rents, a deck of smokes rolled into one sleeve. I thought I was imagining things, I blinked and rubbed my eyes. Yes, it was Stud all right, the trademark Confederate Army cap rammed onto the greasy do.

Stud E. Baker took the cigarette from his mouth and flicked it into the pond. He turned and caught sight of our little circle. Babboo Nass Fazoo continued his philosophizing unmindful, his back, and the backs of the bare-breasted women, to Stud E. Baker.

Stud had just finished stuffing his wad back into his jeans, but at the sight of the fan-wavers he pulled it out and flapped it gleefully. He dropped on to his hands and knees and started crawling towards us commando fashion. The Babboo was reaching the main point of his argument when, with whoops and shrieks, the fan-bearers suddenly tumbled over. Stud E. Baker pounced, he started licking them with puppylike fervour. "I own the pud that boils the blood!" he screamed. There was confusion and thrashing of limbs. Caterwauling and scratching of eyeballs. Babboo Nass Fazoo giggled. (That's when it occurred to me that our spiritual leader was, in fact, severely brain-damaged, the fuzzy little groat will be giggling even as they tan his hide in Hades.) The Babboo's henchmen came to get Danny, they were ex-Australian Rules Footballers, there was very little Danny could do about it, although *I* picked up a fairly substantial stick and managed to open a gash on one of their thick and numby skulls.

Some little newsrat must have infiltrated the camp, because this became big news. HOWL BROTHERS BANISHED FROM BABBOO'S PARADISE. Photographers came to record our mass exodus — Daniel and me, Dewey Moore (leaving behind a spiteful strain of gonorrhea), Sal Goneau, but note that Monty Mann elected to stay behind. With us on the plane, however, was the very addled Starflower. She folded her hands gently, protectively, over her swelling belly. She would give birth to Beth Mann, who would become drunken Daniel's child bride, his final wife.

Daniel stared through the window at the clouds. He turned to me and grinned. My brother had one of the nicest grins ever, even though the Babboo's gorillas had knocked out two of his teeth. "Well, Des," he said. "I guess this plane's headed for the Land of Nod."

"Where?"

"East of Eden."

Daniel held a bottle of Wild Crow, so I discounted all this as drunken blabber.

"Know what they got there, Desmond? Know what they got in the Land of Nod?"

"What?"

"Rock'n'roll, my son. Rock and fucking roll."

"We are not talking," I inform Freddy Head, "we are not talking great maturity. She is in many ways very childish. When crossed she gives a display of petulance that is quite bone-chilling."

Fred is ignoring me. Wait, I am not being fair, he is simply single-mindedly trying to run a patch cord from the front of the console to some rinky-dink machine he's fabricated. I am blocking his way, gesticulating grandly as I speak, waving a cigarette in the air. (Do you know, I think I *will* give up smoking the day after the Whale party, the habit has ceased to be enjoyable and is robbing me of my wind, ill as that wind usually is.)

"Excuse me, Desmond." Fred holds the male end aloft. "The um, er, enhancer." By this Freddy Head means the strange black box that looks as though it either creates fissures in the time-space continuum or dices carrots.

"Enhancer?" I give out with a snotty *harrumph*. "No one uses enhancers anymore, Fred. They are old hat."

"I need it," whispers Fred, "for the delphinoid herald."

"The what?"

"Delphinoid herald," the man repeats, staring at the ground. He blindly lashes out with the cord, hoping that it plugs into something.

"The sax, you mean?"

"Saxophone."

"If you mean sax, say sax, Fred. We have to communicate."

Fred Head virtually shoves me out of the way, he waddles over to his contraption and shoves the cord into a female receptor. He breathes heavily with relief, rubs his fat hands together. Fred looks at me and tilts his head like a bewildered hound. "Very nice."

"Hmmm?"

"*Très sportif.*" Fred grins. He has been taking Conversational French at the loony-bin.

"Oh! Oh, this." I know what he means, I am looking rather jaunty. My lower half is bedecked in jodhpurs (Fay bought us both riding clothes because she'd thought briefly that we might take up equestrianism, a notion she abandoned at her first good snootful of horse) because they are baggy and comfortable around my fat thighs. Mind you, the circulation through my calves is constricted somewhat, greatly if one goes by the purpling of my toes. I couldn't find a shirt to wear, so what I did was, I took an old satin dressing-gown, cut off the lower three feet and sashed it tightly. It looks a bit like a smoking-jacket or a karate *gei*. I am wearing wraparound shades and a pith helmet. I have trimmed my beard. The whiskers are still orthodox-rabbinical length, but they are uniform and approach neatness. Incidentally, I noticed that over half the hairs that tumbled into the sink were grey. I even took a few runs with the scissors into the ears. I have little shrubberies in there, tufts of gnarly hair. I hadn't realized how virulent the aging process could be, I must muster my last reserves of dignity. I suppose Danny avoided all this, the one advantage to attempting manned flight in a silver Porsche.

"Why, um, er?" Freaky Fred is wagging his finger again.

" 'Why, um, er'?" His ineloquence bothers me a bit. "Speak, man!"

"Why are you dressed like that?"

"Why?" I clap my hands together. "No time for idle chit-chat, Fred! We must get this mixed so Sal can master it before he expires. I must say, you're doing a very good job."

Freddy grins and plucks up another patch cord. "I'm going to enhance the delphinoid herald," he informs me.

"Very good."

"It's Mooky, huh?"

"Hmm? Yes, yes. Mooky. He rose from the dead and . . ." I shake my head violently, the fat on my cheeks producing loud *wubba-wubba* noises. The ringing in my ears has started (I suppose it is always sounding, but I identify a sudden increase in volume as commencement) so I reach over and power-on the tape machine. The "Song of Flight" fills the room. "I love those drums!" I scream gleefully. "The snare sounds like seaspray."

Freaky Fred Head sings along, the two of us are beached whales, I join in with baleen harmony, and then suddenly I reach over and whack the bright OFF button.

"Fred," I announce, "I'm going out."

"Out?" Fred Head quakes visibly. "Why?"

"It is no big deal," I claim, fooling no one. "I am merely going out for a constitutional. I shall visit a few of the local emporiums, make discreet inquiries. Perhaps I shall effect some purchases. Groceries, for example. Have you not noticed that you have been subsisting almost entirely on jelly-filled doughnuts, some of which have antebellum best-before dates?"

"When will you be back?"

"I shall be back when — " The time has come for truth-telling. "I shall be back when I find her, Fred."

"How in the world are you going to find her? How are you going to find her in the world?"

"They used to set out in longboats made of reeds. They rode

173

the waves by night, navigating celestially, Cassiopeia's chair to Orion's belt. Necromancers sat at the front of the boat and examined the entrails of albatross, of seal-pups."

Fred Head remains unconvinced.

"The real world holds no fear for me," I assure him. "I know what goes on out there. Kingsley Charlesworth, the scurrilous knave, is secretly bedding his own stepsister Amanda's twin cousin."

"It's not her twin cousin," Fred informs me urgently. "It's *her*. It's Amanda pretending to be her own twin cousin so that she can sleep with Kingsley."

"Deceit! Treachery!" I take a few deep, calming breaths. "Point well taken, Fred. I must never let down my guard."

"But what about the mixing?"

"You can handle the mixing, Fred. Truth to tell, I wouldn't be of any use. I can't concentrate. She is a mousy little girl, for all her vivacity she is as emotionally crippled as the next guy, she causes me consternation and grief, but there you have it."

Fred is thinking. When Fred thinks, he toys with his features quite ruthlessly, as if to rearrange his face. "I had a girlfriend," Fred Head informs me. "Marsha Lem. And one day they took her away. And I thought, go out and find her, Frederick. I packed my bag. I snuck down the hallway at night. I even had a map and knew which road would take me into the city. But the nurse caught me, and I never went. But do you know what, Desmond? I knew the nurse would catch me. I didn't tip-toe, I made a lot of noise, I knew that Mrs. Ames would step into the hallway and say 'Just *where* are we going, young man?' " Fred Head shrugs, finishes his patching job. He flicks a switch on his strange machine and lights flash. "So maybe . . . ," he says — he aligns all the frequency levels, begins to shave off those at either end of the spectrum — "So maybe you're telling me this because you think I'll say no, Desmond, you can't go, you have to stay with me." Fred Head looks up at me. "Maybe?"

"Maybe," I admit.

"I can make myself things to eat," says Fred. "I can go to bed when I get tired. I can mix this music by myself."

"Can you?"

"Go, Desmond. Don't come back without Claire. I want you to promise because you owe me one."

"I owe you one?"

"If it wasn't for me," says Fred Head, isolating track thirteen, Mooky's delphinoid herald, "you'd be the biggest fuck-up ever."

So it's down the golden hallway (platinum, too, in my youth I was quite the rock star) and, laying my hand upon the doorknob, which feels icy cold, into the —

Now is the time to bolt if ever a time there was. Now is the time to race upstairs, climb into nappies and scurry between the sheets.

— real world.

Talk about your bright sunshine, that orb is suspended about thirty feet overhead, it's giving out with a Tarzanian yodel. My eyes, even hidden behind the Polaroids, shrivel into tiny annulated beans. And hot, *phew*, it's like the sun has grabbed me by the collar of my makeshift smoking jacket and is demanding *what did you do with the money, huh?* Still, my eyes will adjust in time, and a few flaps with my arms direct a soothing breeze across my chest.

My front yard is ruinous, three or four species of weed are battling it out for possession, the only competition coming from garbage. Empty liquor bottles stud the lawn (I have vague recollections of pitching dead soldiers out of windows, hoping to outwit Farley and the missus), but I likewise suppose that my yard has become a nocturnal hang-out for alcoholic transients. I don't care. What's the difference between me and alcoholic transients? Several million dollars.

Agh. You remember agh , don't you, the idiosyncratic little kecking sound I make when deeply distressed? I make it now because what has appeared from around the side of the house but a snarling dog, fangs bared and hackles raised. It is a small dog, an unruly collection of mottled cowlicks, but its teeth are pointy and its eyes are red.

I give out with a little of the *nice dog, good dog,* but this mutt is too intent on its yawping to heed me. Then I say, "Excuse me. Do you realize that I am Desmond Howl? I *own* this house. I don't remember retaining you, and if I did in some drug-and/or alcohol-induced state, all agreements are null and void. Now, I beg your pardon."

Curiously, the dog falls silent. It is quite the silliest hound I have ever seen. Its eyes are crossed, its tongue hangs out almost a foot, it is splay-footed, and the fur on its paws is too long by several inches. I haughtily step by it and stumble on my way. Even with shades I seem to be blind as a mole, I must hold my arms out and describe wide circles with them lest I run into the black iron fence that contains my property. And already I am sweating, I haven't gone ten feet, this expedition was a bad idea. How about a nice refreshing flop in the pool, how would that be? But then, you see, what happens is, the mere thought of the pool conjures an image of Claire poolside. Her buttocks presented to Phoebus like an Incan offering. I must keep going.

There is a squeal, my feet get caught up and it is extremely lucky that I don't go tumbling can over tea-kettle. That mutt has gotten underfoot, I curse like the next-door neighbour in a comic strip, "*@★?#!!!" The dog whimpers, and without thinking I shoot a clownish hoof. I catch its belly in the crook of my foot and lift the cur into the air. The pooch adds a high, surprised whine. It executes several acrobatic manoeuvres before collapsing on the pathway. *Whap!* A black iron bar catches me squarely in the face, I reel backwards and flop on my keester. Another squeal, this is not going at all well, my nose is bloodied, my sunglasses are askew, a tooth is loose, and I believe I have rendered a relative innocent into a puppy pancake.

I stand up (after much rolling about) and see that the dog has escaped death. Death likely tossed the scrawny arfer back. The dog stares at me, his eyes filled with world-weariness and philosophy, silently demanding, "Why, oh *why*, did you do such a thing to me?"

"I'm sorry." I dust myself off, try to adjust my shades, but the best I can hope for is to cant my head backwards and hope that they stay balanced on my nose. "I'm off to find Claire. If you care to accompany me as far as the next grocery store, I shall purchase you some Gainesburger." And never fear, I remembered to bring money. You likely thought, oh no, the Whale-man will waddle into the store, cover the counter with stuff, dog food and huge quantities of Whale-man food, and then slap pitifully at his empty pockets. I can see how I must be tiresome at times, but I am doing my best to change.

I open the gate, the hinges howl like something from a grade X horror film — come to think of it, my once palatial estate is looking distinctly Lugosian — and I take a step out onto the sidewalk. This is where the real fear begins. There are other people on this sidewalk. Here comes one now, a bearlike black woman attempting to set a record for most shopping bags carried. She is huffing and puffing, little bits of spit flying every which way, I hurtle off to one side, woe betide the man who interferes with this monumental tote.

Which way do I go? I had forgotten about all the choices one is confronted with. I elect to go left, based on the fact that the action of always going to the left is called *sinistrality*, which is fairly catchy. "This way, dog." The dog turns, a paw shoots out, his legs buckle, this dog is a moron.

Do you know who lives right across the road? Henry Mancini. I've never met the man, but Fay once attended a party over there. This is quite the street I live on. I understand that a tour-bus drives along it four times daily while one of those oversized Barbie dolls intones, "On your right, the house of composer Henry Mancini. The doorbell plays the familiar riff from 'The Pink Panther Theme Song.' On your left, the house of reclusive rock star Desmond Howl. He has a series of Howitzers mounted the length of his sentry gates. Each of the six corner towers is manned by an escaped Nazi war criminal."

Here comes a car of ogling tourists, I can tell by the way it slows, by the way it wanders about the road, the driver distracted by the Mancini mansion. A tiny river has been built across Henry's front lawn, the rapids powered by an underground generator, a huge sign proclaiming it MOON RIVER. I think Henry must be a bit of a dork. Fay reported he was nice enough, claimed that he made a pass at her. Then again, Fay could have a private audience with the Pope and afterwards claim that he made a pass at her.

Fancy this, the car has veered across the road and pulled up to the curb in front of my house. I bolt into some shrubbery, peer through the branches at this. I want to see how my fans are looking these days. A car door opens — what guts, these people are going to attempt a frontal assault — and, *agh*, look who it is!

Dr. Tockette, his long many-shaded hair shooting out from under a Los Angeles Dodgers baseball cap. He politely extends a hand back to the car and out climbs that Mandy journalist person. She is wearing a suit, skirted and tailored for a woman, but essentially a blue pin-striped suit of the sort favoured by the best Wall Street pigfuckers. Who else shall clamber out of this automobile? Aha! A cop. He is wearing street clothes, but even my buddy the pooch here pegs him for a cop and issues forth a low and vicious growl. The cop has a moustache and is clutching in his hand a very official-looking piece of paper. Things are beginning to make sense. Things become crystal clear as Kenneth Sexstone prances out of the car, and if you think it's hard to prance out of cars, you're right, it is necessary that one be Kenneth Sexstone. Oh, Kenny, let me guess. Dr. Tockette has made an official assessment of my sanity, based on facts verified by that Mandy woman, the cop has some sort of paper that enables you to have me thrown into a soft room, whereupon you will have access to all my old master tapes.

Fortunately (not to mention miraculously), I'm not home. You're going to have to catch me, Kenneth.

The dog and I light out for the territories.

The thing about Daniel is — and I tread carefully, for what man can truly say what *the thing about* another is? — he was of two minds. One of them I could relate to. This was the mind that sent him hurtling through life like a slobbering sheepdog. This was the mind that made him vomit in public places. That got him arrested at four in the morning, accused of being a menace to the world as we know it, a threat to the universe as we conceive it. Go, Danny, go. The other mind was alien to me. (As alien as the lithe Torontonian.) This other mind of Danny's decided to rescue and revive — to give the breath of life to — the Family.

He met and wooed, around this time, the famous movie actress Lee B. Bennie. God created Lee B. Bennie when He decided that men in general were breathing too much. *This should put a stop to that,* thought the Almighty, and He placed Lee down somewhere in New Jersey. Immediately, much air was left fresh and unused wherever Lee went.

Daniel courted her in an old-fashioned, chivalrous manner. He brought her flowers and candy. At the end of their first two dates he kissed her chastely and vanished into the night. When they did go to bed together, Danny dug down deep into his memory banks and came up with the old missionary position. How do I know all this? How *do* I know all this? Oh, because he told me, Dan-Dan did, when it was all over, he would hang his head low, consume cheap whiskey and unburden himself of such things. So, anyway, when Dan decided to marry Lee, his course of action was plain. Silly and damned, like the man himself, but plain. He would introduce Lee to his *family*.

So Fay and I received an invitation to dine at a place called Benito's. Thanks, but no thanks, said I. Fay informed me that not going was not an option. And look, this is the kind of insight she had into her lifemate. "But, dorkums," she told me, already dressing for the event, some three days away, draping lace things over her nakedness, "a lot of celebrities eat at Benito's. There's always photographers there. Everybody who's anybody dines at Benito's."

Fay had this strange power over me, I could either do as she asked or suffer in a little hell that made Hades look like Disneyland. I went to Benito's, I even dressed for the occasion in a three-piece suit, sandals, my hair in a fastidious pony-tail. Fay wore something that looked like a chiffon prizefighter's robe. Photographers made our picture as we approached the front door.

Danny and Lee were already seated inside. Indeed, they were the only people seated inside, Danny had squandered his life savings and rented the entire establishment.

"Desmond, I want you to meet the love of my life. The girl of my dreams. My soul partner — "

"Oh, yes, Daniel, but do you mind if I just sit down first? I'm feeling a little faint."

Fay scowled. Fay was a beauty, but a mere mortal after all.

"Hi, Desmond," said Lee, touching my arm, soft as Vermont snow settling on a woodpile. "I love your music."

Those first few minutes were rather pleasant. Waiters descended in a swarm, booze (I shouldn't call thousand-dollar bottles just booze, but, given the way Dan and I imbibed, why not?) was brought.

Fay and Lee engaged in a desultory conversation. Daniel and I drank and told jokes. I recall laughing several times. And then, heralded by an explosion of flashbulbs beyond the single window, the door opened and in walked my mother and her new husband, Maurice Mantle.

Shortly after this, my mother would take to wearing sedate clothes, the pinnings of a businesswoman, but that evening represented one of her last plunges into spectacular dress. *Plunge* being the operative word. Every move my mother made threatened to expose her bosom. The effect was breathtaking, a sartorial Evil Knievel. (Several photographers followed her into the restaurant, only to be shooed out like barn cats.)

There was mass confusion for a while. My mother hadn't known I was going to be there, and she was not talking to me. Her new hubby took control, leading her to the table. Maurice had borrowed God's striped sportsjacket, His beige silk trousers, a shirt rendered out of priceless metals. "Hello, all!" he said. He kissed Fay on the cheek (what?), he shook Danny's hand, his breath caught only slightly in his throat as he was introduced to Lee, and finally Maurice confronted me, proferring that hand. It looked as if he kept it in the fridge, only bringing it out for special occasions. "No hard feelings," Maurice said.

It was neither a question nor a statement, so I said nothing.

"Families," said Danny, "can't do business together. I think we should forget about all that stuff."

"Families," argued my mother — a waiter came with a broom, there was a sneaky little photographer crouched underneath the table — "families are supposed to help one another."

"Families," I finally spoke up, "are supposed to eat turkey and mashed potatoes. I am supposed to shove the peas off to one corner of my plate, I am not partial to them. Families are supposed to watch Ed Sullivan. To moan *en masse* when Ed introduces Topo Gigo, the little Italian mouse. Families are supposed to yawn, to stretch their arms. Everyone puts on pee-jays. The children are ushered upstairs, put to bed with

181

stories concerning fairies and sprites. The parents give each other knowing winks and smiles . . ."

This little speech was interrupted by a voice from outside. A voice that sounded like beavers felling a dead tree. "What do you mean, who the fuck am I? Who the fuck are you?"

Some answer must have been given, because the voice continued. "I *made* the Howl Brothers. Take my photograph. Donna, smile. Take the gum out of your mouth."

The weary pop of a single flashbulb.

Then the door flew open.

"Dad!" exploded Daniel.

"Dan-Dan!" responded the father. "What the hell's going on?"

"Family reunion."

"Shit."

The father was dressed in a manner he thought was hip, a shirt opened to his navel, several medallions around his neck, bell-bottomed trousers and platform shoes. Beside him, Donna glanced around bewildered. "Wow," she muttered, reinserting the gum into her mouth. Donna wore a halter-top and either a minidress or a maxi loincloth.

Had it not been for her, the father would have fled, the evening might have ended. But that young girl knew class when she saw it, probably recognized that this was as close as she was going to get in her lifetime. "Hankies," she said, "Donna's hungry."

"Donna can eat somewhere else."

"No, Donna can't. Donna must eat here. If Donna doesn't, Donna will be weak. *Weak*, Hankies."

"Oh," said the father. He made up his mind. "I'm gonna come sit down over there. But I don't want to talk to none of you. Except for maybe Danny and — " The father looked at Lee for the first time. He collapsed.

The waiters, some twenty-eight of them, began to ferry out food from the kitchen. This smoothed the situation for a little while, everyone sat at the big table and ate. The only talking was done by Donna. "You know who eats here with great regularity? Paul Newman. Old Blue Eyes. No, wait a sec, that's Frank Sinatra. I don't know if he eats here. Probly. But Paul Newman for sure. I love Paul Newman. I've told Hankies, I said, if we marry, which he hasn't asked me to, but if he did and if we did, I would be absolutely faithful. Except for if Paul Newman hit on me. Then Hankies would be history."

As good as the food was, do you know what was better? That's right, the booze. Yummy-yum. Before long I was not using my wineglass, I was picking up those bottles by their necks and draining them. The room began to spin, but pleasantly. I preferred the room spinning. I never had to look at any one person for too long.

Then Danny said, I presume only to make conversation, "Well, Des, I guess next week it's back into the studio with us."

Did Dan-Dan have any idea how wrong a thing to say this was? Could he have? Did he know that my mother, the father and Maurice were going to stand up, all at once, and shout out various pleas and threats? Danny could only counter by standing up likewise and hollering his bit of news, that he and Lee were getting married! Donna demanded loudly to know when Hankies was going to marry her! I started to cry. My wife, in a rare mood of tenderness towards me, tried to quiet everyone. You can probably guess how she did this, by standing up and bellowing at the top of her voice. Lee B. Bennie put her arm around my fat shoulders. It was too late.

The owners of Benito's never pressed charges, only because my lawyers made amends to the tune of many times the actual damage. I awoke in a hospital, strapped to a wet bed. I stopped screaming after a few weeks, and after a few more weeks they released me, after eliciting a promise that I would never again touch liquor or drugs.

I had my fingers crossed behind my back.

I have made a friend for life. Barney here (I have named the dog Barney) thinks I am the finest human being ever assembled, he gazes at me with endless admiration and affection. Don't tell him that anyone could have done what I did, which was to march into a corner grocery store, pick up a box of Gainesburgers and toss some bills in the direction of the proprietor. In Barney's eyes I have performed a major miracle, he has decided to become the first of my disciples, the rock upon which I shall build my church.

My neighbourhood is vanished, I am in a strange new place. Here we have liquor stores and pawnshops. Here we have a sleazy bar. It's hard to imagine such grottiness existing so close to the home of Henry Mancini. Well, perhaps I should begin my detecting. The sleazy bar is called PETE'S. No doubt Pete is a friendly and affable sort. He will wipe at his counter and offer wisdom. I instruct Barney to remain outside. He gives me a doleful look but obeys, hunkering down and applying a long tongue to the tufts of hair sticking out from between his doggy-toes. I push through the front door, which is about a foot thick. Inside exists a sort of Arctic twilight and timelessness. Over in the corner is a couple, a man and a woman, you can tell by looking that they have been nursing their beers since 1956. The man is staring forward, his brow knit in furious concentration, you expect him to snap his fingers and shout, "By god, Einstein was wrong!" A fat bald man sits all alone at a table, chuckling to himself, likely remembering the one fun time he had, in a motel room in St. Louis with a woman named Emma. In one of the bar's darkest corners is what appears to be a small pile of garbage, which has climbed up onto a chair and ordered a shot of house whiskey. And at the bar, perched on one of the high stools, is a black lady. She is dressed in a short skirt and a tank top. Her breasts have given up all hope. Behind the bar, serving her, is Pete. Pete, far from being a friendly and affable chap, looks like he is just waiting for his axe to come out of the shop, so he can get back to mass murder.

Still, I've come this far. I belly up to the bar, smile politely at the lady, offer greetings to the publican. Producing money, I request a beer, which is set down in front of me with all the ceremony of oxidization. This is a place for businesslike drinking, I can see that. I toss it down industriously, belch and ask for another. I take a few sips of the new bottle and then announce, "I am looking for a girl."

"How's about me?" the lady demands.

"I am searching for a particular girl," I rephrase.

Pete stares at me, places a cigarette between his lips. The smoke curls up and forces him to squint his eyes. Too bad. His eyes were the one feature that were even vaguely humanoid.

"She stands about this high," I draw a line some five feet from the grungy ground, "and has long golden hair. Her eyes are green, except for when she is angered, at which time they become tinted ever so lightly with a steely grey. Many people would call her mouth oversized, her lips too full, but this is a matter of taste, I myself would differ. She is slight of build, small-breasted, well proportioned."

"Haven't seen her," Pete snaps.

"Her name is Claire."

"Means nothing," says Pete.

"Imagine a wheatfield. A hot summer's day. Overnight a carnival has appeared, a Ferris wheel and hot-dog stand. A clown races around doing pratfalls."

"Oh, yeah," nods Pete. "She was in the day before yesterday."

"Did you speak with her?"

Pete has softened somewhat, and, if you are willing to grant a certain amount of latitude regarding facial expressions, the man is smiling. "Yeah. She was interesting. Nice kid. Mad as shit, though, at some guy named Dorcus."

"She told you this?"

"Shit, yeah. Said he was a flake. Right nuts, she said. You know this guy?"

"He has certain problems, no more than many people. He is willing to work with a *qualified* doctor, although he will have nothing to do with Dr. Tockette, who is to medicine what Babboo Nass Fazoo is to organized religion."

It's as if someone has set a match to the small pile of garbage in the corner. It begins to zizz and cackle, bits leap with spark, and the small pile of garbage is a raging conflagration. It tumbles to the ground and makes its way towards us. The garbage begins to talk now, it has a voice like Jiminy Cricket on evil drugs. "Bappoo Nass Fatsoo? Ooo are be zaying dis?"

The black lady and Pete the bartender make it obvious that I'm in this alone. Still, self-sacrifice is one of the finer options open to us sometimes morally bankrupt human beings. I address the garbage. "I mentioned the name Babboo Nass Fazoo."

The small pile of garbage giggles. "Pie me a dringkt."

"Hmmm?"

"Pie me a dringkt," the garbage repeats. "Bappoo Nass Fatsoo!"

"Unfortunately," I say, "I was just now on my way. I don't really have time to dally."

"I am gnawing where iss dis garl." The small pile of garbage giggles again. For an instant my heart (*all right*, damn it, I have one, but it is fat and riddled, useless at best) plunges towards my sandals as I imagine my dear sweet Claire being devoured by this small pile of garbage. Then I realize what it has said. "You know where she is?"

"She are bean docking do me."

"She are bean docking do *you*?"

"Pie me a dringkt."

"Pete, may I have one of whatever it consumes?"

The garbage shoots skyward, lands on the stool beside me. At close quarters the features become just barely discernible. This is an old man pretending to be garbage, and a fuzzier, groatier little gnarly-noob I could scarcely imagine. Aha. Once again you have been quicker than I. Just remember that you haven't been waging nuclear war on your brain cells for twenty-odd years. "Why," say I, "it's the furry little four-flusher himself."

"It's Bob," says Pete.

"I beg your pardon?"

"That's his name. Bob."

"Bawp," the small pile of garbage, the erstwhile spiritual leader of millions, says rather proudly.

"Oh." I feel like one of those old Jews who, on a crowded sidewalk in downtown Cleveland, suddenly recognizes the Terror of Treblinka. Still, something softens within me, I even let the small pile of garbage grab my hand. "Pleased to meet you, Bob."

Bob is presented with a small shot of house whiskey, which I pay for and which he tosses back with alacrity. "Yezz," he says, "I are bean docking do dis garl. She are bean zaying dat she are needing an jawwob."

"Jawwob?"

"Verk."

"Employment!"

"Emblowymund."

"Yes. Talk on, Bob."

"I am zaying dat I gnaw where iss jawwobs. Danzink."

"Danzink?"

"Danzink." Bob lifts his arms above his head and shifts some portion of his anatomy lewdly. "Viddowt der close."

"Danzink viddowt der close." I furl my brow, pull on my beard. "Danzink widdowt der close."

The black lady offers elucidation. "Stripping."

"Yowzers!" I grab Bob as if to throttle him, but the worm-eaten material in which he is wrapped comes away in my hands. "You frizzy little pervert." It would be a simple matter to rid the universe of the Babboo, and I am seriously considering it when Barney sends up the most horrendous of howls. It's like Hollywood producers are auditioning for *The Hound of the Baskervilles*.

"That your dog?" Pete asked.

"He is with me, yes."

"Something the matter with him?"

"How should I know? I am not a canine mind-reader!" Even as I say these words, however, I become possessed of a sudden clairvoyance. I lift the small pile of garbage off his stool. "Is there another door?"

Pete points helpfully towards the back of the room. He seems to enjoy this cloak-and-dagger stuff. "Are you kidnapping Bob?" he asks. "I don't think you're gonna get much for him."

"Goodbye." I waddle towards the fire exit carrying Bob — I'd tell you how the little mung smelt but I don't have time — I hit the heavy door with my rear end and as it opens I see Kenneth Sexstone *et al.* rush through the front entrance.

I am in an alleyway, Barney is waiting, we set off at quite a clip. In a few moments I am exhausted and close to throwing up. On the bright side, however, we seem to have escaped for the time being. I set Bob on the ground, lumber over to the curb for a long sit-down.

Barney takes a whiff of Bob. His muzzle cringes so badly that his ears shake. Still, Barney knows how to make the best of a bad situation. He cocks a leg. And listen to what comes out of me, it is unpractised and rusty, but listen to it bloom in the air like a fat and deformed flower, listen to it hit the sidewalk like a drunken cripple. There you have it.

I have laughed.

The last time I laughed — oh, I recall, recently I chuckled at a story my mother told, my grandfather tumbling out of a tree or something — but the last time I really laughed, goofily guffawed, the last time true Bozoisms came pouring out of my bloated carcass, was some years back.

Daniel came to me as I lay in my bed. I pretended I was asleep, but this is useless, you can't pretend you're asleep to your own brother, or he may well do what mine did. My brother disappeared to the kitchen and came back with a turkey baster full of ice-cold water. "Is Des asweep?" he wondered aloud. He gingerly lifted the covers, exposing my suetty tuckus. "Is wittle Des asweep?" I felt the nozzle of the baster being inserted between my hams. I woke up quickly enough.

"Go away! Leave me alone! If I were you, Daniel, I'd scamper into beddy-bye, too. It's fucking *dangerous* out there!"

Daniel said, very calmly and reasonably, "Desmond, let's go out and get a drink."

"You desire drink? Hail one of the nubians."

"No, man, let's go to, you know, a bar. A *saloon*. Let's talk to gimps missing body parts. Let's go see a peeler. Let's *go*."

"No."

"What, you gonna sleep all your life?" Daniel hauled me out of bed — he was a strong son-of-a-bitch — and threw me into my clothes. He stuffed me into the tiny seat of his sports car, he drove downtown, found the sleaziest bar imaginable. He gave me bennies and juice, an old stand-by, very effective nonetheless. The peeler looked like a motel room in need of a paint-job, but Danny turned all wild and woolly and full of fleas, hooting and hollering, and she put on a very good show. Danny reached into his back pocket, removed the Confederate Army cap, rammed it onto his head. "He is here!" he announced to the world at large. "Let the bells ring out and the banners fly, Stud E. Baker is standing by!" Danny climbed up onto the rinky-dink platform, he danced with the now-naked peeler. Things went well until he licked one of her breasts, at

189

which point she screamed demurely and two Sumo wrestlers tossed us into an alley, the moonlight and trash. We laughed until tears came streaming out of our eyes, and then we got up on our hands and knees and crawled away, my brother and I.

Barney, Bob and I are headed downtown. I think that Barney is hoping he is not spotted by any of his little arfy pals. Bob, the erstwhile Babboo Nass Fazoo, has a peculiar way of walking, his hip joints are awkwardly canted, forcing him to swing his little twiggy legs about in semicircles. He also possesses a club foot. In short, the man is crippled, although I never noticed that while I stayed with him in India.

I am attempting small talk. "So, Bob, how have you been?" His response is unintelligible. No matter, the answer is obvious. He is what Momma and Poppa Roundworm point at as they tell their children, "If you don't eat your dung, *this* is what shall become of you." Still, the man seems reasonably happy.

Now I believe he has asked how I've been. "Me? I have not been too well," I offer, "but I think I'm on the upswing."

"Under bruvver?"

"He is likewise none too well."

We are entering the downtown area. Los Angeles has a downtown, and despite the fact that no one ever goes there, it is quite crowded. This is the scuz capital of the nation, it sickens me to think that this is where I shall find Claire.

I need Claire, even though she will complicate my life unbearably. My heart doesn't stand a chance here, I am sending the snivelling coward to war, it shall not avoid pain, injury and possible death. What choice do I have?

We have entered the city. Winos, whores and young people apprenticing to be winos and whores line the sidewalks. Bob is gesticulating at the multitudes, his palsied hands administer benediction. Wait, wait, I am in error, he is pointing to an edifice. A huge sign proclaims, LIVE NAKED WOMEN. Across the face of the building, an artist's rendition of a live naked woman. The genitalia are obscured behind an exploding fireball. Lettering inside the tiny nova announces that there are no less than twenty-six girls, dancing nonstop, furthermore, they will even climb up on tables to do this dancing. My sluggish blood is on the simmer. I am resisting the urge to throttle Babboo Nass Fazoo, but none of this is really his fault. Claire, I suspect, asked him where she could find employment as a live naked woman, her thinking as regards nudity, sexuality, etc., is a touch addled.

Into this place I must go, this place that is called Minos' Bar and Grill.

Barney has raised his hackles, bared his teeth, he is not afraid of the beasts that lurk within. Bob has applied his shoulder to the front door but cannot summon the strength to drive it open. I search my brain for legitimate reasons to forestall the assault. "Very well," I speak aloud. "Let's do it."

I adjust my pith helmet, make sure my sunglasses are balanced on my nose, and I lead my comrades through the front door.

A specimen is collecting admission money. He has no jawbone. He demands fifteen dollars, which is three times five dollars. I am afraid to ask if it is common practice to charge for dogs, fearful that his response will be that he failed to notice Barney was canine. I quickly fork over the money, and the three of us hustle to the most proximate table.

The table is to the rear of the establishment, and beside us is a table full of the LIVE NAKED WOMEN. They are not naked now — they have thrown on dressing gowns, but so little does their nakedness mean to them that breasts and bottoms and many other things tumble into sight. The women drink Diet Sprite and talk about sushi and motion pictures. They smoke many cigarettes and laugh too hard. A live naked woman comes over to take our order. She is an older woman, in most respects she looks as though she could be the den mother for a pack of Boy Scouts, but she is naked. "Give us mescal," I say, for it is the most druglike of potables, slug it back and chew on the worm, you won't know what hit you. She picks up a pencil and writes that down laboriously. The woman has an appendectomy scar, a long cruel one that slithers across her belly. She leaves in a businesslike manner. It is odd to see a naked person walk in a businesslike manner, her buttocks pumping like efficiency experts walking the aisles of a typing pool.

Over there is a young man in a wheelchair. He wears a hat that says JACK DANIELS. He wears a T-shirt that says I LOVE LOU. This is a reference to Lou Gruber, the former dishwasher repairman who has made a fortune by playing old rock and roll songs, including my classic "Torque Torque." The young man's arms are covered with tattoos, crude ones, faded purple ink and misspellings. He rests his hands on the arms of his wheelchair and rocks the contraption back and forth. In front of him, standing on a milk crate, is a live naked woman. She is dancing for the young man, if you can call bending over dancing. That's about all the woman does. She bends over so that her breasts bob in front of him. She turns around and bends over so that, well, you get the idea. When the music stops the woman sits down on her milk crate, has a sip of Diet Sprite, takes a long haul from her ciggie.

"So, do you work, go to school?" she asks the young man.

"Oh," he answers, "I'm on disability."

"Uh-yeah." She nods, looks around curiously. A new song fills the air. "Again?"

"Yeah." The boy reaches into his jean pocket, extracts a crumpled five-dollar bill. The naked woman slips it into a little change purse, climbs back up on her milk crate.

Mescal comes. I drink mine and Barney's before Bob's has hit the table. I ask the den mother for three more. She writes that down.

Bob is grinning idiotically. Barney looks confused. Good for Barney.

There is a main stage set up in the middle of the cave. Actually it is more of a wrestling ring, strong rope girding the edges. In the centre of it a girl is prostrate on a bearskin rug, writhing as if poisoned. She is wearing a cowboy hat, a holster equipped with six-guns, and that is all. Every so often she takes a pistol out and pretends to draw a bead on one or another of the patrons. When the music ends there is a smattering of applause for her act. She climbs to her feet, nods, gathers up her discarded clothing. She puts on a bra and a pair of panties, then slips through the ropes of the ring. She disappears.

Now strange music fills the room. This sounds like the Shriners' Parade on goofballs, an idiotic bass drum thumping at half speed, a strangely strident organ, lush but nasty, the sort of timbre that I have only heard emanate from the Yamaha 666. "Claire," a fairly pleasant voice sings, "the way the moonlight bounces in your hair . . ." Ah yes, now I remember, and it comes as no surprise that Claire is climbing into the ring, dressed in what appears to be Saran Wrap. She does not see us, way to the back and shrouded in shadows. Her eyes are closed as she twists her body in time with the music. Claire doffs the Saran Wrap in nothing flat. She is an inexperienced peeler, the idea is to drag that moment out, we are not even into the second verse before Claire is lying down on the bearskin rug.

The time comes for action. I stand up, make an outraged bellow, and storm the wrestling ring. Surprising myself, I haul my bulk up and squeeze through the ropes. Claire is on her back, her legs sticking straight into the air. She turns her head sideways, sees me.

"Go away," she says. She lowers her legs, spreads them.

"Come with me," I tell her.

"Here comes the bouncer," she says. She flips over on to her stomach, assumes the same position a ten-month-old infant would for a Kiddy Photographer.

"I don't fear bouncers," I say, and I truly don't, I am not alarmed as a thick arm wraps itself around my neck. A hand takes my left wrist, buckles the arm behind my back.

"Okay, buddy," a voice whispers in my ear. "That'll be enough of that."

There is something about the voice, though, that causes me concern.

"Unhand me," I tell my unseen captor. "I've come to take this young lady home."·

"Des?"

"Don't listen to him," says Claire. "He's lunched-out."

"Des Howl?" the voice whispers in my ear.

"That is my name. Unhand me."

The arm loosens off my neck, my wrist is released. Claire is carrying on with her act. I place my hands on my sides, am about to say a stern "Now see *here*, young lady," when I realize that, although I was previously quite famous, there is no way in the world that the fellow behind my back simply recognized me. Claire is doing push-ups on the bearskin rug. I turn around, see a horribly muscled body contained by too-tight pants and a T-shirt. There is the big moustache, the tiny head. I form my hammy paws into fists, I start to circle the perimeter of the ring. "All right, you," I say, "put up your dukes." The patronage sends up a huzzah, they would rather watch fisticuffs than live naked women any day of the week.

Claire sits up on the bearskin rug, crosses her legs. "Des," she says, "what the fuck are you doing?"

"I am fighting," I inform her. "Please get dressed. I'll be with you as soon as I'm through."

194

"Desmond," says my opponent, "you know how much I detest violence."

"I know no such thing."

"It's okay," says Claire. She has stood up, placed a tiny hand on my shoulder. "Come on, Des. You're drunk or something. Let's go home."

"This is unfinished business," I inform her. "This lout has it coming in spades."

"Des —" they say simultaneously. I charge in, my right arm helicoptering above my head in preparation for a mighty blow. Before that happens, Farley O'Keefe pops me right in the nose. I hear a gruesome crunching sound, I begin to teeter, I think I've lost the fight already, a piss-poor showing on my side. My right hand lands ineffectually on Farley's cheek. I'm timbering, Claire tries to catch me, the two of us hit the canvas hard. Still, my punch seems to have packed unexpected power, Farley is screaming and hollering in excruciating pain. I am quite proud of myself until I spot a dangling Barney, the pooch's fangs dug deeply into O'Keefe's backside. Then a huge fuzzball appears on top of Farley's tiny head, which I momentarily recognize as Babboo Nass Fazoo. Stunned by my own ingenuity, I begin to roll towards Farley's feet. I hit like a bowling ball. *Yahoo!* The Whale-man makes Life's seven-ten split! I employ a wrestling maneouvre made famous by Man Mountain Calhoun. I clamber to my feet, take a couple of steps and then lift-off. I spread out in the air as if about to make a beautiful splash in the pool. There is a small *oof* as I land upon Farley O'Keefe.

He is *out*.

The crowd applauds furiously, some even get to their feet. They cheer and wave fists in salute.

Put briefly, the carriage of my life broke under all the baggage. The straw that broke the camel's back — although the camel was a crippled, blind swayback long before — was Daniel's suicide. Accident, I mean. A slip of the brain.

I could not catalogue chronologically the events that have led up to me being here, in this place, this *police station*, being interrogated by a man who fearsomely resembles Broderick Crawford. The man seems to be ingesting cigarettes, he has gone through seventeen in the brief time he has spent questioning me. Myself, I have quit. I decided just now. I tossed my Salems into the wastebasket, all seven packages that I had distributed around my bloated carcass. A filthy habit, cigarette smoking. I feel better already.

The Broderick Crawford clone takes off his jacket, rolls up his shirt-sleeves. He's got me on disturbing the peace and, chuckle-chuckle, public drunkenness. It's as if they found Josef Mengele and charged him with littering. Farley is not filing a complaint. I seem to have put the fear of God into that moustachioed lout. I am concerned about my friends, though, Barney, Bob, and especially Claire.

The detective tries to trick me. He leafs through my folder — I had no idea there was so much information on me — and asks, "When was the last time you saw Eddie Joe Keillor?"

"I am not acquainted with the man."

"He stayed at your house for three months."

"So?"

"So when was the last time you saw him?"

"I am not acquainted with an Eddie Joe Keillor."

"You're not making it any easier on the girl."

Why should I admit knowing Eddie Joe, a man who is to drug abusers what Santa Claus is to little children? Besides, I never knew that he lived at my house for three months. I stay hushed up — I wished I still smoked, so I could ram a butt into my mouth with punkish resolution — but then I make a quick *ack-ack* and demand, "What do you mean, not making it easier on the girl?"

"Well, I mean, the shit comes up to here on her already" — he draws an imaginary line just under his wattles — "and now I'm finding out that Claire has been spending time with a guy who hangs out with Eddie Joe Keillor. Not to mention Quenton 'The Geek' Curso."

"Mr. Curso was in my employ. We were not friends."

"You know where Curso is now?"

"No."

"Curso is *el morto*, Desmond. He got fuggin *hung!!*"

"Hanged."

"It says here that you even know Jerry Lee Lewis."

I search the Broderick Crawford clone's face for twitches of levity. There are none. The Los Angeles Police are mad at me because I know Jerry Lee Lewis. It may be time to vacate the planet.

"Mr. Lewis and I are both musicians, I have encountered the gentleman professionally."

"He played on some fuggin record of yours."

"Yes." This man is a moron. "You see, sir, we needed that sound."

"What sound?"

"A sound like the piano keyboard is a huge dimpled keester and the fingers sailors on shore leave."

"You couldn't get anyone else to do it?"

"When one wants that sound, one needs must have the Killer himself."

Jerry Lee Lewis is called The Killer I think as a joke, although there is a disconcerting similarity in the tragic deaths of two of his wives, both found drugged and drowned in the swimming pool. It is true, he played on one of our records, he played the piano on "Big House," track four, side two of *Reems Street*. That album cooks, oh boy, it features many special guest stars, Mooky Saunders, um, Keith Richards, er, Dizzy Gillespie (has Dizzy's head exploded yet?), and for the song "Big House" we needed that distinctive piano sound. So Daniel got on the telephone — an instrument he loved as much I despised — and a few hours later Jerry Lee Lewis stumbled into the studio.

Jerry Lee had been into the amphetamines. He had the speed-induced dental gnash, the grinders meeting with a pressure of several thousand pounds per square inch. He was also drinking Wild Turkey, wrapping his lips around the bottleneck and pumping like a puppy at the teat. "The Killer has arrived!" he announced, unnecessary heralding considering he entered the studio like a tiny hurricane. He spied the piano and shot the boots, catching one of the corners and sending wood chips every which way. In a single move he devalued the Steinway by about five thousand dollars. "You got show these things who's boss," he explained. "They're just like women, all tits, no ass, if you see what I mean."

Jerry Lee Lewis chuckled, lit a smoke, collapsed onto the piano stool. He polished off the bottle, laid his cigarette down on the keyboard (it burned into the ivory not many moments afterwards), and then the Killer unleashed some music. It was as if he'd unlocked the door of a musical insane asylum, the crazed futzzies stormed into the world defiantly. "This thing's in *tune*," he told us ,"but don't worry, I can work around it." Jerry Lee raised a leg and did his patented play-ing-with-the-heel. This caused both him and my brother Daniel to laugh very loudly. Daniel had found a soulmate. The engineer (Fred had been locked up some time back) placed earphones on Lewis's head, then returned to the console and started pushing up the levels. Jerry Lee popped a thumb upwards and kept it popped, the engineer obediently upped the volume until it matched the exhaust of a Lear Jet. We played the tracks to "Big House."

Big House, on the hill,
I don't live there, I never will.
But I can stand outside the gate,
I'm not worried, I can wait
Outside
The Big House.

Jerry Lee did it in one take, which was fortunate, for the booze and pills in his system conspired immediately afterwards to completely befuddle him.

"I went to Elvis's place," he mumbled. "We're friends, for fuck's sake. Guy wouldn't talk to me. Wouldn't talk to the Killer. So I took out my gun, waved it around, I got thrown into the hoosegow for that. It's not like I wanted to kill the King. I just wanted to shoot his ass. That fat man would have looked good with a bullet between his cheeks." Jerry Lee Lewis laughed and wept in the space of a breath. "Hey, y'all see my cousin Jimmy on the news? What'd he say now, he said that Jews can't get into Heaven. Well, I believe he's right. You want to get into Heaven, you got to live on the right side of the line, man, you got to embrace Jesus Christ and walk with the Lord hand-in-hand. I know that for a true fact. But you do that, and guess what happens. You can't sing for pigshit. Start singing like Jimmy does." Jerry Lee did an imitation of his cousin Jimmy Swaggart. *"Shall we gather at the river...* Tell you one thing, man. Once I got strung out bad, my ass was hung up like the wash, I was playing some dive somewhere. I believe I would have been one dead Jerry Lee but Jimmy come into that place, and he goes up on the stage and picks me up, and people are beating on him and telling him to leave me alone, and he tells them, Jimmy say, you don't care about this man. Y'all watch this man die. Y'all watch this man consign his immortal soul to hell-fire and you don't lift a finger. Shame on you, he says, shame on you. Jimmy took me home and dried me out. He say, cousin, I can't watch you do this to yourself. I say, Jimmy, don't watch, 'cause I'm doing it. All I care about is the music, man, and if you want to sing it right, you got to damn yourself. That's gospel. I ain't going to no Heaven. I am going to Hell, but hey, it may be hot and there may be eternal suffering, but I believe the music should be righteous."

Jerry Lee Lewis rose from the piano bench, collapsed on the floor and fell into a fitful sleep.

Daniel stared at him thoughtfully.

The Broderick Crawford clone's name is Hogan. I know this because every few minutes the telephone on his desk rings shrilly. The man tears the receiver from the cradle, throws it into the loose folds around his neck and clamps head to chest. "Hogan," he croaks, fishing around in his pockets for smokes and matches.

He did this shortly after the remark about Mr. Jerry Lee Lewis. The phone rang, he tore it up and barked, "Hogan." Hogan lit a cigarette. "Yeah? Well, what's the, you know, age of whatever up there? Right. Well, if she left the hospital without her parents' permission, then I guess she goes back. Crime? What crime, we don't need no fuggin crime. Flashing the trim, ain't there some law against that? Yeah. We can think of — Hold on, somebody's here."

Dum-da-dum-dum.

"Desmond!" says Kenneth Sexstone as he curvets into the room. "Have they beaten you?"

"Kenneth," I tell him urgently, "I need to talk to you."

Sexstone's entourage files in. First there is the moustachioed cop, who proffers a sheriff's badge under Hogan's nose. Hogan, not to be outdone, fishes out his wallet and flips it open to his I.D. The sheriff still holds, in his other hand, the official-looking piece of paper, the writ. He waves that in the air, which sends Hogan scurrying for my arrest sheet.

That woman Mandy enters. She holds a tiny tape recorder up to her mouth. "Dank and dreary," Mandy whispers, "the halls of justice do not seem to have changed since the days of Dickens. In one of the darkest corners, Desmond Howl, former glamorous rock star, sits quietly, awaiting the fall of society's . gavel."

Then there's Dr. Tockette, who has fetched along my entire file and is flipping through the pages for the juiciest bits. "What do you want?" he asks Kenny Sexstone. "Sexual aberrations?"

"I want nothing," says Kenneth. "I want Desmond to tell me if he's been mistreated in any way."

"Shortly after his psychotic episode," Mandy whispers into her machine, "Howl entered a downtown strip joint and went berserk, leaping on stage with a dancer and fighting with security."

"Soundly trouncing the bouncer," I suggest.

"Or this," says Dr. Tockette, pulling out a sheet of foolscap. "Still in the note stage, but pretty ginchy, if I do say so. 'Refusal to Acknowledge Same Sex Sibling as Betrayer and Felodese'."

"Kenneth," I repeat, "I really need to talk to you."

"Oh, yes? We've been associated for more than twenty years, I can't recall an antecedent. You need to talk to me. Imagine that."

"What goes on?" Hogan barks, but he has lost control.

The sheriff unfolds the writ, holding it aloft as if it were a Royal Decree and he the Town Crier. He clears his throat and the first word is almost out his mouth when Kenny Sexstone touches him on the arm, silencing him. Kenny is staring at me, his eyes the brightest thing in the room. "All right," says Kenneth Sexstone. "Desmond and I must talk. Alone."

There is resistance from everybody — they've never had so much fun — but Kenneth Sexstone wags his fingers and shoos them out of the room.

"Much of what I do," says Kenneth — I'm in for a dose of the famous Sexstone earnestness — "I do for your benefit, Desmond. An example. I dispatch Monty Mann to your residence. Why? To suggest a reunion. This is not evil. No malevolence there. I wish only to induce you back into the world, Desmond. I send along a journalist. She reports strange claxons. Hideous barks and stridulations. Your personal doctor tells me of retrogression. Your life is informed by squalor, autointoxication and tergiversation. You refuse to seek treatment for your drug dependency, your alcoholism. So. After years of trying to help — of having my offers of friendship rejected, and most recently of being threatened with death — I take drastic measures. I am decidedly in control now. You say you need to talk to me. I can't say that I need to listen, Desmond."

"Kenneth," I say, "you have to help her."

"Her?"

"The girl from Toronto. They want to put her back into a mental hospital. But there's nothing wrong with her."

"I hardly think you're fit to judge."

"I'm fit to judge because I know her. And I'm fit to judge because I've been in those places. You know what happens, Kenny? People break other people — sometimes on purpose, sometimes by accident — and they just throw them away. Into those places. And the doctors try to fix them with Krazy Glue. And I don't want Claire to go there, and I'm asking you please to help me."

Kenneth exhales a bewildered snort. "What do you know? A universe at the centre of which is someone other than Mr. Desmond Howell."

"And I'm sorry if I, um, misinterpreted some of your intentions."

"Hmm!" Kenneth does a little turn about the room. "Desmond!" he calls. "Here's a riddle. What am I not?"

"You're not the, um — "

"Suggestions: ogre, monster, fiend."

"Monster. You're not the monster I take you for."

"Very true. For example: the rectification of our problem with Howl *mater*. I purchased Mantlepiece Records. At a very fair price. Extremely philanthropic, enough to ensure poor Maurice of adequate care. Mind you, I like Moe and your mother. They have always treated me civilly." Kenneth Sexstone gathers in his lapels, adjusts his clothing vigorously. "In your case, it may be a little late in the day."

Sexstone opens the door to the room, the rest of them come tumbling in. Kenneth singles out the sheriff with his index finger. "Read," he commands, and the man unfurls his writ and begins.

"Whereby, in the State of California and on this day, it has been determined by licensed professionals that Desmond Henry Howell is not . . ."

Kenneth snatches the paper away, tears it neatly into many pieces. "Not that. Read this." Kenny reaches into his jacket pocket, removes more official-looking papers, hands them to the sheriff.

"What the fuck is going on?" demands Hogan.

"Oh," explains Kenneth, "Mr. Howl is in violation of his contract. He is supposed to have handed over master tapes months ago."

"This is not a criminal matter," says the sheriff. He has taken a quick glance at the papers, finds them so boring that he doesn't even notice as I remove them from his hands.

"Kenny," shouts Dr. Tockette, "what are you doing?"

203

"Retainer, retainer," sings Kenny, which silences Tockette.

Mandy is babbling nonstop into her tape recorder, but she has ceased to make any sense.

"I understand," says Kenneth, "Desmond's tardiness. He has had some personal problems. In light of which, Mr. Detective, might I suggest that you release Mr. Howl's betrothed?"

"His what?"

"His fiancée."

"He never said nothing . . ."

"Say . . ." I have stumbled upon something interesting in this contract, not that I remember signing it or anything. "Kenneth, here where it says 'unspecified songs of a popular nature.' Now that the work is just about completed, we could name it. Instrumental cetacean compositions, i.e., the Whale Music. Here, I'll just make the change. Would you mind initialling this in front of these witnesses?"

Kenneth leans over, scrawls a quick *KIS*, whispers, "Don't push it, Desmond."

"That quiff," says Hogan, "is nobody's fiancée. She is a Canadian loon."

"May I please use the telephone?" asks Kenneth.

"I guess," shrugs Hogan.

Kenneth begins to dial. "Are you a religious man, detective?"

Hogan considers this briefly, pushing out his lower lip. "Yup."

"Leviticus, chapter 26, verse 21. *And if ye walk contrary unto me, and will not hearken unto me, I will bring seven times more plagues upon you.* Hello, Sexstone here. Legal department, please. *I will also send wild beasts among you, which shall rob you of your children, and destroy your cattle, and make you few in number. And your high ways shall be desolate.* Yes, Edgerton. Full force, code red. Including the SWAT teams. Twenty-seventh precinct. We'll expect you in about five minutes."

"Hold on . . . ," says Hogan.

Sexstone cradles the phone. "My lawyers," he explains sweetly.

"All I'm saying is," Hogan says, sweat beading on his Broderick Crawford brow, "Mr. Howell never mentioned that this young woman was his fiancée."

"Desmond?" says Kenneth.

"Hmmm? Oh. Yes, she is. We are to wed. Kenneth, here where it says 'record shall be released in a reasonable amount of time.' Now that we've almost finished, we could be more specific. We could finalize a release date of, say, two months hence?"

Kenneth Sexstone is clenching his teeth slightly. "Perhaps we could."

"Dr. Tockette, would you mind witnessing this?"

Hogan is trying to light a new smoke, but his fingers tremble and he can't hold the match steady. He tosses the cigarette away. "Maybe we don't need for those lawyers to come."

Kenneth pulls back his sleeve, peers at the forty-thousand-dollar chronometer occupying most of his hairless forearm. "In forty more seconds I shall be unable to stop them. Produce the girl."

"And the dog," I say.

"And the dog," reiterates Kenneth.

"And Bob."

"And the fuzzy one." Kenneth watches Hogan scurry from the room. Then he turns. "Desmond," he scolds affectionately. "You old slyboots."

"I'm sorry, Kenneth. I couldn't help myself." I offer him the contract. "Have your lawyers chew it to bits."

Kenneth shurgs. "The only thing that truly bothers me about that contract is that you are in violation of it. Hurry home, Desmond."

We have been launched into the world again, Barney, Bob, Claire and myself, the Whale-man. Barney is legally mine (I am even required to get him his rabies shot within the next forty-eight hours), the erstwhile Babboo Nass Fazoo is now my *ward*, if you can believe it (I'm taking him down for a shot, too, just to be on the safe side), and Claire is my betrothed.

Claire is taciturn, still upset. The few words she does speak are directed towards Barney, murmured canine praise, "Nice poochie," and that sort of thing. Barney keeps up his end of the conversation with a few strident yawps. The most loquacious of us is my ward Bob, who produces a steady stream, murky water sluicing down a sewer.

Finally Claire pipes up. "That was frigging brilliant."

"I am sorry about our misunderstanding."

"Our misunderstanding when you said that I had no business telling people they could come into our house, like I hadn't been living there, like I was just some bimbo you brought in to do your cooking and give you blow-jobs?"

The little fuzzball cackles lasciviously.

"Do you mind?" I demand. "We are trying to work out our problems in a civil and mature manner —" *Agh.* The poor Whale-man, beached upon the shores of adulthood.

"Des!"

Oh, peachy. Just what I need.

"Des, hang a minute, dude!"

I spin about, brandish the fatty dukes. "Go away, unless you care to tussle again."

"Des . . ." Farley O'Keefe shakes the tiny head wearily. "Would you mind explaining what is going on?"

He hasn't changed one bit, except that his handlebar moustache is longer by a half-inch on either side. His T-shirt advertises a resort in Cancun and he wears Bermuda shorts that are bunched in about the waist, although his thighs threaten to rend the garment to tatters.

"There's no talking to him, Farls," says Claire, that Benedict Arnold.

"You know, Des, I didn't mind when you fired me for no good reason," — Farley has assumed his tone of parental forbearance — "but what did bother me is the fact that you haven't called, you haven't returned my calls, I have even written to you — "

"Learnt to write, have you?"

"Des!" he screams. "Tell me why you're so mad at me!"

"I beg your pardon?" I bridle with indignation.

"We used to be friends, Desmond. We used to talk, we used to laugh, then all of a sudden, I get the can, you lock yourself up in your house, Fay starts calling me in *tears* . . ."

"Do *not*," I launch a finger into his puss for emphasis, "allow her name to vault through your lips."

"Why not?" he demands.

Whooo, what I wouldn't give for a little shot, a little drinky-poo. We're near liquor-store heaven, what's stopping me from merely wheeling around and storming off? Nothing. Let's do it then. And who has chosen to join me? I steal quick peeks to either side. Not a one of them. Fine. Good.

"Just tell me," screams Farley, "why I shouldn't mention my own sister's name?!"

I haul monies out of my pockets, I intend to purchase several demijohns of rotgut whiskey.

"She told me what happened with Danny!"

I am dropping to my knees, the mangled heart turns the valve and the eyes weep. *"Christ!"* I bellow.

"It didn't mean anything to her!" persists Farley.

I'm even willing to buy that, although she certainly enjoyed it, slobbering over Stud E. Baker's prong. Perhaps it did mean nothing to her, but it meant something to Daniel.

"Christ." It is but a whimper, He is not coming, He has had much better invitations.

I will now admit that when I came home that day it was Fay and my brother I stumbled in upon. I knew it was somebody's brother, Fay's brother Nathan adopted the name Farley O'Keefe, who could blame me for getting confused? Now I've got it straight — it was my own brother. Fay immediately began wailing, the tears tumbled upon breasts that were heaving with torment. "Forgive me!" she screamed, but forgiveness was not an option, it clearly states AVAILABLE ONLY TO HUMAN BEINGS. Danny started pulling on his greasy jeans, he struggled into a torn undershirt, he rammed the Confederate Army cap over his curls. Stud E. Baker lit a cigarette and as the smoke snaked around his head he stared into my eyes. Finally Daniel nodded. "That should do the trick," he muttered and left my house.

But it didn't, did it? Danny had miscalculated. He was much more certain when, some months later, he drove the Porsche through the guardrail.

Look what is there on the sidewalk before me. Toes, dainty toes, toes that have been nibbled by trout in crystal clear springwater. Feet that have caressed verdure, the feet that *foothills* were named after. A hand touches the top of my head. "Get up, Desmond," she whispers.

My disordered and defeated heart squeezes with the little it has left.

I believe I once mentioned to you that I have been in hospitals. You may have guessed that it was not my physical well-being the doctors were concerned with. I had a visitor then, and although the import of his words was lost on me, foggy and counter-drugged as I was, they return to me now. "Desmond," he said, in an enfeebled voice. Certainly his voice was enfeebled, this was a man who had been tortured within an inch of his life and starved to his current weight of maybe sixty-four pounds. I lay there in a kind of half-sleep, with no true purchase on reality.

"What is that?" I heard the good professor ask. The nurse responded with the name of some drug, one that even I had never heard of. "Don't give him that," snarled the little man. "Doctor's orders," she insisted. "What do you think I am, bubbie, a refrigerator repairman? I am this boy's personal physician, and I say no more drugs." Professor Ginzburg's Ph.D. was in nuclear physics, but given the way I'd been abusing my body, that more than qualified him to look after me. The nurse left.

"Des," the professor said, "I want you to get up and take a look around. A good, hard look. Without drugs, without booze. I want you to look at *everything*. And then, if you decide you still don't like it, I'll help you. I mean, I'll help you, you know, to leave. I've seen ugliness, I couldn't even make the words come out of my mouth, that's how bad it was. But I've also seen naked ladies. I've heard the music of Mozart. I've caught a fish, must have weighed forty-seven pounds. Me and my friend Karl Oberheim once slept on a hill, and the stars were so close you could reach out and pick them like berries."

I sent up a barrage of spurious snoring.

"Get up, Desmond," he said.

"Get up, Desmond."

"Christ."

I lumber skyward, no big deal, plants do it all the time.

"Well," I say, "let's go home."

So, I have lost my brother Daniel, that is the long and short of it. He was born too late, at any rate. This time is a strange new neighbourhood, no one likes it. It makes no one feel like crocheting doilies that read HOME, SWEET HOME.

The last time I saw Daniel I was in bed. It was not a major bed-going, not in my terms, although I think I'd been there for about five weeks.

Daniel appeared through the bedroom window. That was before I had the thing boarded and barred. He climbed up a tree and launched himself outwards. He broke the pane of glass into a million pieces, lacerated his forearms. He rolled among the shards and then clambered to his feet. He was neither Danny nor Stud E. Baker, he was a drunk and fuzzy combination of the two. His eyes, red and spinning like planets, Danny tried to aim these at me.

"Desmond," he whispered. It was an enticing whisper, urgent, meant to lead me back into the fold. "It's me. It's your brother."

I sought refuge on the outskirts. "I have no brother. My brother died long ago in a car accident."

"Des," he said wearily, "we all make mistakes." He pulled out his bottle, tugged at it, wiped his red lips with the sleeve of his leather jacket. "I got one thing to say. One fucking thing, Des. I am sorry."

I almost — *almost*, I say — lumbered out from underneath the blankets to either strangle or embrace my brother. Of course I did neither. I merely closed my eyes and launched myself into orbit. "You know your way out, don't you?" I spoke quietly. "Second star to the right and straight on till morning."

The good news is, Freaky Fred Head has finished mixing the Whale Music.

I have scuttled down the cliff, I am on top of a huge rock, the waves crash against it and seaspray wets the tootsies. If I cant my head upwards I can see Claire climbing down the rockface. Occasionally I'll shout to her, "Be careful!" but she is very sure-footed. Look up in the rookeries, see what are perched there, *speakers*, huge things with fourteen-inch cones, horns for the high frequencies, louvres to spread the music across the ocean.

Above me, standing on my lawn, sipping cocktails around the swimming pool, are people. My friends and family. I know what you're thinking — "Be careful, Claire!" — you're thinking that I have gone radically fuzzy, that I hurried down the scarry crag to avoid social intercourse. No way, it is in fact social intercourse I am after. Listen as the "Song of Congregation" erupts into the salt air. Yes, I am expecting the Whales.

Claire is just above me now, preparing to join me on the huge rock. "The music's beautiful," she says.

I take her hand, and she is beside me.

But we are halfway through the "Song of Congregation", and I have yet to see a solitary fluke. I was afraid this might happen. There is a great furious flurry of notes — besotten as I was that night, I sure played the hell out of the Yamaha 666 — but on the horizon is nothing but the steady roiling of the water, the slow movement of dark clouds.

"It's not working," say I.

Claire squeezes my hand. "What's the matter?"

"Where are they?" I plop the plump keester down disconsolately.

"Oh, Des," Claire says, and she sits down beside. "The music wasn't really for the whales, was it? I thought it was for us."

The last notes of the "Song of Congregation" fly away, the Beast's cry has gone to die on a lonely archipelago.

From above, from the top of the rockface, I can hear a smattering of applause, but it is a puny human thing.

The new song begins. I am sickened at heart, this music has all the natural majesty of a Veg-o-Matic.

"Hey, Desmond," asks Claire, trying somehow to cheer me, "what's this one called?"

"This?" I look down at the water. People have tossed their garbage into the ocean, look there, a pop can, a cigarette package. "This is called 'Have You Guys Seen Danny?' "

Claire swings her head upwards, her eyes are strange. "No, Desmond."

"Yes. It's called 'Have You Guys Seen a Guy in a Silver Porsche?' "

"No." Claire takes my head between her hands. "No, Des." Tears stream down her cheeks. I, too, start to cry. "Be happy, Desmond. Why can't you be happy?"

I place my head on her shoulder, I gaze out at the desolate sea. "But," I whisper, "I have to tell him that I forgive him."

"Desmond." Claire holds me, we are all alone.

And then the "Song of Sadness" begins. The terrible burden of humanity sits upon me just as that pelican there sits upon the rock, unmovable, unflappable, even though Mother Nature

WHALE MUSIC

dances about as though she were on bad drugs . . . Wait, though.

Something distant, something deep and dark as a mystery, breaks through the waves. Then it's gone.

"Umm . . ." I begin uncertainly, I wipe tears off my chubby cheeks.

A fluke breaks into the daylight, the mighty tail towers above the waves.

I climb to my feet and a huge head rises with me, the eyes large as tires, the bluish maw twisted into what appears to be a smile. It is so close that I could reach out and pet it. Claire screams, and as the monster disappears, her scream turns to laughter.

There is a moment of tranquillity, and then the whales rise all around us.

Scores of them, their gleaming backs black as the bottom of the deepest hole, the bellies preternaturally white and lined with heavy scars. They churn the water, the ocean boils with life.

"Yowzers," mutters Claire.

I am a fat man perched on a rock, the soul God gave me is not much good for anything. Still, I raise my arms towards the sunlight, hold them there for a long moment. Claire leaps up and down, she cries and laughs, she makes whooping noises, embraces me, shakes her fists gleefully in the air.

I lower my arms with all the grace and dignity I can muster.

The whales begin to sing.